The Phoenix Fallacy

Mercenary's Child

Jonathan Sourbeer

VULPINE
PRESS

Published by Vulpine Press in the United Kingdom in 2019
Originally self-published in 2018

Cover by Claire Wood
Cover image by Daniel Fernandez

ISBN: 978-1-83919-293-7

www.vulpine-press.com

For my parents.

It would take a thousand authors a thousand lifetimes to describe what you've done for me.

PROLOGUE
TRASH AND TREASURES

Rarely had there been such a feast in the slums.

Clara sighed happily before approaching the mountainous pile of new trash that had just been dumped into the wastes of Cerberus Corporation. A few trash fires burned here and there, granting a small measure of light to the constant, soft glow from the city above. The highest reaches of the cyclopean buildings that surrounded her were obscured by the smog and smoke that held the slums in an eternal twilight, but the garbage's origin was clear. She picked her way through the mass, her youthful olive skin a sharp contrast to the longstanding filth and despair that surrounded her.

First dibs!

Her bright brown eyes glistened in the dark and her black hair fell to her shoulders, catching the light of the flickering fires despite the grime that caked her clothes and skin. Wrapping her rags tightly around her, she leapt up the base of the rotting mountain.

She was filled with satisfaction. The eternal dark of Cerberus' corporate city seemed just a little less oppressive. Who knew what treasures existed in this bounty? And it was all hers. At least until the Rat gangs showed up.

There was a rustle behind her. She tensed, peering over her shoulder. A figure emerged, clad in tatters, and covered in dirt. It eyed her suspiciously. But it was weak and sickly, and so it quickly slunk back into the shadows and disappeared. It would wait until she was finished. Crowds attracted patrols, and friends were few here. Clara trudged her way to the top, wading and shifting as quickly as she could. Her eyes sparkled as she pulled a large hunk of sheet metal from the jumble.

Heavily rusted, the scrap was nearly as big as she was. Useful metal was rare enough, and the local mechanics would practically kill each other for a scrap this big. She hefted it above her; it wasn't too heavy to carry. Her eyes widened as she considered the possibilities. She might be able to go to E-level and purchase some real food! Her mouth watered at the thought of a few protein packs all to herself. Perhaps she would even splurge on a flavored variety. Clara had never tasted apple. She didn't even know what an apple looked like.

Clara plowed through the mush—she needed to get off the rotting pyramid and sell her treasure before the Rats came along. She was tough and still young enough to fend off some of the single scavengers, but the Rats were nasty. Rats would steal, lie, and kill to get what they wanted. And with the amount of territory they covered, several may have heard the colossal mound plummet into the depths of Cerberus.

As she scurried towards the bottom, however, there was a soft *plunk* from above.

Clara craned her neck back, hoping to catch a glimpse of what had landed in the jumbled waste, but it was useless.

She bit her lip. Opportunities were not to be missed, but was it better to find something extra or return with what she had?

After a moment's consideration, she placed her treasure carefully out of sight and struggled back to the top, slipping and sliding as she went.

She was disappointed.

Nothing remarkable had magically appeared. Or whatever it was had been sucked into the morass. Another noise made her freeze, and she dropped onto all fours. It had sounded like a cough.

Who's there? She knew better than to say it aloud.

The thought of the Rats flashed across her mind and she shivered. After a few tense moments she lifted her head up, peering around. Nothing.

Her mind was playing tricks on her.

...sniff

This time she knew she had heard something. It was to her left, just over the back of the heap. She crept to the edge, where an old machinery press formed a ledge upon the mountain.

A lip had formed, and Clara peered over it. There was nothing but a bundle of blue blankets. *Those might be val*—the blanket squirmed and she jolted in surprise.

It was a baby.

Clara stared at the tiny child lying in the trash for a few moments before pushing the twinge of pity to the back of her mind and turning her nose up in disgust. She had wasted time, energy, and safety climbing all the way up here.

But maybe there's a reward, she argued with herself.

Clara shook her head. She had seen this kind of deed before—usually when one of the elites wanted to remove evidence of an unacceptable relationship. The mother was hidden away, or became "ill" for several months. And after the baby was born, the child would be quickly and quietly removed.

But this child wasn't dead.

That was amazing in itself, considering the fall. That the babe appeared to be well cared for, despite its predicament, was more intriguing. It couldn't be more than a few weeks old. But what did she know about babies? With a shake of her head, she grabbed again for the blankets.

Her hand stopped at the feeling of a small object trapped within the folds.

Carefully tugging it free, her hand opened to reveal a jeweled locket in the shape of a bird with tiny lettering that Clara struggled to read:

To Natalie, From Magnus

Eternal Love

Clara frowned at the locket and fumbled to open it. A small clasp held the locket together, and after a moment's struggle, it popped open, allowing her a glimpse inside. A picture of a woman rested within, carefully painted in deep hues of red, green and brown. She was beautiful. An innocent smile accented her softly angled face, long flowing hair and deep brown eyes.

As Clara studied the mysterious woman, she realized that the opposite side of the locket also held a picture, but the colors had splotched together into a mess topped by a blob of white. Pulling the locket ever closer, her finger traced edges on the back, and she flipped the jeweled bird over to find more writing. The engraving, however, was deeper and rougher, as if scrawled with a small knife:

may Janus remind you

Puzzlement reflected on Clara's face, as she rolled the odd word over in her mind, *Janus*.

Her sheet metal treasure waited. Placing the locket around her neck with one last look at the infant, she sighed and left the blankets. Scrambling down the heap, she made her way as fast as the loose and shifting garbage would allow.

A high-pitched whistling echoed around the dark walls surrounding her.

Clara crouched low, peering upward in a struggle to fathom the dark smog above her. Something was plummeting through the haze. Straight for her.

4

She leapt out of its path just before it made a sickening impact on the hard-packed earth at the base of the mountain of garbage. The charred and smoking armor of a former Corporate Security officer lay broken at her feet. Her mouth hung open in wonder, but her eyes reflected no pity.

The local sergeant controlling this section of Cerberus was a man named Martel, a particularly nasty specimen of a creature. Any slummer who assaulted one of his patrols would be subject to the strictest of military discipline: death. Even the Rats avoided crossing Martel.

Clara was not particularly saddened by the loss of one of Cerberus' finest.

This trooper's armor was only identifiable in its shape. Its occupant and markings were burned beyond recognition. But it wasn't the special modified variant that Martel wore, just standard Cerberus issue.

She peered into the open visor, wondering what could have happened. The stench of burning flesh that struck her was nauseating and she was overcome by the need to escape the odor. She backed away from the corpse just as her ears perked up to the sound of Carrion Eaters, their engines shrieking as they flew through the alleys.

Rats!

She whirled in her search for an escape route, scolding herself for her stupidity. A soldier had fallen into the slums in a fiery blaze. She could think of few things that would attract more attention.

As the whine of their engines intensified, the bile rose in her throat. There was nowhere to go but *up*! Her prize forgotten, Clara scrambled upwards. A squeal sounded from nearby; the patrol had found the poor creature that had slunk into the dark earlier. New urgency overtook her as she clawed her way up the greasy waste, the whine growing louder until it filled her ears.

The Carrion Eaters roared as they raced into the clearing, and she tumbled out of sight over the top of the hill.

She kept quiet, listening as the Rats sped around the small space and then raced off as another cry sounded from afar. *Too close.*

A chill ran down her spine and a new thought flooded through her—*the baby!* If the abandoned child hadn't stopped her, she would have been running down the very same alley that—she wiped the thought from her mind, but compulsively twisted to her left. The blue blankets peeked over the wrapping of a protein pack. She looked away, shaking her head.

A whine of engines echoed softly from between the alleys.

No.

But as she stood, the jeweled locket brushed against her chest, and she stared at it for a moment. With a final growl of frustration, she hustled over to the bundled child, scooped him up in her arms, and took off running down the other side of the hill.

– BOOK I –

MERCENARY'S CHILD

The World Is Changing, Great Executors.

With the fall of Phoenix Corporation, a vacuum has been created within the Corporate hierarchy. It must be clear that Cerberus is a full contender for dominance. I suggest we make use of our mobile forces to secure additional outposts and territory while our opponents are off balance. Our intelligence indicates that we sustained the fewest losses during the recent battle. By engaging in selective assaults against our weakest competitors, namely Titan and Hydra, we may obtain new and valuable territory without raising the ire of the surviving Corporations.

On this note, I must make you aware of the reports of a recent power shift in Titan Corporation's Executor structure. After the catastrophic disease that swept through Titan, a new player has joined the Executor ranks. He is an unknown, although our reports suggest that he was responsible for the large supplies of Immutium alloy that went missing from Cerberus outposts. Increased efforts must be made to monitor Titan's power so that it can never again threaten us. I will be devoting a great deal of my time and resources in the coming months trying to learn more of what has transpired there.

The world is changing, Great Executors. And we must be the ones who change it.

- Letter from *Colonel Victoria Middleton*, Intelligence and Affairs, to the Executors, Cerberus Corporation

CHAPTER 1
CERBERUS

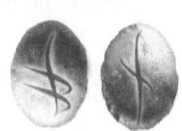

A young man of about nineteen perched on a lamppost that had pitched over and now leaned perilously against the ruins of a long-forgotten building. His hair was a dark brown, contrasting sharply with his sickly pale skin. But his eyes shone bright as he surveyed the scene around him.

"Janus, get down from there, you're too visible."

He heard Clara's exasperated sigh behind him. He missed the days when she'd been able to keep up with him, but he had grown tall. For a slum dweller, at least. Average, perhaps, for one of the upper elite. In the narrow alleys of the slums, the small, quick and lithe had the advantage.

"In a minute," Janus replied. "I'll find something we can sell for supplies. This is the best way to do it. Besides, the Rats could spot us just as easily on the ground."

Every year, the conditions grew worse. And now, the slums had fallen on harder times than ever. No one quite knew why. There was little Janus could do about it other than try to keep the pair of them afloat. Every day, they scoured the slums for new treasures. Sometimes they were lucky. Sometimes, like today, they found nothing.

But the danger was always there. Rats—the scourge of the slums, lurked, waiting for the unaware, or the unfortunate. By scouting ahead, he might just be able to give some warning of an incoming Carrion Eater. Clara hated for him to be the one in danger. If any Rats were to surprise them, he would surely be caught.

"Alright, I'm coming down now, mother…"

Janus kept his back to Clara, but he knew she would be smiling. It seemed so stiff, but he knew she enjoyed hearing that word. He couldn't even use it in protest. It made her feel, if only for a moment, like some highborn Overlord. For all the trouble he gave her, it was the least he could do.

Although she would never admit it, he knew she was slowing down. Just a bit. She was still smarter and faster than most. Her black hair still shined, even in the dark of the slums. But Janus knew that the day would come when only he could safely venture out. It troubled him. She was the only family he knew. And the only person he cared about in the world.

He twisted around on the lamppost, catching Clara fiddling with her locket. It was a beautiful jeweled bird, unlike anything he had ever seen, and Clara's most precious possession. *Next to myself, of course*, Janus thought with a laugh. He only ever caught glimpses of it, when she fiddled with it while worried or distracted. He had asked her about it once, but she had reacted angrily to his queries. She apologized afterward, but he just assumed it was not for him to know.

Janus slid down the pole, leaping off and landing lightly on his feet.

"Something wrong?"

She snapped out of her reverie. His face was a combination of worry and concern.

"No, of course not." Clara smiled.

"Good." Janus turned on his heel and weaved his way between the great heaps of garbage, his footsteps muted by the mush. He could hear her close behind.

"These piles have nothing," he called back softly. "They've already been stripped bare."

It was not unexpected. It didn't take long for any new dump to be picked clean. He stopped at a new pile, waiting for her to catch up. As Clara came around the corner, she glanced at the sky. The last vestiges of light were disappearing from the murky haze above.

"We should probably get back." She bit her lip. "Soon it will be too dark to find much of anything, and the Rats will be out."

Janus scowled.

"Who cares? They're idiots. We can outsmart them."

"They're still vicious, and ignoring them won't help you get out of a situation."

"That doesn't change what they are."

"Let's just get back safely," Clara sighed. "Then we can argue without fear of being caught."

They moved as silently as they could, sticking to the edges of the heaps, and held their breath whenever they heard the familiar *whirrrr* of a Carrion Eater.

Their beacon of safety was a crumbled and sagging structure of wood and concrete. Snaking their way inside, the pair emerged into an ancient and decaying lobby. Letting his eyes adjust to the gloom, he could see the crumbled molding, broken tile, and familiar wrecked elevator wreathed in snapped cables that forever greeted them. He quietly passed an ancient wooden desk where the remnants of a cracked brass plaque hung on a wall, too worn to read. The hole-filled walls whistled with the hot winds of the slums. An ancient stairway, piled in the broken remnants of the ceiling above, protested grimly as he leapt along.

At the end of the hall, around a gaping chasm in the floor, he stopped at room number eight and carefully pushed open the little door. He stopped and listened. The *drip, drip, drip* of the faucet echoed from the sink in the corner. He touched a switch, and a single, dim bulb feebly glowed, illuminating an old armchair and a cracked shelf full of books. A sense of well-being suffused him—their tiny oasis lay untouched. In the corner sat a ratty mattress, which he hopped upon, crossing his arms behind him. He didn't know what fortune had led Clara here—she had found it abandoned shortly after rescuing him. But to this day, it possessed both power and water—precious gifts in the slums. Fusion had made the Corporations lax; the energy required was abundant. It was the maintenance of the pipes and generators that was hard now. Carefully barring the door, Clara plopped down in the chair. Janus propped himself up on his elbows.

"You'll be going to work in the morning?"

"Yes, Miss Middleton wants me to prepare for her party all day tomorrow."

"Middleton wants a lot of things," Janus scoffed. "She doesn't seem to care how she gets them."

"*Miss* Middleton is an Overlord of Cerberus, responsible for the well-being of millions. She can get whatever she wants. And I'm lucky to have work as it is."

Janus looked around the room critically. Clara did not miss his gaze. She grunted irritably.

"Maybe I should spend less time finding books for you then. Saves money, and maybe you won't be so obnoxious."

Janus grinned.

"Too late for that."

Clara cracked a smile, but quickly reverted to a grimace.

"We only have a few hours before the next worker cycle," she said.

"Then we should get some sleep. I'll go with you to the station tomorrow."

"I…" She raised a finger to protest, thought better of it, and instead snatched the blanket beside her armchair.

Janus merely shrugged. Even now, she still didn't like him exploring the slums alone. He curled up on the mattress so that his legs no longer hung over it.

He closed his eyes, listening to Clara's breathing slow as she was beckoned into sleep by fatigue and the *drip, drip, drip* of the faucet.

When she was deeply asleep, Janus rose. Carefully opening the old door and slipping out into the hall, he hugged the side of the old stairway to avoid the groaning steps. Choosing a direction opposite their search this morning, he padded silently through the slums.

The slums at night were nearly as active as the day, and only the world above kept them on any sort of schedule. The haze of the factories and numerous lights from above provided a dim glow that gently illuminated the dusty ground.

One thing was certain. Night was always more dangerous, as the Rats were most active, avoiding the occasional security patrol from above. All around, their screeches, cries, and the whining of their engines made the alleyways claustrophobic. But this was also the best chance to catch fresh garbage, and scout out scrounging spots for the next few days.

Janus' legs powered him quickly over the uneven terrain, his gaze only skimming the piles as he passed. His search was more for information than anything else. *Would prefer not to have to explain any finds to Clara, unless it is something really spectacular.* Eyes darting high and low, he roamed the wastes.

He returned after two hours, his search mostly fruitless. Nothing new had been dumped in the regions he had found, but at least he could discretely steer Clara and himself away from those areas. Leaping over a few of the squeakiest steps, he landed in the hall and silently crept to door number eight. Gently opening the door, he slid inside. Carefully sinking onto his mattress, exhaustion overcame him, and he quickly fell asleep.

He awoke to a dim room, a small amount of light filtering through the many cracks and holes in the walls.

Another day...

It took a few minutes, but Clara finally stirred. Removing herself slowly from the comfort of her armchair, Janus watched her with some amusement as she mentally prepped herself for the long trek to the station. It never changed—she was comfortingly predictable. After a few moments, she stood up and moved easily through the dark to the light switch. He heard the flick of the switch, but the room remained dark.

Her muttered curse was unintelligible.

"Light out?"

"Yes."

Janus bit back his tongue. It would be tough to find a new bulb.

"Here, take your supplement," Clara instructed him.

Janus hated that she used a large portion of her meager earnings each month to pay for a supplement to replace his lack of nutrition. The slums were a notoriously poor place to try and raise a healthy child. There had been a brief period when Janus had resisted the supplement—he didn't think he needed it, nor did he want her wasting the money. But when Clara had continued to purchase the supplement, letting it rot rather than bend to Janus' pride, he'd discovered that his biological parents were probably not the only ones who had put a stubborn streak in him.

"Are you ready?" Clara spoke from the darkness near the door.

"Why wouldn't I be?" Janus said grumpily as he downed the foul-tasting liquid.

"Well, at least I know the supplement is working today."

Janus smiled in the dim light.

"Let's go."

They made their way through the silent slums, focusing on navigating the repugnant obstacles that lay ahead of them.

Trash was both a blessing and curse for the slums. It provided for them, but made the crowded byways a fetid mess. Clara had explained

16

that the real problem began soon after the invention of fusion power. Although recycling was very popular in the days before fusion, it had now become much more "efficient" to produce new products than spend the time sorting the various wastes. Fusion was another double-edged sword for the slums, costing them the few precious recycling jobs that were available, but providing the electricity they needed so survive.

"They've dumped even more trash here since last time," Clara said. "The Rats will be all over this tonight, and pretty soon this whole area will be muck. We'll need a route to the station."

"We can look for one in a couple of days."

"Why not tomorrow?"

"Middleton will want you to clean up after her party, won't she?"

"I completely forgot about that." Clara slapped her forehead.

"Of course, if both of us are busy searching for a new path, we won't have much time to look for things to sell…"

"You may think you're clever," Clara growled, "but I'm not stupid. I won't have you exploring the slums on your own."

"I'm not a child. And I'm better than you at hiding from patrols."

"Yes, but—"

"And I've been making my way back and forth from the station for some time now."

"And you know I hate that—"

"You were on the streets alone for years."

"But—" she sighed. She knew she was defeated. "Fine, you can go. But please…please be careful."

"Thank you, mother." This time it was genuine.

Not another word was said between them as they passed through the slums towards the station, finally arriving at the clearing surrounding it as the hour approached six.

17

Stopping just out of sight, Clara pulled a carefully folded servant's uniform from her knapsack. Slummers weren't technically allowed on the upper levels, and the punishment could be severe if caught. Clara had devised a careful routine to ensure that she at least appeared clean, even if she still needed a shower. As she went into a dark corner to change, Janus stepped onto an old aqueduct wall to look at their destination.

The station had a deep black shine and smooth edges that made it appear as if a giant piece of polished obsidian had been dropped in the middle of the city. Bright lights illuminated the outside, giving the station a strange, otherworldly glow. The light pulsed, giving Janus the sensation that he had stumbled upon the jagged, black heart of some giant creature.

And indeed, the lift stations were the heart of the city. If the people were the blood, the stations kept them flowing. All eleven levels of the city were connected through the central stations. There were seven, scattered across Cerberus. Hardened and protected, the lift stations had been built into the city's design as a defense mechanism. Without control of the lifts, it would be impossible for any ground assault to succeed.

Level Nine, the lowest of all the levels, consisted only of the slums. Long forgotten and unused, the slums were the bowels of Cerberus, the foundation of the great superscrapers that surrounded Janus. It was utterly ignored by the upper castes but for a few exceptions.

Eight, Seven, and Six comprised the factory levels. Sometimes, when the sun was high overhead, and the fog wasn't too thick, Janus could see the crisscrossing bridge-ways of the factories and hear the roaring machinery from the top of a large trash pile. The factory levels produced vast quantities of goods, materials, and even food for the populace of the city. Interspersed between the great factories were quarters devoted to the men and women who kept them running. Worked by millions, they were little better than the slums, but at least provided some element of stability and safety. Whole generations lived and died working the same factories, in what amounted to small cities nestled amongst great furnaces and massive gears.

Levels Five, Four, and Three were dedicated to the Corporate Security Forces, with easy access to most of the rest of the city. The Corporate Security Forces were the largest employer of all. They were the fist of the Executors, maintaining order and stability throughout the Corporation and its outlying territory.

Level Two provided the power and water for the city, supplying the people through its maze of pipes, pumps, and conduits.

And Level One was devoted to research and administration. It was said that little research, but much administration occurred there these days. That the Executors had to focus on maintenance of the Corporation, rather than expansion or improvement.

But Level One was far from the top. Level E was the primary residence of the skilled workforce, and the place where most of the city's commerce occurred. It was the lifeblood of the Corporation in many ways, and played host to millions upon millions, housing those who worked on all of the primary systems of the Corporations—from factory foremen and engineers, to merchants and tradesmen. It was crowded, and rough. But as long as the predominant rule of law and order survived, the Security Forces turned a blind eye. Control and wealth were the concerns of the Executors; the petty indulgences of the masses could be ignored.

And finally, there was Level H. Home of the Executors and their servants: the Overlords, upper castes, and ranking military. It was from there that the Executors ruled. It was also the only part of the city actually subject to direct sunlight.

Emerging from the shadows in her simple white uniform, Clara took the knapsack and her collection of rags and hid them carefully in a loose drainage grate. Motioning she was ready, the pair moved on.

As they crossed the circular clearing that surrounded the glowing lift station, two guards signaled for them to approach. They were Cerberus Security, and truly imposing. Their armor, a terrifying mass of plates and muscle-like ripples, added easily a half-meter to even the most ordinary soldier. Composed of ceramium, the tough, thick, purple-and-black

19

armor was well protected against almost any threat, except for the massive, fearsome Zeus rifles each gripped in their hands.

And set within the heavy helmet was a wide, opaque, Pellucidum visor that allowed the soldiers excellent sight, but gave no glimpse of the man inside—if there even was one.

Janus had heard the tales from other slummers about the inhuman characteristics of the Security Troopers, or STs. He didn't believe them, but he understood why Corporate Security did nothing to dissuade the rumors. Besides, pretending that there was no man inside made it that much easier for Janus to despise them.

"ID?" one of the two guards demanded on their approach.

Clara pulled out her unique Cerberus ID that allowed her access to the upper levels, a rarity in the slums. It was quite possibly the most valuable thing she owned. A simple, partially translucent square, the ID displayed her picture as she handed it over to the guards, and it glowed green as they held a scanner to her arm to confirm her vein structure and identity.

The guard hardly glanced at the scanner before lazily motioning for her to pass through the gate to the station.

The second guard motioned roughly at Janus with his rifle.

"Ya?"

"Was just leaving," Janus stated blandly, ignoring the attempt to intimidate him.

The guard who had inspected Clara's ID turned to face Janus.

"You shoul' show some respect."

Janus gave him a pitying look and then turned with a smile to Clara.

"Have a good day," he waved cheerily.

"You not hear me, mudfish?" the first guard grunted at Janus.

Clara had frozen in the doorway at Janus' reply. She did not wave back, but instead gave him an angry gaze, mouthing *no*. As the two guards advanced on him, her look became desperate.

Janus sighed, and glanced at the first guard, who was in the process of clumsily trying to shove him. The blow from the armored soldier surely would have sent him flying, but the guard was simply moving too slowly. They always moved too slowly. Janus took a step back, easily dodging the simple attack.

"You little—" the guard spluttered as he stumbled forward. Janus smirked and danced away as the guard flung a loose fist towards him. The first guard howled with rage, but the other two laughed.

"Gettin' beat by some kid, Hammer?"

Clara rushed towards the fight, but was grabbed by a third trooper.

"Janus!"

Janus bit his lip guiltily. As Hammer turned to face him, Janus raised his hands in truce.

"Listen, we both know you could take my head off with a punch, so why don't we call it quits for today?"

"Yeah, Hammer, quit while you're only slightly behind," one of the other guards teased.

"Shut it, McKnight," Hammer replied. "You think I'm going to let this kid make a fool of me? Let's see how well you run from a bolt."

Janus felt his whole body tense as the barrel of the Zeus swung towards him, but McKnight quickly grabbed the barrel.

"Might not want to do that."

"Don't tell me you're soft on this mudfish."

"No, but one of the Overlords might be. There's a request for him." He motioned his helmet to the console behind him.

"What?" Clara exclaimed.

"Supposed to send him up with the woman. Come here, kid." McKnight gestured with his free hand to Janus, who eyed him suspiciously. Clara held her breath.

"I was rootin' for ya', remember?" McKnight laughed. "Besides, orders is orders. We can't let you outta sight now."

Janus didn't move.

McKnight grabbed Clara roughly. She gasped in pain.

"I mean it, kid."

Janus scowled, but walked confidently towards the guard.

"That's it. Go on. Straight up to Overlord Middleton." McKnight nodded at Clara. "I presume you know to head there straightaway."

Clara nodded numbly.

"Good. Let them through."

The other guards stepped aside. Janus could feel Hammer's burning eyes through the opaque visor, and he smiled at the angry guard as he passed.

Chapter 2
The Silver-Haired Man

After an interminably tense few moments, the pair passed the checkpoint and entered the obsidian structure. Janus could feel Clara's anxiety, her eyes jumping back to him every few moments.

Janus let his gaze wander over the lift station. The interior reflected the twisted outside, except the walls gave off a darker, redder glow. A Security Officer in a standard black-and-purple Cerberus uniform worked the raised control room in the center of the station, watching the incoming pair through a heavy window. Engraved into the tower wall that extended above him, the Three-Headed Dog of Cerberus howled. Ten heavily armored doors cut into the ceiling designated where each lift would descend, riding magnetic tracks up and down the walls of the station.

Only two of the seven lift stations across Cerberus served the slums, and only one lift within each of those stations ever came down this far. There wasn't much need for more. From what Clara had told him, most traffic hovered between the factory and security levels, anyway.

Janus watched as a flat, heavy platform wide enough for a hundred slummers descended gently to the ground. At Clara's urging, he stepped aboard with a huddled group clustered near the edge. Grease stains and tread marks dotted the rusting surface.

A few troopers manned each of the gates, lazily watching for activity, but mostly looking as though they wondered why they had been relegated to such a position.

"Good morning, Clara."

Clara startled out of her reverie, and Janus whirled around to find a kindly looking old man perched on a gnarled wooden walking stick standing beside her. His face bore tired lines and his spotted hands spoke to his age, but his bright blue eyes peeking out from under bushy white brows suggested a spark of energy deep within him. Straight silver hair was cropped upon his head, and a brown, sharply pressed servant's uniform with two rows of pockets gave him a distinguished air.

"Norm, I didn't see you there."

"I do tend to slip under noses," Norm chuckled.

"Sorry, I was just a little distracted."

"I see." Norm smiled. "And you must be the young Janus."

Janus nodded. He had heard of Norm before, but he had never met him. He and Clara had been friends for many years, and he was the only other person in the slums Janus knew to possess an H-Level ID card.

Norm's face became serious, and he turned to Clara.

"Trouble?"

"He's being requested on the upper level."

"By whom?"

"Middleton," Janus interjected.

Janus was surprised by the flash of panic that appeared in Norm's eyes, but in an instant, it was gone. Norm rubbed his chin thoughtfully.

"Does she know you have a son?"

"She's never asked," Clara said, her eyes searching the floor. "But I suppose she might have heard something from one of the other maids? Or Albert?"

"Perhaps she's looking for a new servant? Since you're so trustworthy?"

Clara's eyes brightened, and as the lift hummed to life beneath them, the pair shifted topics. It had been two weeks since their last meeting, and their discussion ranged from where the best trash piles seemed to be falling to the latest gossip they had "overheard" during their shifts.

"How's Alastor doing, Norm?"

"Bit agitated recently, something regarding one of the other Overlords. You know how it is. They're always at each other's throats. I think the Executors encourage it." He paused, troubled. "Although, I have heard rumors of another draft hitting the slums soon. The Overlords and Executors all seem more focused on their own power struggles now."

He grimaced, turning to look Janus in the eye.

"Their power is slipping. The Corporations are weakening."

They stopped at the lowest factory level, picking up workers from their nightshifts. Even the walls of the station could not escape the pollution of the level, a brownish tinge coating every surface. Clara and Norm pulled out handkerchiefs from their uniforms, tying them around their faces. She handed a spare to Janus, who mimicked them with a few simple ties.

The lift jolted to a start once more and Janus stared in wonder as they rose up through the city of heavy machinery. Clanking hammers rang out, while massive cranes whirred and forges blazed waves of heat. But here and there Janus caught glimpses of darkness. Conveyors that stood still. Empty warehouses with flickering lights. And more than a few rusting hulks.

Clara pointed to an active forge, bustling with workers. A large, tracked vehicle hauled red-hot beams between the forge and an oil bath.

"The Daedulus is back online. They must have finally repaired it."

Janus nodded, though he had never seen one of the intelligent machines before, he was familiar enough with their concept through his books that its appearance did not alarm him.

"Here, lad. Put these on." Norm handed Janus a wraparound visor. "I found these a while back. Why anyone would have thrown them away is a mystery to me."

Janus was dumbfounded by the bizarre sunshade.

"Er, thank you Norm. What are these for?"

"Your eyes are unaccustomed to the sunlight; you'll need them."

"Make sure you wear those whenever you're outside, otherwise your eyes might get damaged. Growing up in the darkness of the slums makes you more susceptible than others. You should also cover up as much as you can, as you are sure to get burned if you stay out too long."

"Thank you, Norm," Clara said, and gave him a glowing smile. Janus was still looking down at the hideous glasses, until Clara dug an elbow into his ribs. He turned away, exasperated.

They stopped once more at the highest factory level, as most of the tired workers filed off. Beside them, a fresh batch of workers crowded onto a lift that had already started down, shoving themselves as close together as possible.

"Attacks have been stepping up lately," Norm said quietly, as the lift departed again. Janus perked his ears up, always eager to hear more about the world outside. From the corner of his eye, he watched Clara lean in towards Norm, stealing a surreptitious glance at Janus.

"Why?" she said. "How many have there been?"

Janus shifted his weight to place himself just a little closer. The lift stopped on one of the military levels, letting off a group of repairmen.

"I heard of at least ten. Mostly just minor Cerberus territories. The Overlords are blaming the Legions, but it's rumored to be the work of one of the other Corporations."

"Legions?" Janus asked quietly, but Clara whistled softly over him.

"There haven't been that many attacks in a long time," she breathed.

"Since before the time you found Janus," Norm said, biting his lip in worry.

Clara stared out at the city as the lift rose steadily. The fog and smoke were slowly becoming brighter. Streams of light cascaded from above.

"We're passing E-level," she said to Janus. "H-level is next."

The sounds of bustling people grew loud around him. She smiled and then turned back to Norm, resuming her whisper. Janus strained to hear.

"I just hope it doesn't spill into the main city. I've heard that can be horrific."

"Yes." Norm paused. "For now, it's a problem for the Executors. Hopefully though, the Corporation will start looking for more soldiers soon."

"I hope not. I know you and I are safe from the draft, but Janus isn't, and the last thing he needs is an opportunity to mouth off to an official."

"Yes, but don't you want him to have more opportunity? And there would be less people picking through the slums!"

"I don't want him sacrificing himself for a Corporation that has done noth—"

Suddenly, the lift exploded through a layer of cloud and a blinding light cut her off. Janus struggled to shield his eyes from it.

They had reached H-level.

CHAPTER 3
BEYOND THE SLUMS

The depthless dark of Cerberus had given way to shimmering gilded towers of glass and marble, crowned in wreaths of white angelic statues and spires lifting towards a bright blue sky. A sudden warmth suffused Janus' skin, and he pressed closer to the edge, struggling to absorb every glorious ray.

The lift slid silently into the station at H-level with Janus squinting upward towards the sky, unaware they had reached their platform. Sunlight streamed through the H-station's glass dome. Gold-fluted columns reached from floor to ceiling, shining brilliantly in the sun.

Clara quickly pulled him off the lift.

"Pay attention," she chided. "You can't afford to lose your head here!"

Norm was already gone.

Janus let his eyes wander the station and suddenly felt extremely self-conscious. Staring down at the ill-fitting rags he wore, he could feel the eyes of the hundreds of elite that surrounded him and hear murmurs of—*can't even dress servants properly*.

"Don't worry," whispered Clara. "People always stare, but it's nothing we can't handle."

She made a beeline out of the station and onto the main thorough-fare, Janus right behind. Despite his appearance, the Troopers made no effort to stop their exit.

He was amazed by the bustling chaos around him. There were never so many people out and about in the slums; a crowd would be a magnet to the Rats. Out of the shade of the station, Janus was forced to narrow his eyes to slits. The crowds gave him a wide berth, but seemed mostly unbothered by his presence.

People avoid each other up here as well, he thought.

Gazing back at the outside of the station, Janus was surprised to dis-cover it was enameled in a deep emerald green. It still possessed its odd angular walls, but the menace was gone. Instead, thriving flora filled the niches, giving the impression the whole station was covered in grass. Gold Cerberus statues flanked the entrances, and the only ST within sight car-ried no rifle, but helpfully directed passersby as they approached.

"Come on." Clara was motioning for Janus to follow her. "We've got to get moving or we'll be late!"

Janus was chilled in the early morning air, his breath rising in puffs as his skin searched for warmth against the thin rags. As they hurried along, a gaggle of children momentarily stopped their play within a cloud to eye them uncertainly.

They were going to see Miss Middleton, but he knew almost nothing about her. Middleton was an Overlord, and a powerful one at that. Only a step below the supreme masters of Cerberus, the Executors. Her home, Clara had said, was the crown of one of the gigantic superscrapers that made up the multi-level metropolis.

And Clara was one of her maids. Janus knew she was thankful for it. Real, non-hazardous work was rare nowadays, and even then, most things were performed by Daeduluses—when they didn't break, anyway. Even when they did work, they lacked the understanding to value the subtle, yet messy, brushstrokes of a work of art. One too many paintings had been "cleaned" for Middleton's taste. And so, Clara was a maid. At least, that was how Clara told it.

An iron-wrought fence of elaborate spirals enclosed Middleton's private hideaway, forcing passersby to steal tempting looks at sprinkling fountains and lush gardens of red, blue, and yellow. Deep jade-green and sapphire-blue walls shimmered in the sun, while gilded frames held sparkling crystalline windows overlooking the lawns.

Clara avoided the ornate gate that stood closed to all but the greatest of dignitaries, and instead made her way to a recessed door in the back. She knocked twice and a stately butler soon answered.

"Ah Miss Clara. Miss Middleton is expecting you and the young man…"

He paused.

"Janus," Clara chimed in with a bow.

"Very good," Albert said, looking her over. "I'm afraid there isn't enough time for a proper cleaning, but may I suggest you consider a change of clothes?"

Clara nodded her understanding, and the butler stood aside to admit her and Janus into a set of servants' quarters. A changing station for most of Middleton's staff, the quarters bustled with maids and cooks who urgently sought to prepare themselves for another demanding day at the behest of their master. Only the head gardener and Middleton's favorite chef had lodgings here. Albert, the butler, was afforded space in the home proper.

Clara joined several women hustling to a set of showers in another room, leaving Janus behind to wait. Albert did not leave his side for a moment. When Clara emerged just a minute or so later, she wore a beautiful, flowing blue gown made of a rich silk.

Janus stared, awestruck. She looked so elegant and refined, as if she were a totally different person. Clara smiled at his reaction, but she did not pause. Carefully, she deposited her plain white servant's uniform in a locker. It would be cleaned and pressed for her when she returned; Albert would make sure of it.

Another maid, wearing the same but in green, emerged behind her, and Albert gave her a sweeping gaze and a tiny nod. She bowed respectfully to Albert and headed out the door.

Clara stopped before Albert with a twirl. Albert tilted his head in acceptance, and with a reluctant sigh towards Janus shooed both of them through the door. Together, the three headed out into the lawn. Clara was careful to avoid sullying or tearing her uniform on the high bushes and flowerbeds. Rushing into the house, they sped up the servants' stairs behind the kitchen, and soon arrived in a small sitting room in front of two great oak doors, gilded handles set deep into the wood.

"Wait quietly," Albert stated, standing stiffly beside the door. Clara fidgeted with her hands. Janus crossed his arms and leaned against the wall. Soft lighting illuminated the hallway, casting a gentle glow on the flowing oil paintings of men and women in prodigious robes, all bearing the three-headed mark of Cerberus. Dark rugs ran the length of the hall, overlaying elegant wood floors, while sculptures and antiquities lined the walls. Awed by the wealth and grandeur that surrounded him, he wondered what it would be like to live in such a place. *Waited on by servants and soldiers...*

"No smart remarks," Clara whispered fervently. "And think about everything you say. Miss Middleton is a very—*grand* woman, and prone to sensitivity."

Albert shot her a disapproving look.

Suddenly Middleton's raised voice could be heard clearly through the thick wood. It was somewhat high, not pleasing in the slightest.

"We aren't interested right now! How many times do I have to tell you? Cerberus needs the extra support for our infantry units! And you charge far too much for everything else!"

31

Janus unconsciously leaned closer to the door, straining to hear what was being said. Albert glared, but Janus ignored him.

"Perhaps...other...could be made...?" a second voice said urgently. The voice was strange, with a thick accent.

Middleton's response softened this time, though it still carried.

"How...offering?"

"Ten per..." the voice said.

"Well...arrangements...suit well."

The great gilded knob twisted suddenly, and the left door cracked open.

"One week, Mr. Ambassador?" The door stopped in mid-swing.

"It would be better if we could make the arrangement sooner, actually," the ambassador said.

"How about tomorrow, then, early morning? I was already planning on making several transactions tomorrow," Middleton said confidently.

"That would be excellent."

"We shall eagerly await ODIN's arrival. In the meantime, I will have someone show you to a room."

"Your hospitality is always appreciated, Overlord Middleton."

Albert stepped forward as the door swung open entirely, revealing a dark-skinned man with brown eyes and silver hair. He wore thick black clothing with a gold-and-red pin on the high neck.

"This way please, sir."

"Thank you," the man said politely, but Janus caught a faint 'hate that damn woman' muttered under his breath.

Before he turned to guide the ambassador, Albert bowed towards the open doors.

"My lady, your maidservant Clara and her son are here at your request."

"Send them in."

Janus stood up straight, uncrossing his arms. Albert glared at him.

"Miss Middleton will see you now."

CHAPTER 4
MIDDLETON

As Clara led the way through the heavy oak doors, Janus could barely contain his laughter at the sight of the woman who stood before him. His first impression of her was that of a pig in a peacock suit. Standing regally behind a cherry-wood desk, Middleton was the most ridiculous creature Janus had ever set eyes on.

Her nose was squashed and snout-like as the fat forced her nostrils outward. Large plumed feathers and sequins decorated the gaudiest blue dress Janus could imagine. A monstrous sapphire necklace struggled to be noticed against her rolling bosom, while bracelets looked fit to burst from her wrists. Her massive jowls gave the impression of a puffer fish, while her bulging body fought to escape the confines of her dress. Fingers like sausages drummed the desk before them, large rings stuck between the second and third knuckles, unable to pass any further. She breathed heavily, like she was in a constant struggle for air. And although her skin was smooth and fair, her hair was streaked with silver, a sign she no longer possessed the youth and vigor she once had.

He smirked, but quickly hid his smile. Clara stood trembling in front of him, and Janus gave her shoulder a quick sympathetic pat before returning his stare to the generously sized woman before him. Her eyes never wavered from the parchment thin computer screen, its appearance like that of dull aluminum foil. Clara fidgeted nervously.

Rich tapestries and paintings hung from the walls, depicting great battles and victories of Cerberus. More than a few were dominated by images of Cerberus troops standing over crushed and broken armies. Lush blue carpet accented the dark swirls and dyes of the paintings and hangings.

Middleton regally raised her head, waving her hand at the screen as it rolled up and closed like a piece of paper. Clara hastily stared at the floor, unconsciously taking a step back, giving Middleton a full view of Janus. The woman froze, a hint of surprise upon her face, but only for a moment. She stared hard at Janus.

"This is your son?"

"Yes, Miss," Clara said with a quick bow.

Middleton looked briefly unsettled, but shook her head.

Clara paled, but Janus didn't blink. Middleton studied him carefully for a moment more then turned to stare out the window behind her desk.

"You're late, maidservant."

"I'm sorry, Miss, the troopers gave us trouble," Clara stammered.

"Do you know why I brought you here?" she asked, still staring out at the grounds.

"No, Miss," Clara said.

"What about you, boy?" Middleton glanced casually at him.

"Well, you don't really seem to be the mothering type, so I don't think you're planning on raining us with gifts."

Clara hissed warningly at him.

The laugh emitted from the piggish snout was uproarious and evil. Janus felt a sudden chill from the sound.

"He didn't mean any disrespect, Miss," Clara said quickly. "He's just a little stupid now and then."

She glared at Janus and made a swift chop across her throat.

"A little stupid?" Middleton turned to them with a smirk on her face. "Your son has developed quite the reputation. If my Troopers are to be believed, this boy here has caused more than his share of trouble. Enough for even the Rats to complain."

"Surely you didn't drag me up here just because some Rats whined," Janus interjected.

"Miss Middleton," Clara hissed at him.

"No, of course not." Middleton smirked. "At least you're smart enough to realize that. I'm more intrigued by other aspects of the reports."

She flipped open the parchment screen again.

"'Boy moves swiftly.' 'Possesses superior speed and agility.' 'Clever, but causes trouble.' 'Can't pin down the damn mudfish.'" She laughed. "That's my favorite. Rats are always so eloquent. And yet, when I tried to bring up the birth files on your son, I discovered he was unregistered. Do you know what the penalties are for not registering?"

Janus flushed with anger.

"How am I supposed to register when I can't even access a lift without an Overlord's order?"

"Do you think that excuses you?"

"Miss Middleton, I—" Clara spouted.

"Do you know what the penalties are for harboring an unregistered individual?" Middleton barked, her smile gone.

Janus stepped forward but Clara yanked him back.

"You belong to Cerberus, boy, registered or not. Do you understand? It's time for you to realize that. I originally summoned you here because of these reports. Cerberus needs more soldiers. I intended to send you for Trooper training."

Janus curled his lip in disgust.

"You think I would agree to be—"

Middleton pushed a button on her desk and cut him off.

"Martel, if you would."

A sudden clomp of boots, and a clawed fist grabbed Janus by the back of the head, forcing him to his knees. He froze, barely breathing. Razor sharp claws surrounded his periphery, and even a slight movement brought them within a hair's breadth of slicing him. A red, two-toed boot was visible between his legs. It was an Infernus Trooper. He had only heard of them, but never seen one. *Still hadn't seen one.*

He became aware of Clara pleading.

"Martel. Please, please Martel."

The pressure on his head was immense. But even in his state, he could feel the delicate control of the Trooper's grip. His head was gently tilted up to face Middleton.

"You'll address me as 'Miss Middleton.'" Middleton smiled pleasantly. "And say it before you say anything else."

She motioned with her head towards Clara, her snout baring sharp teeth.

"I can tell you're the type who thinks you're defiant, so let me make this simple: I'd hate to make an example of your mother. Do you understand?"

Janus blinked in acknowledgement.

"Good." The predatory grin disappeared. "That is enough Martel."

Janus was thrown bodily to the floor, but by the time he turned to face his attacker, the Infernus was already gone. Janus pushed himself up, standing next to Clara. She grabbed him, but did not take her eyes off of Middleton.

"I originally considered fast-tracking you to officer candidacy in the security forces. But I can see now that would be a waste of time. You're far too obstinate and pig-headed," she paused, as if momentarily at a loss, "What was your name?"

Janus seethed, but with a look at Clara's nervous face, he contained himself.

"Miss Middleton—"

Middleton waved him off.

"Honestly, I really don't care. You just need to understand that I control you, and her."

She glanced at Clara, who was now as pale as a ghost.

"And now, with the arrival of ODIN, a far more lucrative opportunity has presented itself to me. You're clearly unfit to be a Trooper, but you might just make the grade as a merc."

"A what?" Janus looked incredulous. Miss Middleton's weariness disappeared and she gave him an angry stare, until he added a quick, "Miss Middleton."

"A mercenary," she began, giving him a wary look, "A soldier we sell to the Legions. Merc Legions are used for less…savory jobs, ones that the Corporation cannot be involved with."

"That's why I'm important?" Janus asked angrily. "You're selling me?"

"You're selling him?" Clara exclaimed.

"Important, hardly," Middleton said with a snort, ignoring Janus' lack of respect. "You're a resource, and we'll be glad to rid ourselves of you."

Janus gritted his teeth and Middleton's smile broadened.

"Of course, that's if you're even capable of passing their test," she added.

"A test?" Janus probed, then hastily added, "Miss Middleton."

"I'm not one for repeating myself, boy. If you pass, you may provide just a tempting enough opportunity to a Legion like ODIN. I have never been much impressed by them, honestly. But in the end, selling to the mercs always turns out to be a good deal for Cerberus."

"But, but, you can't," Clara sputtered. "He's my son—"

"No, he is Cerberus' property," she laughed, "and he may be very lucrative."

Janus' fists clenched. "I'll—I'll make you pay for this—"

"Normally I would have you killed for such a remark," she said, sounding bored. She didn't even glance at the button on her desk. "But your boldness might just impress ODIN. Make a remark like that again, though, and I will string *her* up."

Janus raised a fist, but Clara yanked him back by the neck, pure panic upon her face, and he collapsed to the ground with a cry. He glared at Middleton, rubbing his throat. Middleton sighed, glancing back and forth between Clara's panicked face and Janus' enraged one, and casually pulled her hand away from her desk.

"You wish for your mother to stay alive, correct?"

Janus nodded.

"Then I suggest that both of you go home and grab what little belongs to you. You will show up on Level Four tomorrow at 0600 sharp."

Clara slumped, dejected. Janus stood up and put his arm around her while his eyes blazed hatred at the mammoth woman.

"Good, I'm glad you understand." Middleton scowled. "Now get out of my sight."

Chapter 5
Mother's Dream

It wasn't until they were riding the lift down that Janus spoke.

"I wasn't going to do anything stupid," he pouted. He stared off the edge, avoiding looking at her.

"Even talking back to her in that situation was stupid," Clara scowled.

"Am I just supposed to let her sell me like scrap? Am I supposed to accept her threats?"

The few dreary factory workers perked up at his raised voice, suddenly uneasy.

"No, but maybe if you weren't so damn smug you would be a Trooper now instead of being sold to the highest bidder!" Clara exploded. The workers quickly moved to the far side of the descending platform.

"So this is my fault?" Janus yelled. "You think I'd rather be a Trooper anyway? Doing shakedowns in the slums?"

"Would you rather be sold?" Clara threw her hands up. "At least as a Trooper you might have a future."

"I won't be a pawn! I won't be scum that feeds on the weak!"

"So you'd rather be dead?" Clara pointed to the ground, her voice shaky. "Is that it?"

"Than be stuck following the orders of a tyrant?" Janus shouted.

Clara's voice dropped to a whisper.

"Is life here really so bad? Does nothing here mean anything to you?"

"I'm-I'm sorry," Janus faltered. "I didn't mean it like that. I don't want Middleton to punish you."

Clara shook her head, tears in her eyes. She walked over and hugged him.

"Idiot. I don't care about that. I don't want you to go. I don't know what I would do with myself if I didn't have you."

Janus just stood there, leaning over into the hug. He could feel warm tears on his neck.

"I want you to live a good life. Better than this. I want to know that you're doing something that will give you a future. Not scraping by on bits and pieces tossed your way from above. But you can't do that if you're dead. You can't do that if you can't keep your ego in check for five minutes."

Janus carefully wrapped his arms around Clara.

"I know, mother. I know." He hugged her tighter. "No matter what happens, I'll make you proud."

Clara's head shook, but she said nothing.

A sudden screeching informed them that the lift was approaching the slums lift station. Clara pushed him back, the tears stopped. She swallowed.

"I guess we'll just have to make the best of things. Let's get home, and we'll crack open one of the Passers we've got stored. That'll make a good meal."

Janus nodded, the cold realization hitting that tomorrow might be the last time he would see Clara. A hard, angry lump formed in his throat, but he forced it down with a smile. *I'll meet those mercenaries head on to-morrow.*

The following morning, their journey to the station was quiet. They had stayed up late into the night reminiscing, and there wasn't much left to say. Neither knew what awaited Janus today, and it did the two of them little good to discuss it.

A very nervous-looking guard had let them pass into the station as soon as Janus' face appeared on his security screen. Janus was unsure why he felt so unnerved until he spotted something hanging from the supports above. Grimacing, Janus turned away, feeling his stomach turn. Evidently, Miss Middleton had been displeased with the delay of the previous day. Hammer's skull was apparently not as resilient as his namesake. Janus shook his head, feeling torn by the Trooper's fate.

The station was packed with bodies. Clara and Janus struggled through the crowd to the lift.

"Is it usually this crowded?" Janus gasped.

"I've never seen it like this!" Clara exclaimed.

He could see members of at least a dozen gangs eyeing each other on the lift. Most were big, tough men and women. As Janus looked closer, however, he saw a few anxious individuals who probably survived more on their wits than their brawn.

As they shoved their way through the crowd, it was clear the STs had given up trying to manage the flow of people onto the lift. They shoved on as many as could fit. An ST stuffed the two of them into a walled transport, pressing them against the mass of bodies, holding the crowd in until the last moment as the doors closed. Yells of protest sounded from within.

Edging their way slowly to one side and huddling by the window, they tried to press themselves as close as possible to one another to gain a few more centimeters of space from the crowd.

There was a commotion as nearby Rats muttered angrily at someone who pushed them out of the way. It wasn't long before Janus and Clara saw Norm jostling his way through the crowd.

"Clara, Janus! Thank goodness!"

Norm's face was guarded and he was breathing heavily. He fidgeted nervously at the mob.

"Norm? Are you okay?" Clara asked with concern.

"It's nothing. I just don't do well with enclosed spaces..."

Clara hastily pushed at the throng, trying to make space for Norm. The men and women glared at her angrily, but said nothing. The lifts were not the place to make trouble.

"Thanks, Clara," Norm breathed gratefully to her.

"What's the rush, Norm?" Janus asked without turning to look at him.

Norm paused with thoughtful silence.

"I needed to talk to you," he said, addressing Clara. "What did Middleton want with Janus?"

"She—she's sending him away."

Clara fought to contain herself, but her sudden change of pitch attracted the attentions again of the nearby Rats. But now, they scooted away from her, as if she were contagious.

"She's what?" Norm exclaimed.

"Something, something about soldiers and being sold to—" Clara stammered.

Norm's eyes lit up and he very gently put his hands on Clara's shoulders.

"Is she selling Janus to a mercenary Legion?" he asked, lowering his voice. Clara nodded.

Norm's eyes sparkled with delight and he laughed uproariously, getting more odd looks from the crowd.

"I knew it! They'll regret this!"

Clara stopped her welling tears, regarding Norm with disbelief.

"What?"

"Who?" Janus asked.

"You have been given a great gift, my boy." Norm gave Janus a big smile.

"A Legion is the perfect place for you."

"What are you saying, Norm?" Clara's eyes glowed with a faint ray of hope.

"The boy will have the chance at a life far greater than any a slummer could imagine."

Norm nodded at Janus' doubtful expression.

"Trust me."

The lift slowed, and a voice emanated from the wall speakers.

"Level Four. Military Block. All security personnel and mercenary recruits depart immediately."

The crowd obliged, sending a stream of people swarming into the military block.

"Looks like it is show-time for you and Janus," Norm said. "I'll come by tonight to see you, Clara. Be strong."

He squeezed her shoulder.

"Thank you, Norm." Clara started to smile. "If this is actually Janus' one chance to get out of this dump, then I'll be happy."

"I see that Janus has had as much an effect on you as you have on him," Norm chuckled.

Clara grinned, then hurried to meet Janus at the door of the lift.

Norm raised his hand in farewell.

"Good luck, lad. And remember, it's not how you start; it's how you finish. Make your mother proud."

Janus looked back at the strange man. Norm's eyes were misty.

CHAPTER 6
FACTORIES AND FIGHTERS

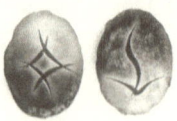

Janus grabbed Clara's hand, and forced his way off the lift and onto Level Four with the rest of the crowd. The middle level of the military block, it marked the final floor of the factories and the transition towards the living spaces. Level Four and Five produced much of Cerberus' arms.

A brownish haze of smoke and grease filled the air, making it difficult to breathe. It was unearthly hot, and the grime clung to their sweaty bodies in the furnace-like heat. They pressed forward into the crowd as it inched along, the horde eager for jobs.

To his left, Janus peered over the mass into the smog, mouth open in wonder at the great factories. Catching a glimpse through a window on his left, he could see liquid metal being shaped into pressed plates of armor. At that moment, the factory ground to a halt, and the last of the plates disappeared down the line. Janus craned to see why, but he was swept along by the tide of slummers.

As they crossed a bridge, a truck as tall as the second story of their hideaway, filled with rocks and earth, thundered along the highway below them. But Janus had no clue where it was headed, and the swarm inched forward, filling the common space shared between several tunnels and railways.

An unarmored officer had clambered to the top of a disused loading arm and was directing the crush of bodies from the station to different areas of the complex. The earth rumbled, as a jawed crane shuttled a thick, ungainly aircraft along the rail overhead, its large wings lording over a cluster of three gigantic engines.

"Dryad," Clara yelled in Janus' ear. "Norm says they're a ground fighter."

The huge craft looked so thick that it could barely get off the ground, but could survive a serious beating.

Janus and Clara struggled forward to the guard, waving to get his attention. The officer looked momentarily confused as the pair shouted, "Mercenaries!" Putting a hand to his ear, it took several tries, but he finally nodded and pointed them towards an arched tunnel opposite the crowd. Janus pulled Clara along, escaping the press and reaching the relatively cool air within the tunnel's thick metal walls.

Two guards were waiting for them inside, a woman in a simple uniform and a fully armored Security Trooper. The woman wore the red cross of a battlefield medic. She looked almost bored as she motioned them over.

"Routine blood test before we ship you out, nothing to worry about," she stated.

After she finished, she gave the other guard the okay and turned to Janus and Clara.

"She'll escort you to Overlord Middleton."

Janus took her word for it. It was impossible to tell anything about what was inside the massive armor. It clomped along, huge boots echoing through the tunnel. The three soon emerged into a small rail station. The air was slightly less hazy, but no less hot. An open-air train car sat hovering slightly off the ground, as electricity crackled through the rail below it. Every so often, a tiny bolt would leap from the track, racing along the heavy air to the edge of the platform.

The car itself was a simple troop carrier. No frills, just seats, as many crammed in as possible.

Just beyond the car, Miss Middleton waited for them in a sedan chair with four STs, one at each corner. Janus had no idea of their rank, but they carried themselves and their rail-guns with a certain level of confidence that suggested they were used to Middleton's presence.

About twenty other would-be recruits glanced around at Miss Middleton and the Security Troopers nervously. The group was huddled near the car, and the variety of clothes suggested that Janus was the odd man out from the slums. He felt slightly self-conscious in his rags.

"There's no one from the elite," Clara whispered to Janus. Janus nodded in agreement; not one wore the finery he had seen from his brief trip to H-level.

Miss Middleton did not look particularly happy about coming down to Level Four, and covered her mouth and nose with a handkerchief that was quickly turning from white to black in the caustic air. She motioned for Janus. He gave Clara a smile and, ignoring the menacing Security Troopers, made his way over to Miss Middleton.

"Now, boy," she said as he approached. "I will not stand for any trouble from you, or that dog you call a 'mother,' Mara…"

"Clara," Janus corrected, struggling to keep his temper in check.

"Whatever." Miss Middleton waved absently. "She will keep you from causing any irritations. You know we won't harm you too much; but make any mistakes and she meets an unfortunate end. Understood?"

Janus made no reply, but stared defiantly at Miss Middleton.

She stood up to address the recruits and cleared her throat.

"It is my unfortunate displeasure that I should be responsible to make sure that all goes well today. You will follow me and do as you are told. That is all."

Miss Middleton motioned for them to get on the car, still covering her nose and mouth.

Janus and Clara clambered in with the other recruits. It quickly became clear that the seats were designed for STs, not people, and Janus struggled to strap himself in. Three of the infantryman took up positions around them, while the fourth escorted Middleton to the front of the car, then hopped into the passenger seat. Middleton fit perfectly.

Another ST came running up to Middleton as she maneuvered her large bulk at the front of the car. Janus struggled to hear what he was saying to her:

"Overlord Middleton…a problem with some of the STs…command of Overlord Alastor…taking…incoming Rats to another section."

Middleton's face turned an angry shade of purple. She was loud enough to hear clearly.

"Tell your men to remove Alastor's troops," she snarled. "Forcibly, if necessary."

"But Miss, Overlord Alastor—"

"I don't give a damn what Alastor says, just do it. I won't have him hijacking another one of my troop divisions!"

"But what will—?"

"Bring in another division and tell them that only under Alastor's direct supervision will you allow those gangs to be redirected. We certainly can't have that slum riff-raff running amok all over the place now, can we?" She smirked. "That ought to keep them busy. I will have this done long before he can intervene."

She glared at the uncertain ST

"Well? Go!"

"Yes, Miss," the ST said in a suitably subdued manner.

Middleton waved him off dismissively, and he jumped down from the car and back onto the platform. Without bothering to check if everyone was strapped in, she pulled a lever, and the rail car jumped forward, rushing into the dark tunnel.

49

The transport whizzed along under great arches of machinery, speeding its way towards an unknown destination. Janus felt a rush of adrenaline. Twisting pipes, gigantic cranes, and dark tunnel walls barely illuminated by the headlights of the train sprang up before them, threatening to smash them to pieces, before the car jerked away, just in time. But Clara clutched the sides of her seat, barely able to control her terror. She kept shutting her eyes, struggling to block out the visions of the car's impending doom, only to turn noticeably green as the car twisted and turned through the city. Janus grabbed her hand. She smiled at him, her terror momentarily forgotten until another hurdling wall appeared and she froze up. But her eyes didn't close anymore. And through the whizzing city, Janus caught snatches of giant armored vehicles and idle factories, marching troops and empty streets. That is, until they flew out of the tunnel and slowed to a crawl, stopping at a large landing platform—and Janus' mouth dropped open.

Before him lay a sight which he had seen only in books. Far in the distance, jagged spires of rocks, dotted with green and capped with white stood out against a bright blue sky. The great peaks sloped gently into a barren plain, which abutted the massive city and ran into an expanse of rolling waves and water. They were at the edge of his known world; they were standing at the edge of Cerberus.

Chapter 7
The Grey-Haired Man

Middleton struggled to pull her ponderous weight from the car and herded the little group forward, gathering them around her. Three of the guards took positions surrounding them, while the fourth moved to the edge of the platform that jutted from the superscrapers out over the plains. The distant call of seabirds made Janus feel as if he had journeyed to another world. A cool sea breeze filtered through the group, and Janus breathed deeply, savoring the clean, fresh air.

After taking a moment to catch her breath, Middleton spoke softly to them. The recruits listened intently, not daring to breathe for fear of missing their Overlord's every word.

"The Legion will be arriving soon to collect you. You will do exactly as they instruct without question. Failure to do so will result in your immediate execution."

She was interrupted by a shout from the fourth guard.

"My lady, the Mercs have arrived."

"Finally," she said.

Gusting wind filled the air. The small crowd pushed forward towards the edge of the platform for a better view, but the STs pressed them back.

In a moment, all activity ceased, and the crowd fell silent. The rushing winds grew louder.

"Incredible…" Janus gasped.

Rounding into view from around the edge of Cerberus, hundreds of meters tall and just as wide, was a massive, floating city. Its shining exterior was a blinding, pearl white. As the shadows of Cerberus encompassed it, Janus could see massive curved windows set into its gently sloping walls. It looked like a floating mountain of steel and glass, a high tower at the center forming its peak. Rounded domes and towers looked like the foothills of the mobile mountain. High in the apex of the city, like a great gleaming eye, was a red window of stained glass. A constant roar emanated from deep below the city's base as huge engines worked in concert with whatever great power lay hidden deep within it to keep it floating gracefully above the barren ground.

As more moved into the shadows of Cerberus, however, Janus noted spots of hasty patchwork and exposed superstructure. A few black scorches marred the exterior, reminding Janus of the nature of the occupants inside the great fortress.

Hurricane force winds billowed through the many alleys of Cerberus as the floating fortress moved closer, buffeting the platform from all sides. Vents opened along the city's edge to compensate for the gale, directing the rush of air down into the slums.

Large bays opened in the sides of the floating mountain, ramps extending to link the two cities. A flood of people emerged from Cerberus to meet the stream of travelers that began to flow down the ramp from the floating fortress. A tiny group broke from the rest, striding purposefully for the aspiring warriors. A man, flanked by two women. Both women were fit and attractive, but their faces were etched with intensity. The man, however, seemed completely relaxed, so much so that it seemed to be an act. A head of grey hair and a handlebar moustache gave the impression of an old gentleman from a bygone era, well past his prime. His physical stature, however, had not diminished with age, and he still looked as fit as he might have 40 years ago. His eyes were grey, too, but intense, belying the calm exterior. He wore two weapons: the first was a silver long-barreled pistol with an intricately carved handle that featured a strange half-moon symbol. Stranger still, however, was the sword buckled across his back. Janus had never seen such a weapon before, at least outside of books. Its sheath was inlaid with a great golden figure of a man wielding a spear and riding some sort of horse. The woman to his left was tall and slim, with long, raven-black hair, and green eyes. She carried a sword and a pistol, although neither had the same intricate carvings. The woman to his right was shorter, though no less fearsome. Her angular face and short red hair gave the impression that she would brook no nonsense. She carried only a rifle, slung across her back.

"Welcome, ambassadors of ODIN," Miss Middleton moved forward, arms outstretched.

"Glory to Cerberus," handlebar replied with a slight bow. He was at the bottom of his bow when his eyes caught Janus. He froze for a moment, gaze narrowing, but then his fierce expression disappeared, and his smile resumed. He stood up straight again.

The smiles were so forced, it was quite clear that even though they obeyed the niceties, they wanted no one mistaking the fact that they hated each other.

Miss Middleton moved forward and spoke quietly with him.

"Why do they carry those swords?" Janus whispered to Clara, glancing at the weapons. "They don't look particularly effective."

Knives were useful for survival, but blades were absolutely worthless against the tough armor of an ST

"The boy wasn't part of the original bargain," handlebar said, loud enough for Janus to hear. "I will not pay ten grams Immutium for him."

"Is that a lot?" Clara whispered. Janus shrugged.

"We will give him to you for half-price. I understand he is quite capable," Middleton bargained.

"If he's so skilled, why ask half-price? Don't try to fool me, Middleton. I'm not one of your half-baked troopers."

I like this guy already, thought Janus.

"How can you even suggest such a thing?" Miss Middleton's face looked as if she was really trying to act hurt but was having a hard time pulling it off. "Every member of our corporation is valuable."

"Don't patronize me. I know all about Corporate citizenship, Overlord," handlebar retorted.

"Fine," Middleton snapped. "Leave him! He still belongs to us!"

"Oh really?" handlebar exclaimed. In a mere moment, the silver pistol at his waist had appeared in his hand.

The world slowed to a crawl. No Trooper had ever moved so quickly. No threat in the slums had ever felt so real. Janus' limbs felt like lead, even as his mind raced ahead of them. For the last thing Janus saw was the flash of the muzzle as the gun aimed straight for his heart.

CHAPTER 8
VALHALLA

Far too many close calls over the years had left Janus with excellent reflexes, but still, he could hardly believe he reacted. Time seemed to slow as he leapt to get out of the pistol's sight. He immediately moved to protect Clara, grabbing her around the waist as he leapt. She did not even flinch, as if she hadn't even registered handlebar's explosive movement.

Clar—Janus screamed in shock.

The round exploded into his shoulder, leaving a scorching black-and-red hole as large as a golf ball.

Time suddenly sped up again, and Janus writhed in agony. Clara was utterly flabbergasted, as were most of the recruits, and all but one of the guards. Miss Middleton, however, turned purple. She pointed a finger at the man.

"You can't ever just take the money and run, can you, Jennings?"

Janus struggled to his feet, wavering against the pain, but ready to run.

Jennings wore a slight grin as he stared at Janus, but it quickly disappeared as he turned to face Middleton.

"Must we go through this every time? When will you learn that I won't take your garbage off your hands? I'm responsible for the well-being of my entire Legion. There isn't anything you can offer me."

Middleton gave an angry scowl.

"Take the ones who passed," Jennings said to his two escorts. "Leave the rest."

The two women saluted, then herded a seemingly random portion of the recruits towards the floating city. Janus felt weak and a wave of dizziness washed over him. He collapsed on the hard metal platform. He was going to be left to die.

A muddled, distant voice said, "Take care of the one on the ground."

"No, you can't!" Clara shouted.

The figure of a security trooper loomed over him. *Goodbye, Clara,* Janus thought, and then darkness overwhelmed him.

Janus awoke slowly. His head hurt. *Where am I?* Warmth seemed to emanate from everywhere around him, and he felt very drowsy. Heavy lids fighting against him, he opened his eyes.

He was in a soft bed. A warm, low light filled the room, allowing his eyes to adjust easily. A gently curved ceiling became large white shades covering a curved window. A closed door stood to his right. Looking above his head, strange machines jutted from the wall, and a glowing white screen showed strange letters and numbers he didn't recognize. Every so often, a green light would sweep back and forth across his body. A strange tube of blue gel disappeared into the wall behind him, emitting a luminescent glow in the semi-darkness. He reached toward the container, but noticed that his hand was unexpectedly gloved in black. He became acutely aware that he was no longer wearing his ragged Cerberus uniform, but a form-fitting black suit, which felt strange and prickly to him. He examined his arm and the glove; they seemed to be of a high quality. He imagined he must look like one of the Cerberus elite.

Clara will be jealous when she sees…

"Clara!" Janus sat up with a start. Everything came flooding back. Middleton's threat, the rail-car ride, the man named Jennings, being shot—

Sweat beaded on his brow; he couldn't feel anything wrong with his arm. Slowly, he turned his head to try to look at the bullet hole. He pulled the uniform away and—the hole was gone. No gaping wound. Only a slightly pale spot gave any impression of his prior injury.

A door in the far wall slid open, and bright light flooded the room. Janus squinted against the bright light, his eyes feeling the burn. A tall shadow stood highlighted in the doorway. It took Janus a moment to realize it was the grey-haired man.

"We weren't sure when you would wake up." Jennings chuckled. "You certainly gave us a surprise."

Janus pushed himself back in the bed, his mind racing as he searched for a weapon. The room was bare but for the bed and the strange devices upon the wall. Janus eyed the man. *No guards.*

"My name is Alexander Jennings." The man smiled, his eyes shining brightly. "You're wondering where you are, no doubt."

"What's going on? Where's Clara?"

"Who? Oh yes, the young lady that you protected. She is fine."

Janus blew a sigh of relief, but did not take his eyes off the man before him.

"But I'm afraid you won't be able to see her."

"Why not?" Janus asked cautiously.

The man seemed genuine, but he certainly wasn't trustworthy at this point. Instead of answering, he moved towards the door.

"Follow me."

Janus sat for a moment; the situation was entirely unexpected. After a brief consideration, he struggled out of the bed. He had a raging headache, but his feet were steady. The mysterious man disappeared through the door.

"Come on, son. I didn't shoot you in the leg."

Janus hurried to catch up with Jennings, jumping into step beside him. More rooms filled with beds and glowing machines appeared to his right. Wide skylights let sunlight stream into the hall. Janus felt an overwhelming desire to stop in the warm patches, but Jennings' quick and steady pace kept him moving. The pair made a left turn, leaving the skylights behind and passing a new set of closed doors. A few were marked with '*supplies*,' while others had strange names he did not recognize. He stopped to stare at a particularly heavy door with several scanner locks on it. It was labeled '*Nanyte Control Room*.'

"You have a very unique name, Janus, do you know that?" Jennings said over his shoulder, not pausing his purposeful walk.

"Are you normally so friendly with people you shoot?" Janus asked edgily, picking up his pace to get back into step.

"No need to be so prickly, my boy." Jennings chuckled. "Clara told me as we loaded you up."

"You spoke with Clara?" Janus asked cautiously.

"Oh, yes. She filled me in on some of the important details about you. A slummer named Janus, found as a baby." He rubbed his chin. "Even Middleton perked up a bit when she heard that. Your name is very interesting to me. You know nothing about it?"

Jennings gave him a curious look.

"No—" Janus replied irritably.

"You seem remarkably well-educated for a slummer, judging by your manner of speech. It doesn't suffer from enough slang," he added. "Clara must have worked hard on you."

"Are you trying to compliment me or insult me?"

"You mistake my attempt to understand you as an attack. Educated as you are, I thought you might appreciate a bit of a history lesson."

58

Janus was silent.

"Your name is Roman in origin. Do you know of the Romans?" Jennings asked.

Janus hesitantly shook his head.

"When the old republics fell, and the Corporations rose to replace them, it was a time of great uncertainty and fear. People looked towards myths, legends, and stories that inspired them. It is from these that the Corporations took their names: Cerberus. Medusa. Titan. Minotaur. Hydra. Chimera. Phoenix."

"Your name in particular is that of a Roman God: Janus, the beginner and ender, the god of gates and doors, peace and war, and the transition between the mediocre and the great. It is a very strong name, and it speaks to Clara's wisdom that she gave it to you. It's always terrible when someone like her ends up in the slums."

"What do you mean?"

"And you don't know any reason why she gave you your name?"

"She didn't," Janus said. "I was named from a note she found with me."

"Someone gave you that name before Clara?" Jennings looked shrewdly at Janus. "That is very interesting…"

The narrow corridors and shut doors of the hall made Janus feel like a rat in a maze. Every so often, he thought he could hear voices through one of the doors, but he had yet to see anyone else. It wasn't far different from the silence of the slums, but at least down there he knew what to expect. He didn't like being led. Ahead of him, the end of the hall opened up into a brightly lit area. The sounds of many more people spilled from the open doorway before him.

"Where is Clara? I want to see her."

"You can't see her because she is still back at Cerberus."

"Back at Cerberus?" Janus sped past Jennings to the end of the hall.

That could only mean…

His eyes fought to adjust to the bright light. Suddenly, his vision cleared, and he stared in amazement around him.

The fortress of the Mercs.

It was unlike anything he had imagined. From the outside, it had been a glittering white mountain. But now, he stood at the center of it. It was as if a solid mountain of shiny pale stone had been hallowed out. The glittering surfaces bathed in sunlight that streamed down from massive windows set in the highest reaches of the peak. Rooms and halls dotted the inside walls—a city inside the mountain. In the center, a huge column stretched from base to top. People streamed in and out of the column at every level. It reminded Janus of a tree he had seen in one of his books; as if a massive trunk had sprouted in the middle of the mountain, its branches spreading out to connect with the walls of stone, forming bridges for the men and women who lived in the city.

Bright rays of sun illuminated tiny islands of green plants, which dotted the trunk and mountain walls, spreading out along the branches of the tree. Waterfalls cascaded merrily down, granting life-giving moisture to the plants.

Janus stood on an exposed walkway. Men and women of all ages flowed past, some talking animatedly with one another, while others had the same grim, purposeful looks he had seen from the two women that had been with Jennings. All were slim and fit, even the elder ones, although none were as grey as Jennings. Clad in the same armor Janus wore, they seemed to blend together as their suits shifted from grey to brown to black. Strange looks followed Janus as he gaped in wonder, making his way haphazardly towards the edge of the wide balcony. Jennings walked a few steps behind him, letting Janus soak in his new environment. Reaching the curvy railing, he peered over the edge, watching the waterfalls spill into a river that weaved around the base of the trunk. Arched bridges crossed the small canal, while benches dotted the edge of it.

Janus ran his hand along the railing; its smooth polished surface looked like a pebble pulled from a river. Tracing the railing with his hand, he stopped at the edge of a branch connected to the trunk, following out across the expanse with his eyes. More branches twisted around the trunk like a set of stairs, granting a view all the way to the top of the city. It made the place seem airy and free, despite the crowd of people.

Janus craned his head back as far as he could. Gigantic glass panes surrounded the top of the pillar, creating the cascade of light that bathed the giant hall. He was transfixed, however, by a huge circular window that dominated the very top of the city. A red, stained glass depiction of a great warrior, having but one eye and clad in fearsome armor, sitting astride his six-legged mount. The warrior held a massive war spear easily at his side, his fierce expression daring anyone to challenge him. Light poured through the window, casting a huge multicolored display upon the grounds below.

Jennings stepped up next to him, raising an outstretched arm.

"Welcome," he said, "to the Avalon-class citadel: Valhalla!"

CHAPTER 9
ADEPTS

"Everything you see here has a purpose," said Jennings. "Despite its tranquil appearance, this entire city was built for war. The seal is our emblem: the great god Odin, astride the mighty Sleipnir, his warhorse, charging into battle."

Janus tore his gaze from the window to look at Jennings.

"But why am I here?" Janus was still wary. "Why did you shoot me? Is Clara okay? Can I talk to her?"

"She's safe at Cerberus. I made sure of that, and as long as you remain here, it will stay that way. Middleton knows better than to test my patience any further."

"As long as I stay here?"

"Yes." Jennings nodded seriously. "You're an ODIN Adept now."

"What if I don't want to be—a what?" Janus asked.

"If you don't want to stay, you don't have to," Jennings said matter-of-factly. "You aren't a prisoner. We won't have anyone who doesn't want to fight alongside us. Would you rather go back to Cerberus?"

Janus took a moment, but shook his head.

"Good." Jennings nodded approvingly. "While you're here, we will watch out for you. And Clara. But I have an obligation to ODIN first; if you leave, my protection of Clara ends. We can't afford to waste any resources, even the slightest influence, on the others outside these walls. Understood?"

"I don't plan on leaving. And I don't plan on dying."

"No one ever does," Jennings replied. "As for talking with her, I'm afraid that Cerberus is out of range by now."

"You must have radios?" Janus asked skeptically. "Troopers have them all the time."

"Of course. But I'm afraid it doesn't work quite like that. There are limits to range, especially with the Corporations controlling what few satellites are left."

"Satellites?"

Jennings pursed his lips.

"It would be difficult to do the subject justice right now. You'll have the opportunity to learn soon enough. But as to why I shot you—my apologies. I didn't mean to kill you, only cause superficial damage. Enough for Middleton to release you to me. Sometimes we find good uses for those not qualified to be Adepts, and I thought it would be far better than your fate as a slummer, or as an ST Admittedly, I didn't anticipate you reacting as you did, trying to rescue Clara. You leapt right into the bullet." Jennings smiled. "But on a positive note, you certainly passed the test."

"You've used that word several times. Adept. What is it? What test?"

Jennings nodded, as if he expected the question,

"I've been studying people for a long time—how they see the world, how they react to new information and situations. For the most part, when something unexpected occurs, something truly terrifying, the majority will simply freeze. Their muscles tense, their minds whirl. By the time they have decided what to tell their bodies to do, it is far too late.

There are select few, however, who can bypass this instinct. Their minds move faster. Their bodies move on their own. Their brains can do the puzzling on the go. These people, they make the only good soldiers there are. The ones most adept at taking control. At decision-making. At survival."

"And you're saying that because I jumped, I'm one of these…"

"Adepts?" Jennings asked. "Sounds better than a mercenary, doesn't it?"

Janus was skeptical.

"For now."

"For now, then." Jennings smiled, raising a hand. "This is the main hall of Valhalla. We are currently located in the medical branch. Each section of the city is connected via bridge to the central pillar, or Trunk, as we like to call it."

He pointed towards the highest reaches of the central tower.

"In the case of an invasion, the base can be locked down from central command, making the city accessible only by use of the Trunk and bridges. As long as the Legion controls the Trunk, we can prevent Valhalla from being overwhelmed."

The pair walked along a bridge toward the Trunk, and Jennings placed his hand into one of the streams of water splattering along it.

"The waterfalls act as a humidity control, irrigation system, and cooling measure, while the windows that provide illumination for the plant life are heavily reinforced plastics that become fully armored blast doors."

He made a motion behind him as the pair walked on.

"As I said, behind you is our medical branch. One of the finest available, I might add. We have an entire lab devoted to Nanyte control and production."

"Nanytes?" Janus asked curiously.

"You will learn more about them soon, but we used them on your shoulder. I think you can see their benefits.

"Next to the ground floor barracks is the mess hall and meeting forums. You will be down in the cadet barracks, across from the main mess. And all the way at the bottom of the city, underneath the main tower floor, are engine control and power, and the arena."

"What's the arena?" Janus asked.

"That, too, you will be experiencing soon enough." Jennings coughed. "Although fortunately, playing in the arena is limited to full-fledged Adepts. Once you join your fellow cadets, you can have the grand tour."

"So I can point out the flaws?" Janus ribbed.

Leaving the tree, Jennings passed through an arched door, Janus following closely behind. Above the doorway, a pair of strange symbols glowed in red light. One looked just like an angular 'R,' and the other was an 'X' between two vertical lines:

"It means 'Chariot of Dawn,'" Jennings explained, gesturing to the symbols. He saw the look of confusion on Janus' face.

"These and the others like them around Valhalla are all that remains of a long-forgotten language. I once knew a man who hoped fervently that there was a place for the brave souls of the world when they passed on. He thought that the Corporations had forgotten something about humanity's soul. I am not sure I believe in it as he so fervently did, but I tend to agree with his assertion." Jennings motioned back towards the Trunk. "This citadel is named in honor of that hope. Valhalla, the halls of the brave."

The door opened to a darkened hall.

"Power preservation," Jennings commented.

Glowing strips of light raced ahead of the pair, extinguishing behind them. Janus peered inside an open door, spying half-completed suits of Trooper armor in the dim glow from the hall. Jennings kept walking, creating a small island of light around each of them. He called out over his shoulder.

"Come on son, I've got something more important to show you than some rusty Trooper armor, and I usually don't give tours."

Janus hurried to catch up, until the two islands of light once again merged into one. At the end of the hall, Janus leaned forward curiously as Jennings waved open a heavy metal door decorated with the seal of ODIN. It slid away silently to expose a wide hanger.

"So why am I getting a tour then?" Janus asked.

"I try not to shoot my own troops," he said, eyeing Janus carefully. "I wanted to make sure you understood that."

The hanger was deathly still, and Jennings' footsteps echoed as he walked across the floor to the huge bay door. Above him, Janus could see a pair of long, sleek shapes, with angular noses, like the prow of a ship. Each had four engines, one situated on each of the four corners of the craft, with the front pair slightly behind the cockpit. The strange-looking vehicle had no wings to speak of, but many hatches: two in the back and along the bottom, and two very heavy doors along the sides.

"Longboats," said Jennings. "High speed armored transport and landing craft."

Jennings pushed a few buttons on a glowing display on the far side of the hanger and waved the translucent panel back into the wall. There was the sound of heavy machinery churning and cranking. The great bay door was opening, creating a platform that slowly extended out of the city, and exposing a setting sun disappearing over a verdant pine forest. The tops of the trees looked like tiny green brushes from so far above. A dull roar echoed from the earth below—the engines of Valhalla as they pushed the city gracefully along.

As he walked out into a purple sky, a fresh breeze swept along the platform, wrapping him in its cool embrace. With his back to the setting sun, he could just make out snow-capped mountains sparkling in the fading light. Janus stood for several moments, still in awe of the outside world, deeply breathing the cool air as the giant city floated its way over the landscape. Turning to stare at the setting sun, Janus' struggling eyes welled up. No matter what happened here, or what Jennings intended, it all would have been worth it. Just for this.

"Is the city always on the move?" Janus asked as he came to stand beside Jennings at the edge. A flock of birds startled from the forest, disturbed by the roaring engines.

"We must always remain mobile." Jennings nodded. "The risk is too great otherwise."

Janus turned and looked back at the city. He could see the scorched and blackened plates upon its pearly exterior, the holes like scars on its beautiful features.

Jennings motioned his arm towards the pockmarks. "But our movement is not strictly defensive. It's for trading, too. Trading keeps us afloat—literally, now that the Corporations have fewer military skirmishes, let alone jobs for us. With the completion of our trading with Cerberus, however, we are bound for the ocean for a while. We have no jobs on the horizon, and it is never wise to become predictable."

He turned away from the city, looking out over the forest.

"Are attacks against the city common?" Janus asked.

"Do you see that down there?"

Jennings pointed down, over the edge, and Janus peered into the creeping dark of dusk. At first, Janus thought he was just staring at more rocky terrain shadowed by the mountains and the setting sun, but he soon realized he was staring at a city. It was a black, twisted mess, and the approaching twilight only made it more difficult to discern.

"That," Jennings said, "is all that remains of Phoenix Corporation. It made the mistake of attacking an Adept Legion."

"That was a Corporation? Like Cerberus?" Janus was in awe.

"Yes. Phoenix was once the most powerful corporation in the world. Many years ago, Phoenix tried to capture an Avalon-class fortress, not unlike this one, and use it as a Trojan horse."

"Trojan horse?"

Jennings glanced at him and smiled.

"A deception of sorts, an effort to make someone believe you have good intentions when you do not."

He looked back to the broken waste.

"It wasn't a bad idea. Corporations regularly trade with us; we're the trusted middlemen, or perhaps, more trusted than another Corporation. A Legion involved in trade negotiations never attacks a Corporation. And a Corporation will never attack Adepts while they trade. Even before Phoenix was destroyed, that was the unwritten code; but Phoenix—Phoenix demonstrated what would happen when that code was broken."

There was a tinge of bitterness in his voice. Janus remained silent, feeling that it would be inappropriate to speak.

"To this day, I'm not entirely sure why they attacked."

"There was no reason for it?" Janus prodded.

"None," Jennings said, shaking his head. "I have many theories, but as for facts, I have few. Some say they needed something. Some say they were testing themselves. There are even rumors that it was integral in some way to Phoenix Serum."

"Phoenix Serum?" Janus asked.

"An elixir, a drug—a mythical substance that supposedly grants super strength, or perhaps wealth, or immortality." Jennings grimaced. "Or one of many things man is willing to sacrifice so much for. No one knows much about it, and even less about the reasons for the battle that day. But I do know Phoenix made at least one mistake. Phoenix underestimated the Adepts. But it has always been that way. Corporations believe Adepts to be nothing more than clubs, brute force weapons like their armies of Security Troopers."

He gave a hollow laugh.

"And no matter what we say, or what we do, they will always think little of us. We are merely an avenue to rid themselves of troublemakers. That is why we leave so many behind in our trades, like the group we left in Cerberus. In the eyes of the Corporations, the best of the best are Executors, and everyone else is rabble. But their arrogance plays to our favor, too. Everyone here is a castoff from a Corporation, and fortunately for us, the Corporations have never realized the magnitude of their loss. It is the reason Phoenix is the twisted heap you see now.

"We Adepts may sell our blades to the highest bidder, but we broke free of the Corporations for reasons very different from power and wealth. And our Avalon fortresses are more than just mobile bases; they are the very homes that we hold dear. Generations of Adepts have been raised in such places, and in many ways, Legions are families. We survive by working together, functioning as a unit. Phoenix did not understand that."

Jennings pointed back down at the wreckage.

"After the battle, Phoenix was left broken and defenseless, and it wasn't long before the other Corporations learned of their weakness and struck, wiping all traces of it from the Earth. This is all that remains of that once mighty corporation; a few blackened and twisted scraps. Many suspected that Phoenix hoped to forever alter the balance of power with their attack. In the end, it did, but not in the way it hoped. After Phoenix was nothing but ash, two major declarations rose from it: The SHADE Continuum, named for the Legion that Phoenix attacked, which was an agreement by the remaining Legions to band together to attack any corporation that attacked one of their own."

"And the second?" Janus asked curiously.

"The Phoenix Declaration," Jennings grimaced. "A proclamation of treaty lines for corporate expansion, and a set of rules to govern how Corporations attack each other, including the prohibition of nuclear weapons."

"And who enforces those?" Janus asked in disbelief. Jennings smiled appreciatively.

"It was a joint agreement by the Corporations. One that has never been tested in the aftermath."

Jennings and Janus stared silently while the city finally passed the edge of the ruins.

Incredible.

Janus watched for as long as he could before the broken Corporation finally disappeared in the dark.

The walk back through the flight bay had been a silent one. For reasons unknown to him, Janus felt as if he had heard a speech Jennings rarely felt compelled to give. They soon emerged back into the main hall, and crossed a branch to the Trunk. Just shy of the massive column, Jennings stopped unexpectedly.

"The Legion doesn't care for a lack of discipline, or an overdeveloped ego," he said. "They tend to get more valuable people killed."

Janus scowled.

"I've never liked that expression."

"Valuable people?" Jennings asked. "Its meaning can definitely change depending on the context—say from a Corporation to a Legion. But it is accurate in this case. Ego has no place here. Clara thought it was important I reiterate that to you."

Janus cleared his throat.

"Who's in charge of ODIN?" he asked.

"The Praetor. And you best watch yourself if you come across him."

"I grew up in the slums—how bad could it be?" Janus asked with a grin.

Jennings came in close to Janus at that moment, his face grim and serious.

"You'd be surprised."

Janus held his ground, but his smile faltered.

"Come on." Jennings smiled, turning away as if nothing had happened. "It's time for you to meet your fellow cadets."

At the end of the bridge, a tight formation of Adepts waited on the lift. All were heavily muscled and toned, and their armored uniforms only added to their bulk. Janus felt surprisingly scrawny next to them. Even the women, who appeared more tone than muscular, were fearsome. And Jennings, despite his age, was no less fit.

As Jennings hopped on, the Adepts stepped smartly to one side and snapped salutes.

"Good morning, Praetor," the men and women chorused.

"At ease," Jennings nodded.

An officer leaned over and whispered to Jennings. "Not often I see you with cadets, sir."

"This one is going to require some special attention, Captain."

Jennings gave the man a wink.

CHAPTER 10
WOURIS

The lift flew downwards, travelling towards the base of the great Trunk. Janus stared at the blur of water and vegetation, while the voice of Clara sounded in his head. *Well, that was a great start*—the voice chided—*next time, try not to stick your foot so far in your mouth.*

The lift slowed and stopped halfway down, and Jennings nimbly leapt off.

"This is my stop; you're heading all the way to the bottom."

Janus wasn't exactly sure what to do, so he awkwardly saluted in the same way as he had seen STs.

"Sir."

"Your new sergeant will be there, waiting to meet you," Jennings said with a knowing smile. "Oh, and it's the other hand."

Janus quickly changed to the other arm, feeling the heat rise in his face. The Adepts behind him said nothing, simply saluted the Praetor themselves. Jennings returned the salute, as the lift started moving again.

"And remember," he called down after him. "It's not how you start, it's how you finish."

Before Janus could respond, the lift sped up, and Jennings disappeared from view.

Janus was the last one to disembark. As the lift had descended, the other Adepts on board had slipped off, floor by floor, without so much as a word, leaving him alone. As the lift slowed and stopped at the bottom of the Trunk, he caught a glimpse of a woman waiting there. Her body was relaxed. She turned towards him, and he could see short red hair framing her angular face, hazel eyes shining like a bird of prey. It was one of the women from the platform. She was toned, perhaps even built, but only in a way that suggested a deep well of strength. Unlike the Adepts on the lift, she wore a red striped suit that bore several stars. Without a second look at him, she turned and started moving away from the lift.

"I don't know why the Praetor is so keen on you, and frankly, I don't care. I saw you that first day, and all I can say is that you didn't move fast enough. What I do know is that he is forcing me to put another slack-jawed cadet into my unit who's thick as one of those security gorillas..."

Her voice was sharp, with a light accent, as if she came from the Cerberus middle levels. Despite the comparison to an ST, Janus felt immediately at ease around the woman.

She sounds a bit like Clara.

"...and I'll be damned if I am going to have some worthless blueback making me look bad."

When she's annoyed.

She swung about on her heel and stared at him.

"Do I make myself clear?"

Janus wiped the grin off his face and stood up straight.

"Yes, sir!"

The woman tensed, her eyes narrowing. Her red hair seemed to bristle. Janus took a step back. He had clearly offended her.

"I'm a sergeant, cadet, and you will address me as such. Call me 'sir' again and I'll make you sorry you were ever born."

"Yes s—Sergeant." He took a quick peek at the name on her uniform. "Sergeant Wour-is."

73

Wouris stepped forward, putting herself right in Janus' face.

"It's 'Worry.'"

The woman immediately turned on her heel and started walking away.

"You're in Section Sigma, with the other new cadets," Wouris said. "Everything you need is already there. You'll meet with your unit tonight. I suggest you make it brief. You're getting up bright and early tomorrow."

Janus was forced to jog to keep up with the woman. Crossing the shallow canal that surrounded the Trunk, Janus watched as water from above cascaded down and merged into the swift creek. To his right, Adepts laughed and joked as they passed into the mess. Recessed lights illuminated their path in the twilight, as shadows crept up the length of the Trunk in the setting sun.

Wouris' path did not deviate, nor did she pause as she passed straight through one of the arched doorways branching from the great hall. Another strange rune stood above the door. It was the two lines with 'X' between them combined with another symbol that looked like an 'M.'

"Men of Dawn," Wouris said simply. "This is where the cadets' barracks are based."

At each intersection, a floor panel would light up with an arrow and display where the branch would go, each of these, too, having a symbol instead of lettering. To his right, Janus passed an armory station, a medical supply room, and a small recreation area. Each was marked with its own rune on the floor. To his left, the floor lit up to tell him he was passing 'α' section. It all seemed surprisingly quiet.

"Where is everyone?" Janus asked.

She glanced back, her face unreadable.

"Legions always grow slowly." She paused. "There are just not enough of us, anymore."

The pair walked further in silence, past 'β' section, to the end of the hall, where a floor panel lit up with a big 'Σ' before a single door and a waiting Adept.

"This is your stop."

The Adept opened up a parchment-thin tablet.

"Yes, Sergeant 'Worry.'"

"You're the one from the hospital wing, right?" the Adept said. "Go to Sigma three, that's your new unit. Just follow the hall, third door on the left, right before it wraps back again. Bunk 'S.' The others are already there. I suggest you make friends fast, because starting tomorrow you live or die by them."

"Thanks," Janus said sarcastically. The man did not glance up, and Janus turned to see Wouris disappear around the curve of the hall. With nothing else to do, Janus stepped through the sliding doors. The lights were dim, and broad windows took up the right wall. He stopped and gazed out at the dark. A tiny pinprick of light held steady above the horizon.

He stared, wondering what it was. Putting his hands upon the glass, he realized that the tiny pinprick was not alone. Hundreds of others shone in the night sky. His breath caught, and he brought his face within a hair's breadth of the glass.

Stars! I can see stars!

Chapter 11
Shared Stories

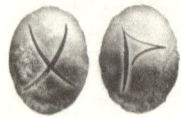

When the door slid open to reveal Sigma three, Janus found a brightly lit room with about two-dozen men and women, laughing and joking with each other. A few appeared to be playing a popular slum card game called 'Mercy.' He hesitated in the doorway. It was a common room of sorts. Round, soft couches and chairs clustered around a few tables. Twenty-six smaller doors ran around the outside of the room, labeled A to Z. A single, larger door stood in the middle of the back of the room, labeled 'Head.' A few of the cadets noticed him standing in the door. Janus felt a knot in his gut.

"Orders?" It was a man with black hair and a dark olive skin-color that reminded him of Clara.

Janus stepped inside and shook his head.

"No—I'm part of the unit."

Another voice spoke up behind him.

"You must be our mysterious missing cadet, then!"

Janus turned to face the speaker and for the second time that night, his breath caught in his chest.

It was a woman, smiling sunnily at him. The most beautiful he had ever seen. Janus was momentarily dumfounded. Just a tad shorter than he, she was thin and curved. She stood on the balls of her feet, as though always ready to spring into action and bubbling with excitement. Her blond hair seemed to bounce up and down in time with her energy. But it was her eyes that struck him. Bright, blue orbs sparkling like the stars.

"Hi, I'm Celes." She stuck out a hand in greeting.

Janus struggled to collect himself, studying the crowd surrounding him.

"Celes," he said, taking a half step back and glancing at her hand, not grabbing it. "That's a strange name."

The surprised looks from the crowd made him shift uncomfortably, but the woman seemed unfazed.

"It stands for Celestia," she said, her hand disappearing without a word. "What's yours?"

"Janus," he replied carefully.

"Nice to meet you, Janus. You don't think Janus is a strange name, too?" She gave him a grin.

"Not really, I've been hearing it tossed around all my life," he said, returning her smile.

"A wise guy, huh?" Celes laughed. The group chuckled.

"Incredibly wise," Janus joked. "And modest, too,"

The black-haired man stepped forward, tilting his head ever so slightly. "The name's Marcus."

Marcus stood half a head taller, straight and proud, but had the same sort of leanness to him as Janus, as if he was used to running. He really did look like a long-lost relative of Clara's, with only his accent creating any discernable difference. It was an odd sort of hardening of the consonants, a softening of the vowels.

"Marcus." Janus nodded conservatively.

Another woman leapt forward, nearly on top of him. She too had black hair, but her eyes were dark and almond shaped, and her skin fair. She was decidedly petite in stature, with delicate features.

"I'm Juliens but everybody calls me Lyn, nice ta meet ya," she said in a breathless string. Janus raised his eyebrows in surprise.

She stuck her thumb at the pale man who sat behind her, who must have been head and shoulders taller than everyone else. Or maybe more. He looked like he could be the size of an ST

"That's Ramirez."

He stood up. Janus drew in a breath. A big ST Lyn smiled at his reaction. Ramirez nodded in greeting, his green eyes staring intently, the hard line that formed his mouth unmoved.

"He doesn't say much," she added. Ramirez nodded again.

The remaining cadets tossed waves his way, some nodding their heads at Janus, others coming to meet him. He recognized a few from the platform at Cerberus.

The rest of the brief evening was spent leaning against a chair, on the edge of the group, listening to the other cadets talk. Celes did most of it, clearly in her element.

Most of the cadets were from the middle castes of the Corporations, but a few, like Janus, remained tight-lipped about their origins. Surprisingly, this included Celes, who seemed to avoid any questions about her past with more comments regarding what she had heard of 'Merc Legions.'

By the end of the night, Janus had associated a few other names with faces: Jones, a stout girl from Minotaur with dark-brown and black hair; a man named Valers, with a broad smile and green eyes; Holloway, a tall, blond-haired, blue-eyed man; Nathans, a young black-haired fellow who looked more boy than man; and finally, Kirsten, red-haired woman with green eyes and a strange accent that apparently marked her as Hydra Corporation. There were many more, but as the night wore on, they all faded together, and the only thing Janus could be relatively certain of was their origin. He kept track of their origins. Each Corporation had slightly different mannerisms and accents. And then there were the few, like Lyn and Ramirez, who stood out, because they did not fit the mold at all.

They all had different thoughts of what awaited them, and what life would be like. Many had been sent without choice, as Janus had, and discussed how much they missed home and its comforts. The floating city had pulled them from their element. Part of Janus agreed.

Eventually, the lights flashed overhead, and a woman's voice sounded over the speaker that 'lights out' was in five minutes. The cadets speedily broke up, heading for their assigned bunks. Janus supposed that they were more familiar with the routine than he. When Janus finally entered bunk 'S' for the first time, he couldn't help but laugh. *Not like home…*

Bunk didn't give it enough credit. A fresh bed was made for him, and newly pressed uniforms were already hung inside the sliding wall panels. He suspected there was more to find, but was suddenly overcome with exhaustion. With a bit of figuring, he worked the lights, waving a hand up and down a glowing green strip to flip them on and off. With a quick wave, he turned them off, and fell back into the new bed.

But falling asleep proved difficult. He was unable to relax his back into the soft foam, and uncomfortably cool in the controlled temperature of the room. Thoughts of Clara drifted through his mind. There was so much he wanted to tell her. About everything that he'd learned so far. About the people he met. About how much he missed her. But mostly that he was more excited and nervous than he had been in his entire life.

Chapter 12
Bluebacks

Janus groggily awoke to the sound of a blaring alarm and bright, artificial sunlight. He instinctively glanced right, searching for Clara in her armchair, but only the empty wall of Valhalla greeted him.

Stumbling out of bed, the alarm shut off as soon as his feet hit the floor. He flopped back into the bed only for the blaring to begin again. Resigning himself to his misery, he planted both feet firmly on the floor and stood up. He grabbed the uniform that slid out from an opening the wall, and pulled it on. He took a moment to savor the experience, even in his groggy state. He was dressed for the first time in a full cadet uniform: black armor with a wide blue stripe running down his front left side, all the way down his leg, and a similar stripe on the back. Janus felt elated.

This elation lasted but a moment, however, as a Daedulus terminal popped from the wall.

"Your dress is poor, cadet," a motherly voice intoned. "Look at the flap on your right side."

Janus stared at the machine, unsure of the strange device.

"Your right side. Look there." A small camera attached to the top of the console zoomed in on his side.

Janus glanced down to see a tiny flap, almost completely flush, but with a tiny curl at the end pulling away from the armor. Janus pressed the flap down, smoothing it.

There was an audible sigh.

"You didn't secure the buttons correctly. It's a wonder anything is straight at all."

Janus gave the glowing console a questioning eyebrow, and moved towards the door. It didn't open.

A *tsk* sounded from the Daedulus.

"Not until you're dressed properly."

Janus waved his hand in front of the door. Tried pushing it open. Nothing worked.

"This is a joke, right?"

"Oh, your dress certainly is, but I am not. I am the Valhalla central Daedulus, currently serving the ODIN Adept Legion. My functions may be limited, but I do certain ones very well. One is teaching cadets how to dress. This program has survived, since before the time of the Avalons, and you can be sure I know what I'm talking about. So we're going to start from the beginning."

"No," Janus said. "This is fine."

"Suit yourself. But I'm not opening the door. And when Sergeant Wouris finds out you were late because you didn't know how to dress yourself…"

"I know how to dress myself! This is perfectly fine. It's not that complicated."

"Au contraire, my young ward. Fine dress is the key to success."

"I don't believe that at all."

"Oh really? Well, I don't know what you want me to say. All I know is, fine dress is the key to success."

Janus turned to look directly at the camera. "Right…"

But the Daedulus wouldn't budge. Eventually, Janus relented, and the device went through a full routine on how to dress, even down to the order of what got put on first. The routine was an ordeal—and almost certainly a waste of time.

Finally, Janus strode irritably from the room, only for the door to slam shut behind him, and just in time for Sergeant Wouris to arrive.

With Wouris leading the way, the entire platoon was soon hustling out into the grand hall surrounding the Trunk. Janus noted that the great seal of ODIN above them remained dark. The sun hadn't yet risen. Now that he was moving, a tingling excitement ran through him. A hard path encircled the Trunk, and Wouris called them to attention as she stood easily at its edge.

"Okay you lot, now I get to see what you're made of. We're just going for a little jog, and you're going to keep up. Simple."

Janus smiled, he was used to running for distances through the slums; jogging would be a cakewalk.

"Anyone who cannot keep up receives a jumpstart from my foot. Understand?"

The cadets grunted agreement.

"What?"

"Yes."

"What did you say?" she yelled loudly. A hesitant cry of 'yes!' sounded.

"Yes, Sergeant Wouris!" Janus said. She nodded in approval.

"What do you say, cadets?"

"Yes, Sergeant Wouris!" the cadets chorused.

"Alright, here we go!"

She took off at what Janus could only describe as a dead sprint. The cadets didn't move, instead watching in stunned silence. Janus was suddenly less confident in his ability to keep up, let alone run that fast.

"That's jogging?" he heard Celes whisper to Lyn.

Wouris had already covered a quarter of the distance when she turned to run backward.

"What are you doing?" she shouted. "Get moving!"

Janus briefly registered between gasps that some length of time had passed, though how much he wasn't sure. Not many cadets were still running, let alone standing. Several had fainted. Many were collapsed on the track, and of those that hadn't, most had trouble moving their legs.

He had tried to keep up with Wouris, but had only been able to go a few minutes before he had to slow down. And then the kicks had started. He'd heard them from the back at first, as cadets had yelled out in pain and surprise, but soon he was receiving them like the rest. The first had nearly buckled his knees and sent him to the ground.

I am...about to die...and Wouris...isn't even...breathing hard...

Wouris ran circles around the cadets, taunting them, while a few Adept bystanders pulled the unconscious out of the way, dropping them on Wouris' order into the shallow river. Most came up spluttering, although a few had to be lain on the stone bank, with the waters lapping around them.

"Come on, you worthless bluebacks. Or I'm going to start putting some weight behind these kicks."

Pain racked Janus' body. He didn't know how Wouris could put more weight behind her kicks, but he didn't want to find out. His bruises throbbed, and his legs felt like lead.

Unfortunately, since nearly every other cadet had collapsed, Janus was now one of a few receiving special attention from Wouris' foot. Originally he had tried to dodge the blows, but that had only made Wouris kick him harder. Wouris' seemed to know exactly how much force to apply to nearly knock her hapless victims flat; just enough to sting and keep the cadets running.

This...is...insane...

His head rolled around to see who was still running, nearly toppling him over as he did so.

Wouris was currently focused on Marcus, the only other cadet still standing. Celes was crawling, Ramirez had finally gone unconscious, and Lyn was grimacing as she lay spread eagle upon the floor. Across the bridge, he could see a crowd of Adepts, chuckling amongst themselves.

Janus was the last cadet to fall.

"Well then, that was a refreshing start to the day, don't you agree?" Wouris said nonchalantly, wiping a few beads of sweat from her brow.

Only a few recruits could muster the strength to moan a reply. Wouris drew in a few deep breaths, savoring the air. To Janus, every breath burned. She struck a pensive pose.

"I suppose that might have been a tad difficult," she said. "You have until 1900 hours to rest up and grab a bite to eat. Return to your quarters. I'll see you tonight."

With that, Wouris turned on her heel and headed for the mess hall, leaving the recruits to tend to themselves.

Chapter 13
Food

When Janus awoke, his entire body ached. After several minutes, he struggled up from the floor and stared at the clock by his bed. Deep red numbers floated in a crystalline block. 1705. He could hardly believe it was still the same day. He vaguely remembered collapsing to the floor, which had felt more comfortable than his bed at the time. His legs barely functioning, Janus motioned for the lights, gathered what clothes were within reach, and stumbled to the showers. His muscles stung with every step.

His first experience with the showers had been a mixed one. He'd been savoring the warm, refreshing feeling until an automatic timer had unexpectedly and very suddenly shut off the hot water, leaving only a frozen stream. The ensuing leap from the shower had resulted in an impressive skid, and a collision with the opposite wall.

"Gah…can't…cold water…" Janus mumbled angrily as returned to his room.

"Cold water," the motherly Daedulus intoned as it lit up. Janus turned to stare at it. "Common cadet keyword. All water in Valhalla passes through a central pumping station, where it is directed to the various branches of the city. To preserve power, heated water is limited in use. After a preset time limit, hot water is redirected to other levels. To compensate for flow, water from sublevel E is redirected to the primary barracks blocks. Sublevel E is located directly adjacent to compartment 56D, the primary cooling tower for the engines."

As the Daedulus shut off, a new scream of surprise echoed from the showers.

The mess hall spanned half of the lower level of the fortress-city. The idea of a meeting place that gave food out freely was a strange dream to Janus, and as such, he was eager to pay it a visit. He had imagined it was how the Executors lived, but to see it in practice would be something.

The first thing that impressed Janus was the sheer size of the room; it suddenly became clear just how many thousands of Adepts actually lived within the halls of Valhalla. Light streamed from huge, curved windows, which wrapped around the length of the mess and cast bright colors across it. Hundreds of tables sat within the massive area, each taking up about as much space as the home he and Clara shared. There were two entrances to the mess, and along the far wall he could see lines of Adepts waiting to pass through the kitchens. Adjacent to the mess lines sat a door marked as the 'Officer's Mess,' closed off from the clattering hall.

Hundreds of Adepts filled the room, all of them laughing and talking. Some were eating or waiting in the mess lines, but others played games and joked. It was clear that this place was the social hub of the city. In the far corner, groups of Adepts gathered around and played a strange game that used no dice or cards, but a board.

"Janus!"

He turned to see Celes standing by one of the tall windows of the mess, waving to him. Behind her, he could see Marcus, Lyn and Ramirez were already scarfing down their meals, replenishing their spent energy reserves.

Celes ran over to meet him.

"Ready to eat?"

"I think that's the idea," Janus said dryly. Celes gave him a pouting look, and he quickly changed tact. "I wonder what they have? I'm not used to getting my meals like this."

The line ahead of the pair moved at a rapid clip. He picked up a fork, holding it by the tines.

"What is this?" he asked.

"You've never seen a fork?" Celes wore a skeptical expression.

"Fork? No, why?"

"How did you eat?"

"Hands work perfectly well," Janus answered succinctly.

"Oh," Celes said, pausing, "Where are you from?"

"Cerberus Corporation."

Celes waited a few moments for him to add to his statement, but he remained tight-lipped.

"Here we go." She turned, and changed the subject. "Now we can see what they've got—"

She stopped as they approached a cafeteria-style buffet line.

"Wait—what is that?" Celes asked, looking alarmed and pointing at a quivering grey mass in the first dish.

"Passers!" Janus exclaimed. "This is great!"

"What?"

Now it was Janus who gave Celes a strange look.

"You don't know what Passers are? Where are you from?" Celes pursed her lips and looked down. Janus waved it off.

"Not important," he said. She smiled.

"It's an acronym," he explained. "PSR Prepared Security Rations. They're a high-protein plant derivative. It's cooked and mixed with different flavorings to make different meals. See, the brown stuff there, that's spaghetti sauce; it's supposed to taste like something called tomatoes. The long white noodles must be the high-fiber variety. And the orangey blocks, that's called Salmon. That's always good."

Celes looked incredulously at the multicolored blocks.

"I can see why they got their name."

Janus began loading up his tray, while Celes hesitantly poked at a few of the different foods with her fork.

"Here, take this."

He handed his tray to her, and took hers, loading it up with a little bit of every food in the line.

"Now you can try everything and see what you like."

"I suppose I'm willing to try anything once." Her smile disappeared as she looked back down at the quivering mass.

Janus followed Celes as she made her way back to the table where Ramirez, Marcus, and Lyn were waiting. The three looked up in surprise at Celes' tray, which was almost teetering over with food.

"Hungry?" Lyn asked.

"I've never had pass…er, PSRs before. Janus says I should try a little of everything."

"Really?" Lyn said. "Ramirez and I would trade for Passers all the time in the Outskirts."

Celes looked up in surprise.

"You're from the Outskirts?"

"Ya." Lyn nodded proudly. "Ramirez and I were born and raised there."

"Outskirts?" Janus asked. He looked confusedly at Marcus, who also seemed unsure.

"Areas outside Corporate control," Celes said. "Officially, there is no territory that isn't claimed by a Corporation. But logistically, it's impossible to control all of it."

Janus and Marcus looked impressed.

"How come I've never heard of them before?" Marcus asked.

Lyn smiled at Ramirez. "Because we're good at hiding."

"And because Corporations don't exactly want people knowing it's possible to survive freely outside their control," Celes said. "When they do find Outskirters, they take the people and destroy the villages."

"Oh," Janus and Marcus said together.

Lyn and Ramirez were silent. The sound of energetic conversations and hearty laughter echoed around the five.

Eventually, Lyn perked up.

"So where are ya from, Marcus?"

"Medusa," he said between mouthfuls of food. "I got here a little over a week ago. It wasn't so bad. I worked in one of the power stations under my parents. It wasn't great, but we survived. I was drafted into the Medusa security forces."

"That's terrible," Janus, Ramirez, and Lyn echoed together.

Marcus looked up in surprise. "Why?"

"Because Security Troopers are bullying scum," Janus said. Lyn and Ramirez nodded in agreement.

"That's true." Marcus laughed. "But it was also my ticket out of there. Military is one of the few ways to move up the ladder. They always need good soldiers, even if they don't admit it. Besides, STs protect people, too."

He looked at Lyn and Ramirez.

"Just because you've seen one side of them doesn't mean they are all bad. And I was only an ST for a day before they decided to make me an Infernus."

Lyn and Ramirez looked even more repulsed. Marcus noticed, plowing quickly ahead. "But I was tested and made a Mercenary right after that. So are you going to try those Passers or not?"

Celes looked down; she had clearly been avoiding her food. Her stomach growled. Tentatively raising a bite of "meatloaf" to her lips, she slid the food into her mouth and chewed as fast as she could. After a few moments, she swallowed, the whole group watching her.

"Not bad." She smiled weakly.

Everyone laughed.

"No really, not bad," she said again.

"Hunger makes everything more palatable," Janus said, nodding wisely.

"Too true," Lyn said. "So let's stop watching her and eat."

When the other three had their heads down, Celes carefully picked up her fork and nudged Janus under the table, silently motioning how to hold it. Janus smiled and emulated her.

Soon all that could be heard was the clattering of trays and smacking of lips.

CHAPTER 14
THE DOVE AND THE HAWKES

The five ran together to Sigma three, just catching up to Wouris as she walked inside for their afternoon meeting.

"Almost late." She gave them a look of disapproval. "Watch it, cadets."

Wouris gathered the unit around her.

"Alright bluebacks, tomorrow you begin your real training. This morning was just about getting a feel for you."

Many of the cadets wore looks of relief, while a few gave knowing looks and grins. Wouris couldn't expect them to run the same distance every day; it would be suicide.

"Tomorrow, we'll start with the same run, but stragglers will start losing their free time."

Their smiles faded.

"Then, you'll begin your hand-to-hand exercises, tactical lessons, and weight training. Eventually you'll be expected to work on these on your own." The cadets' faces and shoulders drooped. "All of these are the basics. You will have much more to learn if you want to survive the final test."

One of the cadets chimed in.

"Will we have another chance to complete the test if we fail the first time, Sergeant?"

"What's your name, cadet?"

"Kwandis, Sergeant."

"Incorrect," Wouris replied. "Your name is cadet until I call you otherwise. And you misunderstood what I said, *cadet*. I said if you want to *survive*. Your final test will be your first mission. Survive and you will be accepted as a fully-fledged Adept. If not, well, you certainly won't care, will you?"

She grinned cheerily.

"See you in the morning."

Janus tumbled out of his room the next morning bleary eyed and exhausted. The prospect of being thrown straight into his first mission was a bit anxiety inducing. Looking around the common room, he was not the only one. Wouris lined them up for roll call, then quickly took off. In no time they were jogging around the Trunk, huffing away. Despite Wouris' warnings the night before, their exercise that morning was lighter, and although some of the cadets definitely struggled more than others, no one had collapsed by the time she called for them to stop.

As they recovered, Wouris ran down the schedule of the rest of the day's lessons.

"Alright, listen up. You're due with Colonels Keats and Hawkes for Tactics at 0700. Don't eat too much; you'll pay for it later. Just grab a bite and meet me at 0650 in front of the Beacon. At 1400, you'll have thirty minutes to eat before we start running. At 1600 you'll report to Major Northcott for weapons training. At 1800, you get the pleasure of meeting with me. I'll see how you've progressed today with some one-on-one combat."

Janus glanced at Celes, who remained impassive at the announcement. Behind her, Marcus leaned into Wouris' words.

"Then at 1900, you can eat without worry because 2030 is sack time. Except for you and you." She pointed at two cadets named Hughes and Kwandis.

"You'll meet me outside Sigma at 1930 for some extra endurance sessions. We can't have you falling behind now, can we? The rest of you will have a chance to review your lessons, which I strongly recommend. Any questions?"

Hughes and Kwandis tried to speak but Wouris cut in.

"No questions? None at all? Good. Now move out!"

Strategy and Tactics was held in a domed extension of the city, designated by two rune symbols that looked like the front of an arrow and a curved line bent at each end.

It meant "Beacon of the Tree." Wouris had told the cadets there were two more Beacons in the city, all designed to serve a multipurpose role. What that role was, Wouris did not elaborate, but the room seemed innocuous enough. As Wouris led them inside, it appeared to be nothing more than a large auditorium. Seats rose towards high windows that flooded the room with sunlight, and currently provided a spectacular view of the open ocean. A large, translucent disk was set into the floor of the room. Janus was still studying the glass-like plate when Colonels Keats and Hawkes joined them.

Colonel Keats was the tall, slim woman Janus had seen at Cerberus. She walked with the ease of flowing water, her long black hair cascading down her back. She had a strong, but gently rounded jaw. She radiated serenity and strength, her friendly smile brightening the room. Her bright green eyes, however, seemed even more intense than Janus remembered, as though she were a coiled spring, waiting quietly for the perfect moment to explode.

Colonel Hawkes, on the other hand, was none of these things. Short and stocky, he stomped around like he was crushing insects beneath his feet. He wore a scowl that made an angry Wouris seem carefree and pleasant. He carried numerous scars across his face and neck, just below a fierce cut of hair. He looked like he could crush a skull in his bare hands, his muscles rippling whenever he moved.

"Good morning, Colonel." Wouris nodded to Keats.

"Good morning, Sergeant," Keats said with a friendly nod. "Keeping the cadets on their toes?"

"You betcha, but I'm expecting you to get their brains working." Wouris smiled and turned to Hawkes. "And I'm expecting to get them back in one piece. If someone's going to kill these cadets, it'll be me, Colonel."

Hawkes returned the smile with an ugly grin.

"I'll see what I can do."

"Alright, cadets," she said. "Sit down, shut up and maybe you'll learn something. I'll return at 1400."

She saluted and marched out of the room at a sharp pace.

Col. Keats addressed the cadets while they sat in the raised seats. She spoke softly, but with a command in her voice that bade all to listen to her.

"Greetings to all of you. I am Colonel Keats, and this is Colonel Hawkes. We will be training you in the basics of tactics and strategies, and the execution of these strategies, both physically and mentally. We will cover everything from using your terrain, to silent communication, to Corporate tactics. Colonel Hawkes will be responsible for your physical tests."

Janus saw a light flicker behind Hawkes' eyes that suggested this was something he was looking forward to.

"Lights!" she shouted suddenly, and the room darkened, shades coming down over the windows. "Projection on!"

The translucent disk began to glow, filling the room in a pale bath of green light. The strange device rose upward, revealing many identical, thin plates, all stacked on top of one another. The device pulsed, as if alive, and hundreds of tiny motes of light appeared, hovering within their prison.

"Map Valhalla," she said. A tiny Valhalla appeared, suspended inside the translucent glass. Janus leaned forward in his chair. It appeared to be an exact replica, down to the tiniest detail, from the huge engines keeping the city aloft to the four docking bays, all the way to the very top spire of the floating fortress-city, where the nerve center of the base resided. As the map rotated slowly, mimicking the movement of the city itself, Janus could see one of the bay doors was open, and tiny Adepts worked diligently inside, while transports and fighters flew in and out of the bay.

"MuDis like this one are extremely useful for examining a battlefield before going in," Keats said.

Janus leaned in to Celes, whispering, "Muddies?"

"MuDis," she said, as though it were different. "M-u-d-i. Multidemensional Projector."

"You will become well acquainted with them over the course of your training," Keats said.

"Enhance location," she continued. The model of Valhalla expanded, closing in on one side of the city. The view passed through the wall and showed an image of the cadets listening to Keats, while Hawkes paced beside them. Janus found the experience somewhat surreal. Keats noticed Hawkes pacing in the picture and looked up at him.

"Is there something you would like to add, Colonel Hawkes?"

Hawkes returned her gaze, but he didn't cease his pacing.

"I'll wait."

She eyed him momentarily, before turning off the MuDi. It retracted back into the floor, the room returning to normal.

"Please."

She motioned to the center of the room.

Hawkes seemed to think about this for a moment before making up his mind and stomping back in front of the cadets. The vein in his forehead seemed ready to pop.

"Fancy technology is all fine and good," he said, "but we're here to show you that it doesn't replace good old-fashioned strength and know how. But none of you have that yet. Not one of you. I can see it. You're weak. Untrained. Incompetent. And if you want to learn how to set foot on the battlefield and not be immediately killed, then I expect absolute discipline from all of you, all of the time. If you choose not to follow our orders exactly, someone *will* die. And I won't stand for it."

His speech was met with shocked silence, a reaction that seemed to please him.

"Today I get a chance to see what you're made of." He cracked his knuckles menacingly, a twisted smile on his face. "Show you how far you have to go. Now, bring me down. If you can."

Without preamble, the chairs retracted towards the walls and the cadets were forced to scramble out of them. Janus caught a glimpse of Keats sliding gracefully from the room, and was sure he heard Hawkes sigh as they ineptly lined up. The cadets looked hesitantly at one another.

"Sir?" Celes piped up in confusion. "Are we fighting you?"

Hawkes' grin grew larger.

She looked at the others and then back at Hawkes.

"So who goes first?"

"First? There isn't any first. It's all of you versus me! When I say go, you fight!"

"But sir—"

"Ready Set Go!" Hawkes grabbed the closest cadet, who happened to be Ramirez, and threw him over his shoulder. He had two more cadets down before the rest finally sprang into action.

CHAPTER 15
WEAPONS

When Wouris joined them at last, it was well before 1400 hours. Keats had decided they'd had enough. No cadet was without a bruise, cut, or broken limb. It had been a massacre. Wouris quickly revised her earlier plans, and directed everyone to the medical branch.

Out of all of them, Lyn suffered the least. Her flexibility was outstanding, and had kept her mostly out of harm's way. Ramirez had fared the worst. His size quickly made him Hawkes' favorite target. Janus, Marcus, and Celes had all survived in slightly better shape than the rest. Janus had been doing well until Hawkes managed to catch him on the wrist and spin him hard onto his back. The dislocation and subsequent relocation of his shoulder had left him feeling slightly nauseous. Before tossing him onto a group of cadets, Hawkes had shouted down Janus' ear.

"Come on, boy, back into action! You're doing well!"

It was no wonder Wouris called them bluebacks.

Marcus, sporting a swollen eye and bruised ribs, followed directly behind Wouris. Celes hopped on her right foot, using Janus' good shoulder for support. She had unexpectedly requested his arm while recovering from Hawkes final offensive, and hadn't let go, much to Janus' chagrin. He wasn't used to people being this close in the slums. Occasionally she was forced to lean in to adjust her hand, and he would awkwardly twist his head away to avoid putting his face so close to hers. But even as battered as they were, he couldn't help but notice how different she smelled from anything he had known in Cerberus. It reminded him of a flower that had once somehow miraculously sprouted not too far from his home.

When they reached the Medical Wing, Major Yalla, head of ODIN's medical branch, dutifully situated the young cadets. Wouris had explained on the walk over that Yalla had served as a soldier and a medic for many years. But his time was past. Now a thin man with greying hair and a gentile disposition, he no longer served in any military capacity, but was still highly valued for his wisdom and knowledge from years of bravely saving lives on the battlefield.

For the first time, Janus had an opportunity to watch Nanytes in action. But Yalla distributed the blue Electrogel with the eye of a miser. Filling an injector with the tiniest of doses, Yalla targeted Janus' shoulder, and sent the blue goo directly into his arm. He was even more disappointed to realize there was nothing else to see. A warm sensation and strange tingling filtered into his shoulder.

"Two weeks' limited rations," Yalla said.

"What?" Janus asked in surprise.

"The cost for your dose. While you're a cadet, your wages are your food. But we won't let you starve. It'd be worse if you were a full-fledged Adept."

Janus was dumbfounded.

"Why?" he finally asked.

Yalla gave Janus a patient smile. He pointed to the blue tube emerging from the wall.

"Inside this goo are millions of microscopic pseudo-cells. The Electrogel keeps them alive, so to speak, until they enter the body. They'll do their job, die off after a few hours, and be flushed from your system. Make sense?"

Janus nodded slowly.

"But why are they so expensive?"

"It's not cheap to manufacture them. Neither in materials nor crafts-manship. And they can't be recharged or reused, so we have to transport them in Electrogel. That in itself is expensive and mildly carcinogenic, but the Nanytes take care of any ill effects. You're just lucky the Praetor covered that bullet wound. A cadet like you would have been paying that off for a while."

Janus nodded, moving his arm around. His shoulder was already feeling better.

"Does the Praetor get injections regularly?"

"Oh heavens no," Yalla chuckled. "Even the Praetor would go broke. More expensive than Immutium. But even if he could, he wouldn't. Nanytes are dangerous in high doses. They over-repair and over-build the body's systems."

"That doesn't sound too bad," Janus commented.

"It is if your heart and lungs become too big for your chest. And Nanytes can't save you from that."

Those cadets fortunate enough to have injuries that didn't require Nanytes avoided them. Marcus' eye was taken care of nicely without much additional aid, and Celes received a 'fast cast' that allowed her foot enough movement to perform, while helping it to heal. Ramirez was told that he would have to stay overnight. He would be on limited rations for quite a while.

With Yalla's permission, Wouris took the survivors for exercises around the Trunk. Even injured, the cadets were not allowed to stop. After many hours of training, she instructed them to eat and rest for the next day. Their introduction to Major Northcott would be postponed until tomorrow.

One blaring alarm, one chiding Daedalus, and 100 laps around the Trunk later, the cadets, with a recovered Ramirez, followed Wouris towards weapons training.

"Alright, listen up," she said. "You are about to meet Major Northcott. While performing your weapons training, obey Major Northcott's every command. He puts up with even less than Colonel Hawkes. This is for good reason; you will be training with some of the most dangerous weapons available to us. You'll be outside, on one of the landing platforms. Remember: this isn't a game, so be careful. We don't like having to replace you."

Weapons' training was held outside the bay marked with two runes shaped like an 'R' and an 'M.'

"Chariot of Voyages," Wouris explained. "This is the main launch platform for all ODIN missions."

Longboats waited in silent rows, suspended high above them, while mechanics worked on a few of the vessels on the ground. Walking by one at eye level, Janus suddenly realized how big they were, and how powerful their engines must be. Each was nearly as tall as he was.

"They only need one engine to fly, two to hover," Wouris interjected, as if reading his thoughts. "Between the reinforced prow and the strength of their engines, they can ram holes in the sides of buildings."

Janus studied the craft for a moment longer. But when the bay door opened to the outside, all thoughts of Longboats vanished from his mind.

It was just the second time that Janus had gone outside the base, and although his eyes still hurt, he adapted quickly to the bright sunlight. Janus drew in a sharp breath as he stepped out. He remembered the ocean from the edge of Cerberus, but now that he saw it up close, it was much more intoxicating. Hovering along the coast, Janus took a deep breath of salty air, listening to the calls of wheeling seabirds. In the distance, over crashing waves, sheer cliffs rose higher and higher, a clash between earth and water.

He lined up with the other cadets in front of a very irritable Major Northcott. It took Janus a moment to realize he was the ODIN ambassador he had first seen at Cerberus, fleeing from Middleton's office, recalling the same dark, black hair flecked with grey, the bushy silver mustache, skin the color of deep mocha. Behind Northcott sat a tripod and two large metallic cases.

"You!" He pointed a finger at a cadet in the back, a lanky boy with brownish-blond hair. "Name!"

Northcott's accent was thick and strange to Janus.

"Roderick, sir!"

"Roderick? Get over here. Move!" He made a motion towards the tripod set up behind him.

"Sir, yes, sir!" Roderick rushed out of line, nearly tripping as he scurried over to the tripod.

"Bluebacks," Northcott muttered. "Alright, cadets. You're here to learn how to use weapons, whether they're yours, the man's next to you, or the enemy's. I'm Major Northcott. If I give you an order you will obey it instantly, or you may end up with your head blown off. If you are not fortunate enough to blow your head off, then I will be happy to do it for you. Out here, my word is law, and you would do well to remember it. Do I make myself clear?"

Janus was unshaken by the bluster, but a few others looked less sure, the encounter with Hawkes still fresh in their mind. Yet despite their unease, every cadet responded clearly.

"Yes, sir!"

Northcott didn't seem to register the nervous looks at all. He simply turned and opened the case to his left.

"This," he said, hefting the huge weapon from its housing, "is a Zeus rifle."

Janus knew the look well. The rugged Zeus was a single beam of black steel sculpted and molded into a weapon. Thick, solid, and rectangular from stock to tip, the Zeus had no definitive barrel. The pistol grip and trigger were huge, made for the large hand of ST armor, and the stock of the gun was longer than usual, maybe a half-meter out, to accommodate for the suit's lack of flexibility.

"Over one and a half meters long and capable of carrying 4,000 rounds in single clip, the Zeus is one of the finest, most devastating weapons ever made. First mass produced by Hydra Corporation during the Shinai Outskirts Rebellion. The Zeus is hands-down the best infantry weapon available. Semiautomatic, firing 16-millimeter hollow rounds that can penetrate anything except a plate of Immutium."

Northcott traced a line along the barrel with his thumb.

"Unfortunately for you, you won't be using it. The batteries and capacitors required to power it make it unbelievably heavy, and the recoil would send you flying."

He put down the Zeus, and reached into the case, pulling out a compact, dull-metallic rifle. Its shape from the barrel to the stock suggested a triangle with rounded ends, and it shifted colors as he held it.

"In battle, you will be using the Skadi rifle. The Skadi is a fine weapon, valuable for Adepts because of its weight, size, and ability to match the active camouflage of your armor. Using electro-thermal rounds, it's powerful, but still vastly inferior to a Zeus' power, capacity, and accuracy. And unfortunately for you, the Zeus is the standard issue Security Trooper weapon."

Northcott dropped the Skadi back into the case and lifted up the Zeus.

"It is incredibly accurate. Each bolt is fired from the electromagnetic rail system at thousands of kilometers an hour. Deviation is less than a millimeter per kilometer traveled. To make things worse, its unique ammo design and massive capacity makes it virtually free of reloading, jamming, or even maintenance."

He pulled out the clip of ammunition to show what appeared to be a stack of pointed metal cups.

"In fact, the only good news is that you will rarely find an automatic version of it, because of the incredibly heavy power requirements. Roderick!"

"Yes, sir!"

"I will mount this weapon, and deploy several targets into the air. I want you to destroy them as quickly as possible. Understand?"

"Sir, yes, sir!"

Mounting the Zeus on the tripod, Northcott stepped over to the second case. He opened it, pulling out a long, metal tube, and resting it on his shoulder.

"Ready?"

Roderick looked down to check the weapon and Northcott immediately pulled a trigger on the tube, launching a long silver shape high into the air. Propelled by a rocket, it flew rapidly away from the city. Northcott added four more behind it. In a flash, the silvery shapes burst open, leaving their rockets behind and morphing into spinning discs that flitted upward and away from the city.

Roderick whipped the turret around and began to shoot wildly at the hastily vanishing discs.

"He's almost as bad as a Trooper," Janus whispered to Celes. "Maybe worse."

She gave him a scolding look, but the edges of her lips curled slightly.

The five discs were completely unharmed, becoming tiny specks in the distant sky, until they slowed, reaching the top of an extreme arc. High above the group, the discs were momentarily frozen, suspended for a brief moment from their fall, waiting to begin their long descent to the ground. But before they had fallen even an inch, all five suddenly veered, twisting in mid-air and making a beeline straight back at Roderick and Northcott. As they moved closer, they gained speed, darting rapidly from side to side. Roderick fired gallantly at the whirling discs, vainly trying to knock but one from the sky.

Major Northcott watched for a few more moments, then screamed into Roderick's ear.

"What are you doing? I'm glad you're not in the field, you'd probably hit me! Aim, boy, aim!"

Beads of sweat formed on Roderick's brow, as Northcott continued screaming. A palpable whirring filled the air, and the discs accelerated faster towards the platform. Janus felt his whole being become acutely aware of the five discs hurtling towards the group, and as he did, the world around him seemed to slow ever so slightly. He took a step back, and looked around. He was not the only one. The other cadets had done the same. Northcott was shouting again.

"Shoot, boy!"

Then he yelled to the cadets.

"This is a prime example of what you will likely face from Corporate Security Troopers. Absolutely pathetic. Move boy!"

Roderick scurried out of the way as Northcott forcibly grabbed the turret.

"This is what happens when you have a skilled hand."

He whipped the turret onto the first disc and it exploded in a flash of silver. Within moments three other discs were nothing but smoking remains as they fell from view over the edge of the platform. The fifth and final disc disintegrated completely as Northcott fired his final shot. Northcott turned away from the destruction without hesitation to look at the students. His voice was hard as he spoke.

"Do not underestimate the power of the weapons I show you."

Janus no longer thought Northcott was full of bluster.

CHAPTER 16
THE BEACON OF NEED

Sitting in the common room that evening, Janus felt waves of exhaustion wash over him. He had chosen a large leather armchair in one corner of the room, by himself. Despite his protests, the door to his room remained locked, so he had few other places to retreat. He imagined it was part of ODIN's efforts to instill unity through forced interaction.

As he stared through the skylights at the stars, he had to admit it might be working. The intensity of the past several days had planted the seeds of friendship between the new cadets. Sharing in mutual suffering did wonders. But for Janus, to be surrounded by so many people was a new, exciting, and frankly somewhat uncomfortable experience. Being in such close quarters was totally alien to him. But with hardly the chance to breathe, he hadn't been able to give it much thought.

Now, with a moment to think, he thought about the slums. They would be still and quiet at this hour. Clara would already be in her own armchair, getting what sleep she could before the next day. This would have been a perfect time to sneak out for more supplies.

"Ha! Beg for Mercy!" Lyn shouted at Ramirez, startling Janus from his reverie. She leapt up on a chair in the middle of the common room, standing triumphantly in celebration, and threw a card at the square table in front of her. The other cadets didn't even bat an eye. Janus wondered if she had done this more than once already. Ramirez, who though he was sitting was still about eye level with her, remained expressionless.

"Don't give me that look!" Lyn said. "I won fair and square."

Janus wasn't sure what look Ramirez was giving her, if he was registering anything at all. He had no idea how Lyn interpreted anything from Ramirez. He glanced around. Celes sat at the opposite end of the room, listening to Marcus as he told a story to several cadets.

Marcus appeared to mime an ST, suddenly pretending to look at an imaginary rifle in deep confusion. The raucous laughter that erupted filled the room. Kwandis leaned on Hughes, nearly doubled over. The other cadets, including Celes, laughed heartily at the joke.

Janus felt his throat go dry and rough.

"Oi! Janus!"

Janus startled again as he realized Lyn was yelling at him.

"Want ta play Mercy with us? Ya've been watching us play from over there for a while."

Janus glanced at the door to his room. It remained closed. He shrugged, and lifted himself from the armchair, moving to one of the couches at the center of the room.

"Do ya know how ta play?" Lyn asked.

"Five card? High crowns? Colors and suits?" Janus retorted with a smile.

Lyn grinned back.

"Finally got a player here, Ramirez. Can stop goin' easy."

Ramirez sat up, but still remained expressionless.

"Mind if we watch?"

Janus looked up to see Celes standing beside him. Marcus was right behind her. Lyn beamed, motioning to a seat.

"Want ta join? Five's no problem."

Celes sat down on the couch, and Marcus pulled up a chair. Other cadets followed in interest. Lyn shuffled the deck.

"Have you played before?" Janus asked.

Celes shook her head. Marcus nodded.

"It's pretty simple. The goal is to get rid of your Mercy."

"Sounds pretty cold," Celes smiled.

Janus laughed.

"That's the trick." He looked at Lyn. "Five card high crowns?"

She nodded.

"Everyone will start with five cards in their hand and a card face down on the table. You can look at your hand, but not at the card on the table. That's your Mercy card. The game is about deducing your card and other's hands based on what's been played. More players mean more options, but more information. Once your hand is empty, you flip over your Mercy card for everyone to see and then try to play it to win. If you can't, well…"

"Everyone else knows what it is," Celes interjected, "and will try to play around it for as long as they can while you 'beg for Mercy.'"

"You got it," Janus said. "The other rules are all about the variants of how you play cards. 'High crowns' means that you can connect low aces to any card with a crown."

"What do you consider a crown?" Marcus asked.

"Got burned by that one, did ya?" Lyn asked.

"Lost a day's wages to a cheat." Marcus replied.

"Happens to everyone." Lyn nodded knowingly and riffled the deck. "Me and Ramirez once lost our best catch because we didn't ask before we started. Never mind the fact he was aiming to play another way until we started beating the pants off of him. We'll play all crowns, any face card, for first games simplicity."

"Yeah, have mercy on me," Celes joked.

The cadets groaned.

"Sounds like they're beggin' for us ta start!" Lyn cried. Ramirez shook his head. And the games began.

An hour later, the group was perched over their cards, as the entirety of the cadets sat around to watch.

"You should play your last card, Celes," Janus said. "You've got a good chance of winning right now. Don't hold that card just because you don't want us to play on it."

Celes looked at Janus skeptically, pulling her remaining card close to her chest.

"How do you know what I've got?"

Marcus nodded sagely.

"He's right."

Celes looked around at the group.

"Does everyone here know what I have?"

Janus, Ramirez, Lyn, and Marcus all nodded. Everyone else did not.

"How do you all know?" Hughes asked.

"Celes has been shuffling that card around since the beginning," Janus said. "Marcus and I have both played sets that should be connecting in numerous ways, but they don't, and there are only a few options left. My guess would be that Celes is holding the eight, and that means she can play almost any card left, unless it's the three, five, or two."

"Lyn's got the three," Ramirez grunted.

"Hey! I don't talk about your tells!"

"Do ya know any?" Ramirez asked curiously.

Lyn stuck out her tongue at him.

"Which means that Celes only has a one in five chance of not being able to play and win immediately," Marcus concluded.

Celes carefully looked around at the cards on the table, and nodded in understanding.

"Well, I suppose I should get this over with then."

She placed down her eight next to Janus' nine and reached for her face down card. Janus could feel the collective group lean in to see her card.

Celes pulled the card to the edge of the table and— the lights shut off.

"What happened?"

"Can anyone tell what's going on?"

"What's her card? Did she win?"

A scolding voice sounded from above.

"Lights out! Return to your rooms now, or I will notify your Sergeant."

Bright lights came far too early for Janus' taste the next morning.

"Sergeant Wouris will be arriving shortly. Promptly ready yourself."

Janus shielded his eyes from the light. "What time is it?"

"0200 hours."

"Why is she showing up so early?"

The Daedulus remained silent.

"Is it that you don't know how to answer, or you won't, Val?"

"That is not an approved designation."

"Nope, not at all," Janus sighed, readying himself.

When she arrived, Wouris gathered the group, and whisked them across the city and upwards along the Trunk, many floors above the mess hall. Crossing a lonely bridge that sat separately from the ordered structure of the other branches, the cadets were greeted by a heavy, silent door.

109

Inside it was dark, but a large skylight and a ring of windows created a glass dome through which starlight filtered softly down on the cadets.

"This," she spoke in a low, clear voice, "is known as the Beacon of Need. It's a place any cadet, Adept, or officer may come at any time. You may use it freely, but know that it is dangerous if not handled respectfully."

Janus furrowed his brow.

Dangerous?

He looked around the empty room, turning to Marcus and Lyn on his right. They shared a mutual confusion. Wouris turned and walked into the center of the room.

"Lights!"

The room brightened slowly as the walls and ceiling came to life with a soft glow.

"This place will help you train. It is a place where you can face your fellow cadets, or test yourself."

She spoke loudly and clearly to no one in particular.

"Rotate, slow!"

The floor slowly rotated clockwise, moving the cadets in a circle along the outer wall, while Wouris turned slowly in the center, watching the cadets stare in wonder at the room. Celes looked unsurprised, but Janus found it difficult to conceal his fascination. Wouris spoke to them with a slight smile on her face.

"Of course, it can do much more than just go in circles, so feel free to come here when you have time off and experiment with it. All stop!"

The room slowed and halted, and the cadets were left standing on the other side of the room.

"This week, each of you discovered that your current combat abilities are woefully inadequate to take on someone like Colonel Hawkes.

Tonight, I hope to improve your odds. Remember, you always want to force your opponent to fight on your terms."

"Maybe Wouris isn't so bad after all," Lyn whispered to Marcus and Janus. "Especially if she can teach us how to stop Hawkes from killing us."

Wouris took them each through one-on-one training, showing them simple blocking maneuvers, pointing out errors and weaknesses, and demonstrating how to use an opponent's movements against them.

Marcus excelled. Whether it was something to do with his background, or just that he was a natural, he clearly knew his way around a fight. And while Ramirez was the biggest and strongest, it became clear he hadn't had much opportunity to practice. Janus doubted anyone had ever been brave enough to fight Ramirez head on. And he suspected that Ramirez would have avoided it anyway.

When it came time for Janus' turn, he quickly found himself covered in sweat, as he struggled to evade Wouris' attacks using what he knew and what he had seen from those before. Years of evading close calls in the slums had given him excellent agility, but he hadn't had much occasion to do more than that, so he found it difficult to find an opening to use any of the simple offensive maneuvers against Wouris.

"You're using too much energy, Janus!" Wouris said, delivering a punch that barely missed his shoulder.

Janus struggled to counter with a punch of his own. Wouris batted his arm aside, and delivered a light palm to his chest, setting him off balance and staggering backwards.

"You need to be better at seeing the whole. Where are the anchor points of the body? Where is the center? How am I moving? When you can see these things, you can know where I'm going before it happens. You can react to avoid anything."

Janus gasped for air as he leapt back to gain space. Wouris reacted immediately, pushing into Janus' space with powerful strides. Janus could see her cock her arm back for a powerful strike, and he raised his arms in a desperate block for his head.

Wouris' strike stopped just short of his face.

"Good. You saw it coming at least, even if you couldn't do anything about it."

Janus dropped his arms to his side, feeling like his heart was going to explode in his chest.

"Roderick you're next."

Roderick timidly stepped forward, as Janus dropped into line to watch.

Celes whispered to Janus, "She really worked you over."

Janus, still clutching his chest, nodded.

After an hour or so, Wouris returned to the center of the room.

"I have a few more lessons for you this morning. Marcus. Janus."

Marcus and Janus stepped forward and glanced at one another in surprise. Wouris looked at all the cadets.

"If you want to survive as Adepts, you will need to learn to adapt as a group, without the help of the officers. On the battlefield, things can get chaotic quickly. You will need to become comfortable training and learning on your own. This means instructing one another. I want all of you to watch this next exercise carefully and see if you can pick up anything from watching just Janus and Marcus move. Training circle segment twelve!"

A large glowing circle appeared on the floor, surrounding Janus and Marcus.

"This is a mock fight," she said. "No punching. No grabs. Open hands only. Touching the head and the blue stripe on the chest of your uniforms is worth two points. Touching the chest anywhere else is worth one. First to three. Leaving the circle is an automatic loss. When I say 'break,' you separate immediately. Understood?"

The pair nodded.

"Take positions."

Janus and Marcus turned to face one another. Janus felt his blood start pumping rapidly. This was a fight he could win. He raised his hands. Marcus smiled, raising his arms as well.

"Ready?" Wouris stepped out of the circle, looking back and forth between the two. "Go!"

Marcus leapt forward immediately, and Janus dodged to the side. *He's fast.* Fighting against Wouris made everyone look slow, but Marcus was more than keeping pace as Janus moved in a semicircle, skirting the edge of the circle.

Watch his body.

Janus knew he couldn't keep up the dodge routine forever. His earlier bout with Wouris was catching up to him. Marcus kept pressing him, however. But he was more predictable than Wouris. With every step Janus took, Marcus matched it one for one.

Wouris' voice cut across them. "Are you cadets just going to stare at this slack-jawed? Or are you going to talk about what you're watching?"

Janus momentarily lost focus as the cadets suddenly started chatting about the fight. Marcus closed in on his face and Janus pushed himself harder, catching a gloved hand moving just in front of his vision. There was an audible intake of breath from the crowd. Janus leapt back a few steps, his breath fast. He glanced at Marcus' face. He was smirking. Marcus was trying to make him tired.

Janus took a step back, but as he did so, he planted his foot early, and stretched his right arm out. Sudden surprise appeared on Marcus' face as he struggled to stop. But he was already committed.

But Marcus reacted quickly, extending his own arm. Janus felt a firm push in his chest as his fingers brushed armor.

"Break!"

Janus and Marcus stepped back, breathing hard.

"Two points to Janus. One point to Marcus."

The cadets whispered more.

"Marcus is fast. And he doesn't look tired at all."

"But did you see that move Janus pulled? If Marcus didn't have a longer reach, he would've hit him clean."

"Notice their movements," Wouris interjected. "Marcus. Janus. Return to center."

The pair readied up again.

"Go!"

Marcus followed him more carefully this time, and Janus knew the same trick wouldn't work twice. He would have to beat Marcus fair and square, and quickly. But he was up a crucial point. He could sacrifice a body shot for a body shot. Janus suddenly stopped again, and Marcus instinctively dodged to the side. Janus went right after him, pushing Marcus this time. It was significantly easier, and he realized Marcus must have known this all along. He could push the pace, and he didn't have to react. So he tried going more aggressive, watching Marcus' feet. Marcus skirted the edge like Janus. Janus glanced up. Marcus wasn't smiling this time, as he intensely watched Janus' arms and legs. So Janus flicked a hand out to the side, as if he were attempting to cut him off. Marcus raised an arm to block and stretched out with his other hand. Janus quickly realized he had underestimated Marcus' reach. Janus ducked, hoping to get inside. But as he planted his leg, his boot slid on the floor, and he careened forward, into Marcus' waiting arm. Marcus caught him on his forehead, stopping his fall.

"Break! Two points to Marcus!"

Janus pushed himself up and away in frustration.

"Close," Marcus said, stepping back.

"What happened?" Wouris asked the cadets.

"Janus slipped," Kwandis interjected.

Wouris glanced at Janus.

"True. But did you see more?" She stepped back a few steps as she spoke, watching the cadets. The morning sun had finally arrived, and she stood within a large circle of sunlight, highlighting her.

Celes raised a hand.

"Marcus had reach, and Janus misjudged it because of the first round. Neither of them were watching the ground, only each other."

Wouris nodded.

"Very good. As Adepts, your awareness is one of the keys to staying alive. You must watch your opponents, your teammates, and your environment at all times. Otherwise, the best laid plans will fall apart. In battle, even the slightest positional advantage can turn the tide. Never allow the battlefield to be decided by your opponent."

Wouris took several more steps backward, back into the darkness.

"Even on good pretenses."

Something in the tone of her voice unsettled him, and Janus felt a pit forming in his stomach.

"These advantages can include height, distance..."

He became suddenly aware that Wouris was now blocking the only door out of the room.

"Or even something as simple as an exit."

She stood there, smiling vaguely at them, waiting for their dawning comprehension.

"Each of you has had some defensive training, but how will you do on offense? If you manage to get out of this room, you are free to go, including you two, Hughes and Kwandis."

The pair looked flustered as the situation slowly dawned upon the group.

"Now let's see what you've learned!" Wouris raised her voice. "Chamber Test: Wouris I. Lock."

A disembodied female voice replied.

"Command registered. Now accepting commands from Sergeant Wouris. Initiating test sequence: Wouris I."

The door behind her locked and the room came alive with a strange hum.

Suddenly, the floor dropped out from beneath the cadets, falling about a meter, sending the group sprawling. Wouris' half of the room, on the other hand, rose upward, granting her the high ground, and a small plateau with which to fight off attacks. She looked completely at ease, not even taking a fighting stance as she stood on her circular hill. Without hesitation, Janus pulled himself to his feet and rushed her. Marcus was right beside him. Wouris just watched the pair rush the hill with a smile.

Just steps away from her, Wouris raised her arm, showing the back of her hand and made a brushing motion towards them. Janus felt the floor burst upward, sending Marcus and him flying backward. They slammed painfully into the floor and slid across it, stopping just short of the other cadets, who watched them, eyes wide.

The cadets stepped backward, trying to get closer to the wall. But Wouris shook her head.

"Will you stay there like frightened rabbits? Will you let me control you? Will you wait there all your lives?"

She made a simple gesture with her fingers and the wall behind the cadets sprang out, knocking them forward. Her expression took on an evil smirk.

"What if I don't let you?"

Her hand became a blur of motions, and the room sprang to life. The cadets went into a panic, as walls, floors, blocks, and bars sprang forth, attacking them from all directions. Cadets separated, trying to avoid the storm of blows, watching as some were swallowed by holes in the floor, others lifted high above their comrades.

"Come on, you worthless Bluebacks!" Wouris yelled. "Are you Adept or not? Anticipate!"

Janus leapt about the room, trying to stay ahead of the shifting onslaught. Out of the corner of his eye, he caught glimpses of others that were not so lucky. But Janus focused on Wouris. She waved her hands constantly in front of her. Sometimes up, sometimes down, sometimes making circular motions with her fingers. It was a blur. But yet, the longer he watched, the more he started to sense a pattern.

"She's using the same motions!" he exclaimed. She twitched in a new direction and a part of the wall slammed painfully into him, knocking him sideways. But he managed to keep his feet and saw another wall retract.

"We've got to attack her all together!" he yelled out to the other cadets. "She only has two hands. She can't make the room do everything at once!"

Some cadets looked uncertain, but Celes, ducking out of the way of another pillar that flew a hair's breadth over her head, yelled and waved her hand to the rest.

"Come on!"

"You four with me!" Marcus said, pointing at Roderick, Freeham, Bynes, and Kwandis. "Janus, I'll take the right!"

"I'm going left!" Lyn yelled. Ramirez leapt beside her, and the pair jumped just in time to avoid a wave in the floor.

With the rest of the cadets at least temporarily roused to follow, they leapt and dodged across the room, charging towards their quarry.

Janus repeated the mantra in his mind. *Watch her body.* He glanced over a rising block to see Wouris coolly watching him. *Anticipate!*

"Jump!" he yelled.

Janus wasn't sure why he said it. Whether it was because he deduced it, or it was a reaction to the slightest twinge of Wouris' fingers, or simply a feeling. But he shouted it.

117

And the cadets listened, just as the floor gave way.

Everyone cleared the gap, avoiding a disastrous fall. And suddenly, Wouris' face became hard and grim. She held her hands flat and the chamber became still. The cadets still charged forward, urged onward by their small victory. But then she did the unexpected; she charged, too.

Janus smiled inwardly. They had her; she would be overwhelmed.

Her hands flew out like she was pushing against air and suddenly the floor sprang up, launching her into a high-speed flying kick. Janus felt a sharp, unexpected pain, as her heavy boot connected with his gut. He was launched backwards, and the rest of the cadets rushed by in surprise.

Janus slid to a stop with Wouris right over him. He coughed up blood.

"You have a lot to learn, Janus."

She reached down and roughly hauled him up by the neck.

"You all are free to go," she said, making a motion with her hand. The door slid open. Through Janus' hazy vision, the door seemed so far away. "Except Janus. He's earned a few more lessons from me about the price of leadership."

She slugged him in the jaw, knocking him back to the ground. The cadets looked uncertainly between Wouris and the open door. No one moved. Yanking Janus back up by his armor, she spoke over her shoulder at them.

"Unless, of course, you want to see what surprises I have from this side of the room."

She opened her free hand towards the cadets, and the chamber immediately reacted, the floor dropping ominously. Her eyes never left Janus. He could hear footsteps moving towards the door.

"That's bett—" Wouris began, but something made her shift her weight suddenly, and her hand twitched. The floor exploded upward behind her. There was a flash of blond hair. It took Janus a moment to realize Celes had come to rescue him. But Wouris was ready. She grabbed Celes by her injured foot, bringing her painfully to the ground.

"You're going to need a bit more than that to—"

Wouris dropped Janus and Celes, leaping backward as Marcus and Lyn flew in.

"Ramirez, grab Janus—we'll block her," Celes yelled as she leapt to her feet.

Janus felt himself hauled bodily up, and heard an acknowledging grunt.

"That won't be necessary," Wouris cut in, standing up with a grin. "Chamber Test: Wouris I complete."

"Register," the chamber responded. "Test complete."

The light immediately dimmed again as the room went quiet, its dull hum disappearing. Only bright sunlight streaming from above illuminated the environment.

Wouris smiled, looking around at the cadets, who had come charging back across the room. Ramirez still held Janus up by the arm, supporting his weight. Celes, Lyn, and Marcus stood in matching defensive positions, still wary. But Wouris was totally relaxed.

"You passed," she said. "All of you. The final lesson of the morning. There will be many more trials before you become true Adepts, but this was a good first test. You learned something here today. Something that separates an Adept from a Security Trooper. Yes, your speed, your knowledge, your anticipation—these are important. But your loyalty, that is what defines an Adept, it is what keeps us alive and whole; not just physically, but spiritually."

She walked over to where Ramirez and Janus stood, and threw Janus' other arm over her shoulder.

"Now it's time to get our fearless leader here back to medical for another two weeks of limited rations."

Janus groaned.

CHAPTER 17
NEW HEIGHTS

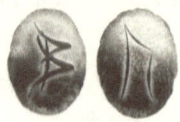

Keats was waiting for them alone in the Beacon of the Tree, and the cadets all breathed a sigh of relief. Wouris had let them free as promised, with the expectation they would arrive on time for their strategy lesson. Janus' jaw was a bit sore still, but he was already feeling a better from another round of Nanytes. Though Colonel Yalla had warned Wouris to ease up a bit, as he would only provide more injections in the most dire situations. Wouris had demurred, however, and Janus sincerely hoped that such concerns were unnecessary.

Keats motioned to the desks as the cadets lined up to salute her. They quickly sat, as Keats summoned the MuDi from the floor.

"Today will begin the first of many lessons on Corporate battle tactics. As all of you are aware, we have a unique relationship with the Corporations. And as such, it is important we understand them inside and out. We'll begin with something I'm sure all of you have seen."

The MuDi lit up, displaying a Security Trooper.

"Standard-issue corporate Security Trooper armor. The backbone of Corporate security and warfare. This particular version is a Mark VI Aries."

Janus leaned forward. It was fascinating to see the armor in a situation that didn't involve some hotheaded Trooper trying to push him around. Keats made a motion with her hand and the armor began to rotate within the MuDi.

"Refined over a century of warfare and use, Trooper armor provides a tremendous battlefield advantage over regular troops. We believe the first model was developed at Minotaur nearly one hundred and fifty years ago, but it proved so effective that it quickly proliferated around the world. What are some of the advantages this armor brings?"

Kwandis spoke up. "Enhanced strength and stamina."

"One of the biggest advantages it provides, actually."

"Chemical weapon and environmental protection," Ramirez grunted. Lyn seemed to avoid looking at him.

Keats' eyes lingered over Ramirez for a moment and she nodded.

"Armor?" Roderick asked.

"Not so much, I'm afraid. That might have once been true, but most modern weapons, including the Skadi rifle you will all be equipped with, will easily penetrate the plating of Trooper armor." Keats smiled. Her expression became more serious. "It is quite effective for riot suppression, however."

Roderick gulped.

"For good or ill, you all seem to be generally familiar with Trooper armor. But can any of you tell me some of its disadvantages?"

"Reaction time."

"Lateral movement."

"Blind spots."

Janus, Marcus, and Lyn all looked at each other. The other cadets, minus Ramirez, stared at them.

Keats nodded appreciatively.

"Very good. Yes, Trooper armor has evolved over the years to meet the needs of Corporations that have less and less reason to engage in guerilla warfare, and have pursued more public displays of power. These are the weaknesses that we will teach you to exploit when you engage them."

Hughes raised a hand.

"Yes, Hughes?"

"I know that we will eventually be asked to fight against Corporate Troopers on missions. But do the Troopers ever attack us?"

The cadets all looked silently at Keats. She sighed.

"It's very rare, and not something you should generally be concerned about. But it has happened. Generally, we are considered 'non-optimal' targets. Attacking us provides no territory. No real resources. And at the very least cuts off the Corporation from viable trading partners. But there is one well-known example of a Corporation attacking a Legion."

"Phoenix," Janus and Celes said together.

Keats looked sternly at the pair.

"Cadets, I allow this forum to be more informal to promote discussion, but I would prefer not to be interrupted. You are correct, however. Phoenix Corporation once attacked the SHADE Legion."

Celes raised a hand.

"Yes, Celes?"

"Does anyone know why?"

Keats cocked her head, as if considering how best to respond.

"There are theories. But ultimately, no. All we know is that Phoenix launched a surprise attack during a regularly scheduled trade."

"What happened?" Lyn asked.

"Both SHADE and Phoenix were destroyed."

"Just like that?" Valers asked in shock. "An entire Corporation?"

If Janus hadn't seen the result, he would have been just as shocked as the others.

"It involved a bit more than that," Keats said calmly. "But SHADE did enough damage that the other Corporations took the opportunity to burn Phoenix to the ground. But for now, let's return to our lesson, so we're prepared for anything that might come our way."

Over the next several hours, Keats broke down the armor, piece by piece. There was much to learn.

The next day dawned clear, and Janus found himself less groggy when Val woke him up. After their normal run and exercises, Wouris escorted them back to Major Northcott and the Voyages bay. The mechanics were hard at work, as usual.

"How long does it take to repair the ships?" Janus asked aloud. It didn't look like the mechanics had made any progress.

"Weeks," Valers responded from ahead of him. "If they're anything like Behemoths, they're durable, but proper maintenance requires a lot of effort. Shrapnel can end up anywhere, and the last thing you want is to be surprised by a failing engine at a critical time. I suspect the mechanics here meticulously check every piece after any sort of engagement. And if we were waiting for parts from Cerberus, some of the repairs would have only just started with so many birds to service."

Janus was impressed. "How do you know so much about it?"

"Mechanic family." Valers shrugged. "Been servicing Behemoths at Minotaur since I was little. Good at crawling into the small spots, you see."

"You're from Minotaur, too?" Celes asked curiously.

"Yeah. Wait, did you grow up there?"

Celes cleared her throat. "I know Jones is from there."

She motioned towards the dark-haired woman behind them. Jones leaned forward.

"What about me?"

Janus nodded towards Valers.

"You're both from Minotaur."

"Yeah." Valers smiled. "But we never met before coming to ODIN. It's a big place, I imagine like the other Corporations. We were basically from opposite sides of the city."

Lyn shook her head and looked back from a couple rows ahead of Janus.

"I can't imagine living in a Corporation. Not knowing someone living in the same place. Valhalla is huge as it is. When we first laid eyes on Cerberus, I couldn't believe that anything could be that much of an eyesore."

She glanced at Janus. "No offense."

"Trust me," Janus laughed. "I don't disagree. But home is home."

"Cadets!" Wouris yelled. "Fall in!"

Janus looked forward to see Northcott just in front of them. The cadets immediately stopped their chatting and jogged forward, falling into line.

"Major." Wouris saluted.

"Sergeant. I'll take it from here, thank you."

Wouris turned on her heel and left the cadets with Northcott once again. Northcott eyed them for a moment, and then gruffly began pacing along the line.

"Last time, I introduced you to the standard issue Security Trooper weapon, the Zeus. You'll have many more chances to experience it in the future...but for now, it's time to acquaint you with the backbone of the ODIN Legion: the Skadi."

Janus felt there was something decidedly ominous about the way Northcott paused there, but he quickly focused on the triangular rifle that Northcott produced from a set of nearby crates.

The Skadi did not shift colors this time, instead appearing as a simple matte black. As Northcott brought the rifle forward, Janus realized how small and compact it was compared to a Zeus.

"The Skadi, along with the larger Vidar sniper and Fenris pistol," Northcott began, holding the weapon toward the ground, "is electro-thermal, making it a considerably smaller and more manageable weapon. Unlike the Zeus, the Skadi fires cartridge-based rounds, using an electric charge to propel the ammo forward. Because of this, Skadis can be managed by someone not wearing powered armor like Security Troopers. Can anyone tell me the biggest advantage Adepts have using the Skadi?"

Roderick hesitantly raised a hand.

"Roderick!"

"Sir, the electro-thermal nature of the rifle!"

"WRONG!" Northcott whirled on the hapless cadet. "It's discipline! Which is exactly why none of you have a rifle in your hands right now. I don't plan on getting shot by some blueback who doesn't know how to handle a weapon. Discipline keeps us cool in battle. Discipline keeps us from making mistakes. Discipline is the only way any of you are going to survive your first battle."

Northcott kicked open the crates in front of the cadets. Janus could just see a line of Skadis within each one.

"These weapons are unloaded, to prevent you from hurting yourselves or others. We're going to cover the basics. Has anyone here ever operated a rifle before?"

Marcus confidently raised a hand. Celes did too.

"Cadet!" Northcott barked at Marcus. "Come here."

Northcott grabbed a rifle from the nearest crate and shoved it into Marcus' arms. "Show me your Trooper training."

Marcus looked down at the rifle.

"Sir?"

"Pretend you're going to shoot."

He waved to a far wall. Marcus pulled the weapon up to his side with one arm and aimed down the sights.

Boom!

Janus nearly jumped at the sound, but forced himself to stand still. Marcus had started, but mostly kept calm. Janus looked around. Most of the cadets had jumped, but Lyn and Ramirez were crouched, as if ready to run. Celes had not moved. Janus followed her gaze to Northcott, who was holding his rifle out towards the open sky. Waves of heat radiated from the barrel as he lowered the weapon.

"What are you doing?" he yelled. "Are you trying to kill someone?"

"No sir."

"Then why didn't you check your weapon first?"

Marcus swallowed.

Northcott shook his head. "Medusa Trooper, right?"

"Yes, sir."

"They haven't done a good job in years."

Marcus bristled, but Northcott put a hand on his shoulder.

"Nothing personal, son. You're doing as you were taught. Which unfortunately, was all wrong. Troopers can get away with a lot, and wearing armor can easily teach bad habits. We'll fix it up."

He turned to the cadets, who were starting to relax again.

"Never assume a weapon is unloaded. Never assume it is working as intended. Discipline always! As Adepts, your weapon will be your life on the battlefield. If it doesn't work as it should, if you don't know its state at all times, you might as well be dead. Knowing whether you have one round left or none could be the difference between victory and defeat."

Northcott looked at Celes.

"Cadet."

Celes stepped forward. Northcott took the rifle from Marcus and handed it to her. She immediately pointed the weapon at the ground and checked the chamber. Northcott nodded in approval.

"How would you fire this weapon?"

Celes stepped past Northcott, towards the open bay door. She crouched on one knee and pulled the Skadi into her shoulder.

"Father or mother?"

"Father," Celes replied succinctly.

Northcott smiled, and then pulled the magazine from his own weapon. He tossed it to Celes.

"Demonstrate."

"What am I aiming at, sir?"

Northcott looked up and down at Celes' positioning once more. And then he picked up the expended round casing from his weapon.

"There are five rounds left in that magazine. Hit one of these while I toss them out."

"I'll try, sir."

"Ready?"

Celes nodded.

"Begin."

The casing flew out from Northcott's hand, over Celes head and into the open sky, glinting in the sun.

Boom!

The casing continued its fall, but Northcott had already snatched the next case from the air and tossed it forward.

Boom!

Another miss. A third flew further out this time.

Boom!

The glinting case suddenly tumbled and veered sideways.

Boom!

A short throw continued to fall.

Boom!

A long throw flashed to the right.

Celes pulled the rifle from her shoulder and checked it was empty.

"Whoa," Valers said. Janus was inclined to agree.

"I don't think anyone in my division at Medusa could have done that," Marcus added.

Northcott rubbed his chin in satisfaction.

"Very good. We'll shorten that reaction time so the close ones don't escape."

"How many did she hit?" Jones whispered from down the line.

"Two," Lyn said. Ramirez grunted in agreement.

"Third and Fifth," Roderick said meekly.

Northcott looked back at the group.

"I'll soon expect even better showings from all of you." He looked down at Celes, who was still crouching, and chuckled. "For you, we'll aim even higher."

CHAPTER 18
SIMPLE TASKS

A week later, the sun dawned with clear skies over an open ocean. Janus leaned against a wall of the Longboat he sat in, waiting for a sign they were close to their destination. He had been stuck inside the practical, but not particularly comfortable craft for nearly five hours.

There were four Longboats in total. Three held the entirety of ODIN's new cadets, plus the pilots. The fourth held Sergeant Wouris and two officers: Captain Rogers, their instructor for the day, and Major Winters, the leader of ODIN's scout corp. Major Winters was overseeing the cadets' first outdoor foray, and on the lookout for individuals with potential. Rogers would be leading them while Wouris watched from the sidelines. From what Janus had overheard in the mess, Rogers was one of the finest blade masters in Valhalla, whatever that meant.

"Head's up! Target in sight." A boisterous voice came over the intercom.

Janus' Longboat was piloted by a woman known as Glory. She was a veteran who had been around for many years, and had streaks of silver in her black hair.

"Cadets ready up!" Glory exclaimed. "Get ready to deploy."

Janus leapt towards the front of the Longboat, peering through the cockpit.

"What do you see, Janus?" Kwandis asked from the back.

"A beach."

Clear blue water lapped against white sand, highlighted by bright dawn light, with a dense tropical jungle just a few hundred meters away. Dense hills rose up in the distance, culminating in a cliff several kilometers away.

Janus felt his stomach drop as the Longboat swooped low and nearly plowed into the sand nose first, just skirting the beach. A green light illuminated on the right side of the Longboat.

"Right side deployment!" Hughes said.

The cadets moved into line on the right, and Janus moved to the back of the line.

"Remember, back to forward," Janus yelled ahead.

"Hit it!" Glory yelled.

The armored door on the right side of the Longboat flew forward and out, creating a wall that blocked their forward view, but gave them a clear view of the white sand and water. The Longboat was still moving speedily across the sand. Janus steeled himself and jumped, tapping the shoulder of Jones in front of him as he went. He landed, stumbling on the heavy sand, but kept his feet as the Longboat moved away from him. Jones landed stumbling in front as well, and the cadets leapt neatly in a running line, the door of the Longboat providing cover for them.

Until Hughes, that is. As Kwandis jumped, she tapped Hughes, but he hesitated at the moving Longboat, and froze. After a moment, Hughes recovered, but it was too late. Janus could see the tops of trees in front of the Longboat, and it veered, sending Hughes and the remaining cadets tumbling back inside as it sharply banked up and away. Janus stopped running to watch, and realized that his group was not the only one to properly deploy.

Celes, Lyn, Ramirez, and Marcus also stood on the beach, watching their own Longboats as groups tumbled back inside for failing to deploy quickly enough. With a better angle, Janus could see the shock and surprise on Valers' face as the Longboat rolled unexpectedly away from the sand.

"What happened?" Jones asked. "Did Hughes freeze?"

Janus nodded.

"Only for a second."

"But that is more than enough," Wouris interjected, coming up behind them. She, Rogers, and Winters watched as the Longboat doors slammed back shut and proceeded to perform a difficult set of evasion maneuvers.

Rogers shook his head knowingly.

"That's right painful." He slapped Janus on the shoulder. "Best way to learn though. Never miss your window."

Janus took in the man. He was lean, and had brown hair speckled with grey. But his face was still very young. Janus wasn't sure if the man was old or just prematurely grey. His brown eyes had a hint of merriment in them as he watched Glory's Longboat do a set of barrel rolls. Jones winced at the maneuver.

"Well, we'll have them down soon enough. The pilots know full well they still have training to do today," Winters said. She was a small woman, with strawberry blond curls and freckles.

"Right you are, Major. And then the real fun can begin," Rogers added, clapping his hands together.

Janus had a flashback to his first run with Wouris, and his stomach dropped.

"Logs?" Lyn asked.

She eyed the three massive wooden logs that had been stacked on the beach, laid out in front of the cadets. The first two were long, and looked massively heavy. The third was even bigger. Rogers smiled.

"That's right."

"You want us to carry logs around?" Roderick asked.

"Yes."

"That's kind of primitive, isn't it?" Jones asked. "Sir."

Rodgers laughed.

"There are a few conditions."

Marcus folded his arms over his chest.

"You'll have to work as a team. I know some of you are stronger than others." He glanced over at Ramirez, who was testing lifting one of the smaller logs by himself. "Much, much stronger. But most of you will not be able to lift these on your own, so you couldn't move them without help, even if you wanted to. However, that's not enough. Moving these logs has rules."

"And what are those, sir?" Celes asked.

Rogers looked around at the group of cadets.

"You'll be divided into groups of seven, similar to how you were in the Longboats. You can only move a log if the seven of you are touching the log, and only if it is above your shoulders. Dropping your log before you reach your destination will result in consequences."

"And where are we moving these logs?" Janus asked. He regretted the question as soon as he asked.

"Why, right over there." Rogers pointed with a laugh. His finger traced a line upwards to the top of the cliff. An audible whimper sounded from somewhere.

"Now as for teams: Marcus, Roderick, Naka, Browning, Zhao, Nathans, Bynes. Grab that first log there. Hughes, Alexis, Young, Kirsten, Byron, Lyn, Freeham. You're on log two."

Ramirez looked towards Lyn in surprise. Rogers looked over at the two teams. "What are you waiting for? Get that log up and moving!"

"Cadets! Move out!" Wouris barked, and the two teams swiftly surrounded the logs.

"Janus, Celes, Valers, Jones, Holloway, Kwandis, Ramirez. You get the big 'un." Rogers chuckled. Janus looked at the log and grimaced. It was huge.

"Stop staring and get moving cadets!" Wouris shouted.

Janus bent down and strained; the log barely moved.

"Work together!" Rogers yelled. "This isn't an individual exercise!"

Ramirez reached down and hauled the log up, straining visibly. Janus quickly moved under the log to help, and between the seven of them, they held the log up above their heads.

"Good." Rogers smiled. "Now get moving."

The seven began marching across the sand, holding the log in a mishmash of ways. Ramirez had to stoop a bit to let the shorter cadets reach the log without stretching too much. They had barely moved fifty meters when Janus' shoulders began to throb. His feet shifted in the sand, and beads of sweat covered his face. The sun rose higher and higher in the sky. The log crushed down on him.

If I could just shift the weight a little…

He pushed on the log, trying to get a better position.

"Ugh!" Celes' grunt from behind him made him stop.

"Watch it, cadet," Wouris said. "Your companions might not appreciate that log moving around too much. Looks like some of your companions are struggling."

Janus looked up and realized Jones was drenched in sweat directly in front of him. He had been so busy focusing on the ground just trying to walk, he hadn't even noticed. The two of them were at the front, so he had no idea how the rest of the line was doing.

"How you doing there, Jones?" Janus breathed.

"Fine. Just peachy."

Janus turned his head to shout back. "How's everyone doing back there?"

"Real great, Janus," Celes grunted.

He took a brief moment to look around. The other teams were slightly further behind them, but struggling equally. The cliff was impossibly far away. And Wouris, Rogers, and Winters were all watching them, as if waiting for something.

"Cadets, halt," Janus said.

The group of seven stumbled to a stop.

"What are you doing, Janus?" Wouris yelled.

Janus ignored her. The other two groups stumbled to a halt as well, watching.

"Jones. Tell everyone exactly how you're doing right now."

Jones gritted her teeth and shouted, "I'm about to die, Janus, so if we don't get this log moving shortly, I'm going to haunt you in the afterlife."

"I'm hurting," Janus shouted back, "but I can carry more weight."

He was glad Celes was right behind him, especially when she chimed in.

"I'm with Jones. I can't carry anymore."

Ramirez was in the middle. "Can carry more."

"Everything hurts."

Valers.

"I'm not sure if I can take more."

Kwandis.

"It hurts, but I can continue."

Holloway.

"Ramirez," Janus shouted back. "Can you take a bit more for a moment? I'm going to reposition myself, and then grab a bit more weight. Then you reposition yourself as best you can, then Holloway, you do the same."

"Done," Ramirez grunted.

Janus felt the log get noticeably lighter, but he heard Ramirez' strained breathing. He quickly repositioned himself.

"Ready," he said, and the weight came back. It got heavier, but only for a moment. Janus could hear Holloway moving, and then the weight felt lighter all around. Janus pushed his shoulder into the log a bit more. He could hear sighs of relief from the others, and Jones looked a little less tense.

"Everyone ready?" he shouted down the line. "March!"

Their pace doubled. That wasn't saying much. But Janus could feel the whole group become more energized. They had only gone a bit further when he could hear the voices of the others doing the same. He caught a glimpse of Rogers nodding and smiling.

But Janus quickly realized the worst was yet to come. The dense jungle lay ahead of them. The sand was bad enough, but the idea of the jungle seemed impossible.

"Lyn," Ramirez grunted from behind him.

"What?"

"We need Lyn."

Janus was confused, but Ramirez seemed to read his mind. "For the jungle."

Janus looked at Lyn's group. They were struggling the most, even with the adjustments.

"Can we help them?" Celes asked.

"The rules say we can't drop the log, and we can't move it unless all seven of us are touching it," Valers interjected.

"So don't move it," Ramirez said simply.

"Cadets, halt," Janus said.

The group stopped more smoothly this time.

"Can we hold this log up with six?" Janus asked.

There was a pause.

"I think we can," Celes said.

"Aye," Jones seconded.

There was a chorus of agreement from the others.

"Kwandis. You still feel okay?" Janus called out.

"Ready to go."

"Everyone else ready?"

The agreement was quick and loud.

"Get to it, Kwandis."

As Kwandis slipped out from under the log, Janus could feel even more weight pressing down. It was bearable only because they weren't moving. Kwandis took off across the sand, finally reaching Lyn's group, lagging meters behind them. She jumped into the middle, helping to hold their log. The look of relief on the team's faces was palpable, but they still weren't moving that fast, and Janus could feel their own log biting deeper into his shoulder. The sun was starting to beat down upon them. Significant time had passed just to move them a few hundred meters down the beach. The log shifted slightly, and several grunts rippled down the line.

Marcus had slowed his group down, and as Lyn's team pulled next to them, they fell into line together, and offered a few free arms to help lighten the load. The pace of Lyn's team increased dramatically, and soon they had almost completely caught up to Janus and the rest. After a few more steps, Kwandis extricated herself from the group, and returned to Janus' team. Her return was greatly welcome.

"Ya' been waiting long?" she quipped through gritted teeth.

"Usual," Ramirez responded. "Need a path."

Lyn peered ahead and shook her head.

"Not here. Need a game trail."

"You sure?" Marcus huffed out.

"Don't want ta go that way."

"Doesn't look bad," Jones gasped.

Lyn gathered a breath before raggedly replying, "No trails means there's something we're not seeing."

"Not sure...how much more...we can take," Kirsten said between heavy breaths.

"Going to stand there all day, cadets?" Wouris called from behind them.

Marcus looked around.

"Any ideas?"

"Let Lyn scout," Ramirez said. Lyn nodded in agreement.

"Stop until I find us something."

"As in...hold this thing...while you go off?" Kirsten asked in disbelief.

Janus looked around. Everyone was struggling, well, except maybe Ramirez. But even he looked strained.

"This isn't supposed to take all day," Rogers chimed in.

"I don't know if we can hold for that long."

"Let's try going forward here anyway," Marcus said.

Lyn looked doubtful, but said nothing.

"We'll go first," Marcus added. He looked at Janus and the rest of his group. "Can you help hold the other log while we go ahead?"

Janus tilted his head back and heard a series of affirmative grunts.

"Sure."

After a few moments of maneuvering, Marcus' team was free to move into the jungle. They marched forward cautiously, wary of underbrush.

The growth was dense, but not impassable. The ground seemed surprisingly smooth. Janus peered into the shadows, trying to follow the path of Marcus' team. Rogers and Winters moved carefully forward, watching the group. Suddenly, there was a sound of suction, and Naka cried out from the front. The log tipped to the left in slow motion, and Janus fought the urge to dash forward. Suddenly, all of Marcus' team pitched over, and the log came crashing down.

"Aaargggh!" Nathans screamed.

"Ramirez!" Marcus cried from the front.

Nathans was pinned to the ground underneath the log, and his arm was bent at a bad angle.

"Ramirez, we need you now!"

Ramirez started to move the log to the side, and Janus could feel the crushing weight coming down. He could feel everyone in the group getting ready to drop it.

"Don't you dare drop that log, cadet!" Wouris shouted.

"Janus! Go!" Ramirez said.

Janus felt the log lift up, and he dashed out and forward. Nathans was in pain, but Marcus' voice told him that wasn't the problem. He burst through the bushes to find Marcus and the others stuck in mud and struggling to lift the log.

"Naka! He's under it!" Marcus shouted.

Janus could see Naka's flailing arm, but not his head. He was buried in the mud. Janus looked for a brief moment around. Winters was standing nearby, counting.

"Thirteen…fourteen…fifteen…sixteen…"

Rogers nodded in time with her, but made no move to help.

Janus looked at the closest spot to Naka, and braced to jump.

"Not there!" Lyn came bursting out of the bushes.

"Over here!"

138

She leapt over to a patch of grass and grabbed the log, heaving. She only sunk an inch or two. Janus jumped after her, and together with the others, they pulled the log off of Naka, shoving it back towards dry ground. Marcus hauled Naka up, who sputtered and spit mud. Nathans moaned to one side.

The cadets huffed and bent over their knees recovering.

"You cadets appear to have dropped your log and do not appear to be picking it up," Major Winters said simply. Janus and Marcus looked at her in disbelief.

Wouris appeared.

"Cadets, pick that log up now!"

"But Naka and Nathans!" Marcus protested.

Wouris gave a once over on Naka, who was white as a sheet, but did not appear to be injured.

"I'll look at Nathans," she said. "You look fine to me. Pick that log up."

"But we're down a man!" Marcus said.

"Are you questioning my orders, cadet?" Wouris said, stepping forward. Marcus swallowed hard.

"No, Sergeant."

He, Janus, Lyn, and the other cadets hauled up the log.

"Let's get this moving. Janus, Lyn, mind helping us clear the jungle?"

"And where do you think you're going?" Winters asked.

"We're going to look for another way around," Marcus said.

"Not without Nathans, you're not."

"What?" Bynes asked incredulously. "His arm is broken."

"Do you think that stops you from following orders? Do you think an enemy is going to care that you broke an arm?"

"I thought we were supposed to support each other?" Marcus looked towards Wouris. "Not just watch while one man drowns and another suffers."

"We do." Rogers stepped forward. "Which is why Major Winters and myself are watching closely. Which is why when we saw Naka take a breath right before going under we knew we could count off a few seconds before jumping in, in the hope that you would figure out how to make things work."

Wouris looked up from examining Nathans' arm.

"You'll recover with an injection or two. We'll splint it soon enough."

Nathans was breathing quickly through gritted teeth, obviously in pain. He struggled up.

"Put a hand on the log, Nathans," Roderick said.

Nathans did so, his other arm hanging limply, and Winters nodded.

They emerged from the jungle a few moments later, to a scene that seemed hardly more believable than the last one. Ramirez was down on one knee, supporting the large log entirely by himself, muscles bulging with strain. Celes and the others were helping support Lyn's log, looking as though they could barely stand.

Rogers looked up at the sky. The sun was already nearing midday.

"None of you are going to make it today. Best return those logs and we'll try again another day." He turned and shouted to the group. "Ready up cadets! I want those logs stacked before we can go home.

Janus knew that if he let go of Marcus' log, the whole group would collapse again. Ramirez gave him a nod. He turned his head to Marcus.

"Let's hurry and drop this off, then we can rush back and help the others."

Marcus nodded, and Janus caught a glimpse of Nathans squaring his good arm under the log, struggling to add as much power as he could.

Janus barely remembered getting the logs back. Once on the Long-boat, he drifted in and out of sleep amidst the vivid dressing down Wouris gave Lyn and Ramirez for not speaking up more about their misgivings, and how that had nearly gotten someone killed, while Nathans grunted in pain from standing at attention. For once, he sorely wished he could be on half-rations for another week, if only so his shoulders would stop burning.

CHAPTER 19
BREVIS BELLUM

Janus no longer required the alarm to wake him up in the morning. His muscles no longer ached every day. He just wished sleeping had gotten easier.

His armor today was thicker, protecting him against the frosty weather. Valhalla was moving north again, and winter was upon it. Wordlessly, Val showed him a screen to the outside, where frozen seas churned and swelled, the wave caps adding an appropriate white tinge under grey skies. He glanced at the chronometer; he was up early again.

Today he and the other cadets would perform a field-training test in a joint weapons and tactics session. Flopping back into his bed, Janus reflected how the time had flown by. How long had it been? Months? More?

Wouris' rigorous training had pushed them to new limits of physical toughness, and he had learned all about the variety of Adept weapons: the Skadi rifle, the Vidar sniper, the Fenris, and many more. They had learned the ins and outs of Corporate tactics and strategy, and studied ST armor, learning its weaknesses and its strengths. But with everything Janus learned, he realized there was much more he did not know. Every part of a cadet's life was devoted to learning. Every spare moment Janus could find he spent poring over Valhalla's database. Every Longboat voyage made for hours of study. Math, science, literature, history. How humanity and the Corporations had changed each other, and how humanity had once been so much closer to the stars than they were now. All of them mattered to the life of an Adept, and Janus gobbled it up.

He put his hands behind his head, staring out at the grey-green. Each cadet had developed his or her own specialties and strengths, learning to rely on the others to eliminate their weaknesses. Celes was the go-to sniper. Lyn, their scout. Ramirez could carry a small army's worth of heavy weapons. Out of all of the cadets, only he and Marcus seemed to be the odd ones out. They varied, not unexpectedly. But neither had been able to set themselves apart as exceptional in any particular thing.

Over the past few months, he had realized years in the slums had made him more methodical.

The slums. Clara. How is she?

He thought about their days of picking through the trash. Struggling to survive. To his days of run-ins with Cerberus security and always getting away by being too clever for them to handle. By helping them beat themselves. Making them look like fools was always worthwhile, even if it cost him a bit later.

In his mind's eye flashed Clara's disappointed gaze, followed by the sickening end of the ST named Hammer. Janus grimaced, and pushed the image from his mind.

The image of a Security Trooper brought Marcus to mind, and he focused on that. Marcus was bigger and faster, preferring quick, unexpected attacks. To strike hard, and without mercy. He firmly believed that speed was the key to victory, and to preventing unnecessary losses

These tactics carried over into the board game Janus had seen his first day in Valhalla and the pair now frequently enjoyed. It was like a variant of chess, a game called *Brevis Bellum,* or 'short war.' What made it different from chess is that it could involve anywhere from two to four players, all fighting for domination over an octagonal board. He and Marcus were closely matched. Their games attracted quite a crowd, and a number of challengers, including some of the officers.

A seabird that had perched upon Valhalla's exterior now launched forward from below the window, as if it had been magically commanded. As if it were a pawn on a battlefield. A sudden rush of swells gave the impression of a marching army, and Janus pictured Marcus looking at him from across the waves.

It was a four-player match between himself, Marcus, Lieutenant Forrenza, and much to Janus and Marcus' surprise, Major Northcott. Despite their initial skepticism regarding Northcott actually playing games, they had quickly discovered that the Major was one of the finest players in all of Valhalla, second only to Keats and the Praetor.

The goal of Brevis Bellum was to capture and hold certain strategic points upon the board. Only by holding the strategic points could one achieve victory; pure destruction of the enemy was usually not the goal. Each player had a certain number of 'deployments' that could be used to purchase units at the start, each of which had unique advantages and disadvantages. It made each unit choice crucial.

Unfortunately, it also made each unit loss a devastating blow. And Janus and Marcus had lost many units today. Individually they were fierce, but they had been at each other's throats for the entirety of the game. Northcott had kept his forces reserved, only grabbing what points he could, without sacrificing units.

"Brevis Bellum is a game of understanding the different forces at work on a battlefield, especially through the eyes of an Adept," Northcott instructed, with a bored look on his face. "I'm afraid that both of you are missing a key concept right now."

He grabbed his Fafnir gunship and advanced it six spaces, destroying another of Forrenza's Hoplite infantry. Forrenza miserably glanced at her remaining Hoplite.

"I would figure it out gentlemen, or you'll soon face a fate similar to mine."

Northcott advanced his own Hoplite two spaces, eliminating Forrenza's final unit.

"Shut out," he said. "I believe that's double rations for me, Lieutenant."

Forrenza sighed.

"Geez, Forrenza, when are you going to learn?" a spectator called out.

"I'll get him eventually!" Forrenza shook her fist. "Besides, he actually has to win the game first. That's a condition of the bet."

But she looked doubtful of her chances even as she said it.

Play returned to Janus, who advanced his Jormungand assault platform, his sole remaining unit with any real chance of doing damage. Other than that, he only had two surviving Hoplites. He moved them behind the Jormungand, using it as a shield. There wasn't much more he could really do.

Northcott's force was still essentially untouched, with three Garm tanks, a Fafnir, and a Hoplite. He had only five strategic victory points to Janus' eight and Marcus' nine, but Janus knew that would quickly change. Northcott had moved all three of his Garms towards the rightmost control point.

It was Marcus' turn. He had two Fafnirs and a Hoplite, perhaps the fastest remaining force, but the least powerful. He pushed his first Fafnir forward, to a position where it could strike Janus' Jormungand and Northcott's Garm tanks. His second moved left, to a flanking position on the Garm's.

Northcott's turn. He barely looked at the board as he moved his Fafnir only three spaces, well within striking distance of Janus' Jormungand. The move was shocking. Positively boneheaded. Janus wondered if Northcott was getting lazy. With one shot, he could eliminate two enemy Fafnirs: Northcott's and Marcus'. Of course, if he didn't destroy the Fafnir, he would be exposed and would need to retreat or lose his assault platform to Marcus. He reached for his Jormungand, and Northcott suddenly sat up, as if seeing the board for the first time in a while.

"Whoops. Well, that was a mistake on my part."

Janus froze. His hand hovered over his Jormungand. Putting his hand on the piece would mean he was committed to moving it. He pulled slowly away.

Northcott looked at him skeptically.

"You don't like free units, cadet? Aren't you trying to win?"

Janus looked at the board, and then at Marcus, who was grimacing at Northcott's decision-making. He had banked on his Fafnir being a particularly unattractive target.

Janus returned his gaze to Northcott, and he understood. He smiled.

"Yes." He turned to Forrenza. "You owe the Major double rations if he wins, right?"

Forrenza nodded.

"Would you give those rations to Marcus and me if we beat him?"

Forrenza laughed approvingly. "Absolutely."

Marcus' eyes went wide, and he nodded in understanding. Before another moment passed he glanced at Janus with a smile of agreement. But Northcott remained impassive.

"Bold words. How do you plan to do that if you don't start taking out my units?"

"I won't do that by eliminating your Fafnir. At least not yet."

"Oh?"

"Destroying it is exactly what you want. It will eliminate Marcus' gunship, too. And if that weapon goes down, the whole line we have between the two of us will be broken, and you'll overrun us with your tanks."

"And what about Marcus?" Northcott said, unsmiling. "Your Jormungand is exposed. If you retreat, you'll lose what small gains you've made. He'll take everything from you over the next few turns. Destroying your opponent when you can, is that not how you play the game?"

"Things change," Marcus interjected.

"Common purpose unites us," Janus added with a joking smile.

Marcus slapped him on the shoulder.

"Namely, stuffing our faces with extra rations."

When all was said and done, Marcus was declared the winner. Janus' Jormungand couldn't stand up to both Fafnirs after Northcott's Garms had been cleaned up by their combined efforts. But as Northcott stood up, gracious in defeat, he nodded to Janus. "Now you're thinking like an Adept, and a leader."

A knock on the door brought him out of his reverie.

"Janus, ready?"

It was Ramirez. He too seemed to suffer the same trouble with sleep, and for several weeks both he and Janus had woken up before the others.

With a nod, Janus opened his door, and the pair disappeared into the dark.

Chapter 20
Tidings of War

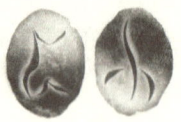

When Janus and Ramirez reached the mess, Praetor Jennings was sipping his morning coffee in a corner, looking out through the giant, frost-covered windows. The two cadets were surprised to see him, but moved through the empty breakfast line, and made their way to their own table in the back. As the pair sat down with their trays, however, the Praetor appeared beside them.

"Fine morning, isn't it?" Jennings asked exuberantly. Janus and Ramirez stood up immediately and saluted.

"At ease. May I join you?"

"Of course, sir." Janus motioned across from him.

The Praetor sat and leaned back, clearly relaxed.

"You two are up earlier than I would expect. Do you usually get up at this time?"

"The last few weeks we have, sir," Ramirez spoke.

Jennings nodded.

"Always good to see cadets waking up early for a little extra training."

Ramirez and Janus exchanged a glance.

"I'm only kidding." Jennings smiled. "I usually come down to enjoy my coffee in peace."

"We didn't realize, sir," Janus said. "We haven't seen you down here before."

"That's because I'm not usually up so late." Jennings winked.

"Why the change today? Is it because of the field training exercises?" Janus asked.

"No, no—I was just concluding a difficult negotiation last night," the Praetor said. Janus and Ramirez leaned forward and a slight grimace appeared on the Praetor's face. "Nothing to get worked up about. Just a little out of the ordinary."

"How so?" Janus asked.

The Praetor sat his coffee down, looking pensive.

"I suppose you'll find out soon enough," he sighed. "Adepts don't keep secrets very well, at least to one another. Besides, I like rewarding earnest young cadets, and this is something all of you should know."

Janus nodded eagerly. Ramirez leaned forward. The Praetor chuckled, and then became serious.

"Well, for one, the representative came here. Normally we negotiate during regular trading. We've been picking up air scouts tracking Valhalla for nearly a week, so when he finally contacted us, we nearly blew him out of the sky. But I'm not one for starting a fight unless absolutely necessary. Also, the representative was an Infernus. A fairly intelligent one at that."

"An Infernus?" Janus exclaimed. "We've discussed them in strategy and tactics, but I've never seen one."

"Where was he from, sir?" Ramirez asked.

"Didn't say. No markings on his armor, either. Not that it was a surprise. Large operations are always planned in secret, and Corporations sometimes seek out Legions directly for important jobs. It takes time and resources to track us down, but it is the best way to avoid undue scrutiny. He asked only that we call him 'Martel.'"

Martel. The name sounded familiar to Janus, but he couldn't place it.

"What kind of scrutiny, sir?" Janus asked. "Other Corporations?"

The Praetor nodded. "Sometimes. But Corporations are large. Enemies are not always found outside."

A flash of Middleton's angry face on the rail platform appeared in Janus' mind. The Praetor blew lightly on the cup, and a puff of steam rose from the surface.

"He offered a hefty sum. We pick up the first half of the payment in a few months. A transport will meet us at a designated location to the South, give us the final target, and we will have a few weeks to prepare and launch the attack."

"Isn't that potentially dangerous, sir?" Janus asked. "Meeting them directly. Not knowing the final target until later? You said yourself it was odd."

The Praetor took a sip of his coffee.

"Perhaps. But what we do can never be considered safe. We choose this life for the freedom, not the safety. If you want safety, go back to the Corporations." He paused, looking at Janus. "Well, some enjoy more safety than others. I can assure you that the officers have thoroughly discussed this matter."

He spoke this last sentence with a note of finality that suggested a new topic was warranted.

"Will you be present at field training, today, sir?" Ramirez asked.

"Yes, I will." The Praetor leaned back comfortably again. "It's scheduled for this afternoon, correct?"

"Yes, sir," Ramirez replied.

"Well, be sure to eat a light lunch," the Praetor chuckled. "Eating too much is never good for intense training. Though as Adepts, it is always important to be ready for unexpected developments."

Janus lowered his fork.

"Sir?"

The Praetor waved the question away as he stood up.

"On a completely unrelated note, you will soon begin your advanced training, and I can assure you it will be far more interesting than any field test."

He looked at them then, a mysterious smile on his face.

"Your class is advancing more quickly than we could have hoped. You may be taking on your first mission sooner than expected."

Sometime later, Celes, Marcus, and Lyn joined them, heavily laden breakfast trays in hand. Janus and Ramirez sipped tea and watched dryly as their fellow cadets stuffed themselves with food. Ramirez snorted at the display. Janus put his legs along the bench and looked at his three friends.

"It's a good thing the field test is scheduled for late in the day. Normally you'd have to wake up as early as Ramirez and me to digest all that."

Celes glanced up at Janus from her tray, inhaling an 'egg' in the process.

"It's a good thing we don't. We normal people need sleep, you see."

She gave Janus a wink and began shoveling her food again.

Janus smiled.

Ramirez folded his arms across his chest as he spoke sternly to them. "Ya, it's a good thing. Because Sargent Wouris and the officers would never suddenly move training from the afternoon to the morning, would they?"

Janus stared at the ceiling, smirking. At that, Celes, Marcus, and Lyn collectively looked up from their food and glanced at one another.

"You know," Marcus grimaced, "I don't think I'm hungry anymore."

He pushed his tray away from him. Celes and Lyn did the same.

"I wouldn't have told them, Ramirez," Janus chuckled.

"Thanks a lot, Janus!" Lyn exclaimed irritably and tossed a piece of synthetic bacon into his hair.

"Well, we know who our real friend is, don't we Lyn? Thank you, Ramirez."

Celes gave him a light peck on the cheek. Staring at Janus' scowling face, Ramirez couldn't help but grin.

CHAPTER 21
MONSTERS AND DEMONS

Wouris appeared like a lightning bolt, yelling as she marched into to the mess.

"Form up, Cadets! Field test is cancelled for today! It's time for a run! Move it!"

Confused, the group stood from the table and followed her. For the first time in months, only five cadets were able to finish the daily run.

Afterward, when most of the cadets had finally recovered, Wouris addressed them.

"Field training will resume tomorrow. Today, you've been deemed ready to start ODIN's advanced training. We'll start sorting out who can push themselves further in ways only an Adept can. Of course, ready and able are two very different things."

The 'Chariot of Hail' bay, the largest of Valhalla's launch bays, was positively bustling. Despite the length of time Janus had been at Valhalla, large swaths of the city remained unknown to him, and the 'Hail' bay was no different. A cadet's time was extremely structured, and left little room for even simple freedoms like eating, let alone exploration.

Mechanics yelled, tossing tools back and forth as they scrambled to keep ODIN's Valkyrie fleet up and running. More than ten of the sleek and curvy craft littered the cavernous room. Janus had never seen them so close. They were superiority fighters, much faster and better armed than Longboats, but not nearly as armored. Small, pointed noses gave way to long, slim frames and cockpits. Four wings, offset at forty-five-degree angles, swept back from the rear corners of the craft. The two upper wings were smaller and shorter than the lower. Together, they surrounded the central booster, which was actually three smaller engines, recessed and protected behind a large nozzle that gave the Valkyrie its rocketing speed. More so than anything else, they looked like they belonged within Valhalla's halls, with their glistening, pearly white exterior. Janus knew from his studies, however, that this was not how they would ever appear in battle. They had an uncanny ability to become a dull blue, grey, or even brown, and absorb active sensors when the situation warranted. Janus wondered if Valhalla had the same capabilities.

Pilots moved in and out of their cockpits, communicating with the mechanics on maintenance issues. High above, Valkyries glided along through the air as giant arms of metal reloaded their weapons. At the edge of the platform, fully stocked Valkyries awaited in silent, suspended rows, ready to be deployed at a moment's notice. As the cadets passed, two blast panels swept down behind the forward fighters. Firing their engines, the Valkyries disengaged from the chutes that connected them to the pilots' barracks above, and sped out of the city, two more Valkyries moving forward to take their place.

Celes leaned over and whispered in Janus' ear. "Wouris has had me run a few errands down here before, but I've never seen it so busy."

Praetor Jennings and Captain Rogers were waiting for them at the far corner of the launch bay, away from the hammering and yelling of the mechanics. Jennings wore the slim sword on his back he'd had at Cerberus, and there was a Skadi rifle and a disc launcher in the open case beside him. Rogers had donned a full set of ST armor, faceplate open, making him stand head and shoulders over the Praetor. Two heavily armored suits and a plate of ceramium sat behind him. The right suit was standard Security Trooper armor, just as Rogers wore. The left Janus knew immediately. Though he had never laid eyes on one before, the horror stories from the slums told him exactly what it was.

Infernus armor.

It looked like something born from a nightmare, almost demonic in appearance. Tinged red, the armor was broader and taller by a full head than standard ST armor. Thick, sharp-edged plates descended towards massive, split-toed boots. Zeus cannons and flamethrowers mounted on each arm came together on vicious, clawed hands. But nothing was quite as terrifying as the strange, disturbingly angular helmet, centered on a red, V-shaped slit of visor.

Wouris saluted Jennings while Janus and the cadets fell into line. She leapt over to the Infernus armor, disappearing behind it.

"Today, you begin advanced training," Jennings said. He grimaced as he spoke. "I always like to teach this particular lesson to cadets myself, to demonstrate how important it is, and what you are capable of. Captain Rogers and Sergeant Wouris will assist me."

Rogers touched a console on one side of the bay, and the launch platform slowly slid out beyond the hanger.

"All of you have seen standard Security Trooper armor." He pointed to the right. "Each suit is an exoskeleton; a strength-enhancing, hostile-environment suit that allows Corporate Security forces to use a variety of heavy weapons, including the Zeus. It's powered by a battery and micro-capacitor system that can easily last for several days. But it also has several distinct disadvantages."

Rogers stepped forward in his suit, twisting and turning in it. His movement was encumbered and ungainly compared to his natural grace.

"Namely, a distinct lack of mobility, even with an experienced soldier inside. The suits rely on internal manual inputs to respond, making them slow. STs can run fast, but only in a straight line. They have to build up a head of steam, so to speak. They also possess another disadvantage."

Jennings picked up the Skadi rifle, turning on the empty suit behind him. He shot three times through the middle of the unoccupied suit. Light filtered through the newly created holes.

"You will not find the same weaknesses with Inferni," the Praetor said dangerously. And at that, Wouris stepped forward in the terrifying armor.

"Inferni are top of the line," the Praetor said, walking around the suit where it stood, Wouris somewhere inside. "They are faster, stronger, more flexible, and possess a powerful capability."

He tapped at the cloven boots with his foot, then stepped back. A moment later, Wouris the Infernus leapt into the air, activating a set of boosters. Three jets on each foot and two larger ones on the back carried the suit to the top of the hanger before it finally flipped over and came crashing down, landing on its feet with an earth-shaking rumble.

"Their visors detect heat, light, and a dozen spectrums in-between. And as for weapons," the Praetor added, picking up the disc launcher and launching a set of five silver discs, "Inferni feature a fully integrated arm-mounted Zeus cannon."

Wouris raised an arm and blasted two from the sky.

"And dual flamethrowers"—two discs were engulfed in flames and disappeared over the edge—"specifically designed for engagements with light infantry like Adepts."

The fifth and final disc shot off, flying as fast as it could away from Valhalla.

"Finally, for some advanced variants, shoulder mounted heavy ordinance, ranging from grenade launchers to a light anti-aircraft package."

A launcher snapped up from the shoulder, firing a missile. The silver disc sped away, detecting the missile, but to no avail. The missile closed in like a cheetah on its prey. The disc juked left, and with lightning speed and accuracy, the missile reacquired. Janus found himself willing the disc forward, trying to help it hang on for just a few seconds longer. But the disc could not outrun the fierce predator, and made a desperate dive. It was too late—the missile crashed into it from above, obliterating it in a flash of heat and light.

"Just one Infernus," said Praetor Jennings, turning back to face the cadets, "can turn a successful Adept into a dead Adept."

He tapped the shoulder insignia of the armor.

"Inferni have their own rank and command structure separate from normal Troopers, and are headed by their own Commandant in charge of all Infernus operations, known as the Commandant Novus. Below the Commandant are lesser Novus, Volcanus, and Pyrus ranks, terminating with the basic Infernus trooper. But make no mistake, all of them should be respected as opponents."

In an instant, he whirled and fired a three-round burst at Wouris.

"Wait!" Janus cried.

The other cadets gasped, unable to stop the Praetor. But the rounds bounced harmlessly away.

"No penetration," the Praetor said. "None. Your Skadi rifle is completely ineffective against the armor of an Infernus. Constructed of the heaviest grade ceramium, only a Zeus or equivalent weapon has any hope of penetrating an Infernus chest plate. But speed, skill, and stealth are the keys of the successful Adept. Your abilities will allow you to destroy any Infernus you come across."

Wouris removed the odd helmet, making her head seem strangely small within the massive suit, and tossed it high into the air. The Praetor whirled again, firing three shots into the heavy visor, shattering it completely. He snatched the broken helmet from the air as it tumbled down, and turned back to them with a stern look on his face.

"The visor is the only vulnerability on an Infernus. A relic of design, and a counter to corporate weapons made to knock out its vision, you must hit this spot every time"—he pointed a finger at the center of the shattered helmet—"or you will die. This is why we select so few for training. This is where you learn how much better you are compared to the riffraff that the Corporations put in the field. This is what makes you Adepts."

Whispers emanated from all the cadets, but ceased immediately as Praetor Jennings cleared his throat.

"Don't worry, you will be ready," he chuckled. "Of that you can be sure. Of course, you won't always have a good shot at the visor, especially in close combat. In those cases, I turn to this."

He drew the slim sword on his back from its sheath in one smooth motion.

There was a sharp intake of breath from the cadets. The sword was unlike anything Janus had ever seen. Double-edged and straight, the weapon glowed blue, and had an almost ghost-like translucence to it. It seemed as if it wasn't even really there. The two edges were thin, sharp, and separate, with a long empty channel running between them, connected only at the handle and the point of the weapon, almost like a loop of wire. But it was straight and did not flex. Outside of the sheath, it came alive, suddenly turning white-hot. It looked like glowing glass.

The Praetor tapped the plate of metal that stood between the Infernus and the ST with the flat of the blade.

"Alpha-grade ceramium, twice the thickness of Infernus armor."

He spun, bringing the weapon through an elegant arc. In a flash, the top edge of the ceramium plate detached from the rest, and spun through the air. The Praetor had already sheathed the blade. Wouris caught the flying debris, holding it emphatically in her hands.

Walking back towards the cadets, the Praetor took the blade and sheath off of his back and heaved it with both hands to Janus. Janus caught the sword by the handle, and was immediately knocked onto his back, staring in amazement at the weapon. The cadets watched in confusion as he struggled to his feet, still fighting with the weight. Praetor Jennings chuckled.

"That blade is made entirely of Immutium. An alloy of Silver, Gold, Steel, and Titanium, it is nearly indestructible. It exhibits several other unique properties, as well. Some of you may know of its importance to fusion, but may not entirely know why. One of these reasons is that it maintains its shape until the moment it reaches its melting point, but becomes nearly translucent at higher temperatures. This property, along with its use as an assassination tool has given the weapon its nickname. Ghostblade. A small generator in the handle heats the blade to extreme temperatures, allowing it to cut through an Infernus like butter. It has about ten minutes at full power."

Janus flipped the weapon over, looking at a chronometer on the pommel that read 9:50 in tiny numbers.

"But Ghostblades have their drawbacks, as Janus just discovered. Immutium is deceptively heavy."

He pointed at the intricate sheath that held the weapon.

"The sheath is unique, designed for each blade individually. It must hold the blade at the handle to prevent contact, and interact with the power supply, cooling the weapon when not in use. An Immutium blade is in many ways useless, even a liability, without a sheath. Ghostblades require extremely precise techniques; even the simple act of sheathing the weapon takes skill. I have known many an Adept who has nearly lost a limb because they failed to treat their weapon with respect."

He gave them a grim look.

"The Ghostblade is an archaic weapon in many ways; excellent in stealth or close combat, but not an incentive to charge an enemy. It is a weapon of skill and of last resort."

Lyn raised her hand.

"Yes, Miss…Lyn, wasn't it?"

Lyn was momentarily taken aback, surprised the Praetor knew her name, but quickly regained her composure.

"Sir, what is that?"

She pointed to the monstrous suit that had emerged from high above them, suspended by wires. Or at least it looked like a suit. As Rogers directed the crane holding it to the ground, Janus realized it was taller than even the Infernus. Its frame was less fractal, with a rounded helmet, and larger visor. Gold and silver etchings of a Minotaur stood out clearly on the arms, while huge ivory-colored horns sprouted from the head. Those surfaces not covered in gold and silver gave the eerie blue sheen of Immutium.

"Executor armor," Celes whispered beside Janus. He gave her a questioning look, but before he could ask her what she meant, the Praetor answered Lyn's question.

"That is Executor armor," the Praetor said, "or command armor. I am afraid you won't see too many of those. They've gone somewhat out of style, fortunately for us. We were able to procure this shell in a surprising deal with Minotaur."

"I'm sure the Minotaur Executors were only too happy to sell it," Celes said, with disgust in her voice. All the cadets gave Celes a strange look, and she blushed.

"Command armor was designed for Executors, and rarely, Overlords when they engaged in battle. It comes equipped with specialized communication equipment. The horns hide the antennas in this particular model. They, like Inferni, have jump jets and enhanced power supplies, but do not carry flamethrowers, and usually no heavy artillery. It is also the only armored suit that is fully actuated; it does not require the pilot inside to move.

"You might wonder why Executor armor should be so feared then? Carrying fewer weapons, ornate as it is?"

160

He paused, looking around the cadets for an answer, but they remained silent.

"Executor armor is hardened with a thin layer of Immutium, capable of deflecting Zeus fire. Even the visor has been strengthened to ceramium toughness, making them immune to your Skadis. To compensate for the weight, the suit is both stronger and faster than an Infernus, sacrificing a few minor weapons for truly terrifying speed and toughness. The only weapon with any real chance against it is a Ghostblade, or a Zeus in the hands of skilled marksman. Pray that you never run into one."

Lyn gulped, and many of the cadets looked nervously at each other. But the Praetor continued.

"As you have discovered over the past several months, Troopers are lousy shots, but not because of the Zeus rifles they fire."

"Yes," Rogers chimed in, "it's more the fact that they're just a bunch of gorillas crammed into clumsy suits."

The Praetor's grey eyes gave him a disapproving look.

"Your training will hone your reactions and senses, giving you the offensive advantage you need to face the larger forces of the Corporations. But there are other advantages, as well. Refining your skills will allow you to judge where an enemy ST is aiming. This advantage is more meaningful than you might realize, as each Zeus round has approximately a one half-second delay between shots. As an enemy ST unit brings his or her weapon to bear, you will have a short amount of time to react."

"Are you telling us that you can dodge Zeus fire?" Roderick looked dumbfounded.

Marcus whistled.

"It's actually quite easy once you realize how much time a half-second really is during a pitched battle." Jennings smiled at Roderick.

"All you have to do is stay away from the barrel's cross-section, a tiny width. Of course, there is a difference between dodging one and dodging many, especially from more than one ST It all comes down to the question of how good you really are."

He looked over at Wouris, who wore a smug grin on her face. She stepped forward.

"You hear that, cadets?" she said. "You better rest up tonight, because starting with tomorrow morning, we're going to find out."

It was clear and starry that night. Janus shivered in bed. He was freezing. It was never this cold in the slums. Was he getting sick? He took a deep breath, exhaling. A large bloom of steamy air emerged from his nose and mouth. He recoiled, then remembered a book he had once read that showed pictures of people in cold weather.

"Val!"

The terminal sighed audibly.

"Yes, Janus…"

Val had long since given up on trying to correct him, and had reluctantly agreed to his naming convention.

"Why is it so cold?"

"The planet's axis of tilt combines with natural solar orbit to create periods of cooler and warmer weather. Depending on the time of year, one hemisphere may receive more or less sunli—"

"No! Why is it so cold in here?"

"Valhalla has moved far to the North, and Sergeant Wouris ordered all temperature controls removed so that the air temperature inside the cadet barracks should mimic the outside," Val said.

Janus swore he heard a snicker in her voice. He groaned and wrapped himself up tighter in his blanket. The lights flipped on and Wouris' voice came over the speaker.

"Rise and shine, cadets! We don't have time to pamper you with late starts anymore. You have five minutes to meet me in the commons."

162

Janus sat upright. The biting cold immediately gnawed at him, and he regretted his decision. But ten minutes was barely enough time to ready up and give everything a double check. He needed to move quickly. He stepped out of bed, and looked towards the closet. His cold weather suit was gone. Only a thin pair of leggings and his boots hung in its place. A chorus of groans sounded from the rooms nearby.

Four minutes later, Janus and the other cadets stood shivering in the common room. Even the girls had not been spared much more than a simple exercise top. Janus looked over at Celes. She had wrapped her arms around her torso, and huddled next to Lyn, who leaned on Ramirez for warmth. Janus met eyes with Ramirez, who seemed mostly unaffected by the cold, feeling a pang of jealousy. The warmest piece of gear anyone had was their boots, and Janus hopped up and down desperately trying to get warm. Wouris, dressed in much the same way, strode in, looking as if she were comfortably warm. She shook her head at them.

"Yesterday, you seemed so eager to get out of the heat. Have you changed your minds? Fortunately for you, I've got plenty of things to keep your minds off the weather."

Once they got moving, Janus felt a little better, but only for a bit. Wouris quickly led them to the 'Voyages' bay, and they soon stood outside on the extending platform, exposed to the elements.

"Form up!" Wouris shouted to them. The cadets fell into formation, barely controlling their shivering as they stood exposed to the elements. Wouris did not shiver at all.

"From this point forward, you are hereby prohibited from speaking. Adepts work in silence. They work as a team in silence. So you will learn to act in silence. To communicate in silence. Today, I will introduce you to one of ODIN's unique specialties. A language that only we use."

Janus' interest was piqued, even as his teeth chattered. She raised her ungloved hand out in front of her.

"What do you see when you look at my hand?"

She paused, but none of the cadets made a sound. She held her palm out, letting all the cadets see it.

"This is the greatest tool humanity has ever had. We have taught you to use this tool as a weapon, just like your other weapons. Now it is time for you to learn how to use this tool for communication. In battle, you will frequently encounter situations where you cannot speak, but you must still communicate with your fellow Adepts. Occasionally, you may even need to express multiple ideas at once. Your hands can do all of this for you. Today, I will teach you the basics."

Janus felt his body temperature dropping, but he continued to stand in formation. His knees felt like they were shaking. If Wouris noticed, she did not act like it.

"There are two forms to this silent language. Long form, which uses both hands, and short form, which is quicker and easier to use in battle, but less specific, and requires only one hand. Now some of you may wonder why you are being subjected to the cold while trying to learn a new language. But it's quite simple. This language is highly contextual. It can be dependent on timing, on positioning. It is used in situations where it must be used quickly and without error. So you are going to learn it here, through exercises that will subject all of you to longer bouts of freezing cold the more you mess up. To hands that won't respond as they grow numb, but must."

Janus suddenly realized his own hands felt very numb.

"Because the first rule you must remember is that you must not signal the wrong message." She held up her hand to her chest, palm towards her heart, with a single finger extended.

One.

"Show me the number one."

All the cadets repeated the gesture.

One.

"Good. Now take a lap to warm up, and then we'll begin."

164

The sun dawned bright over melting snow several months later. Janus emerged from his room late this morning to find Celes leaving her room as well. She made the gesture for 'you' across her torso.

[Hey] you.

Janus smiled and signed 'take' and 'food'.

[Wanna] grab [breakfast].

"Sure."

After a grueling stint of several weeks' forced silence, the cadets had finally been given their voices back, and been issued comms for the main ODIN channels. They had also finally been given a day off, so Janus had decided to catch up on some sleep. It hadn't mattered much, as he had still woken up long before dawn. But he and Ramirez had solemnly agreed not to go to breakfast early today, and so he had spent the time trying to fall back asleep. Finally, after an hour or so, his body had relented, and he'd snatched another forty minutes. It was surprisingly refreshing. He had woken up just before dawn and had decided that he couldn't avoid the day anymore.

The pair meandered towards the mess, enjoying the warm sunlight streaming into Valhalla's main hall. High above them, light from the red 'eye' of ODIN fell upon the highest reaches of the trunk. The light shining on her hair pulled his attention away.

"How much longer do you think our training will last?" Celes asked as they walked, watching the light reflect off the stream in the trough that surrounded the trunk.

Janus pulled his eyes away from her and looked forward, but remained silent, thinking. He suddenly felt ill at ease.

"It is so different being here. Not knowing what lies in store."

Janus wasn't sure whether to agree. It was different. But too many times, the slums had been unpredictable in the worst of ways. Not knowing where the next meal would come from. Here he had food. Even half-rations were better than the best he had in the slums. He felt as if he were moving towards something here. Not just stuck in a place with no hope. Like Clara.

"It's nice here."

Janus nodded. He felt a wave of guilt. It didn't matter he knew that she would have wanted him here. He couldn't quite stand the thought of her left behind. With Middleton.

"Is something wrong?"

Celes had stopped, watching him.

"Oh, sorry. No, just thinking…" He paused.

A group of Adepts in full gear were rushing out of the mess just in front of them.

"Deployment in five," one said to another. "Winters wants to know where that ship went."

He exchanged a curious glance with Celes, and the pair proceeded into the mess, which seemed mostly undisturbed.

Grabbing trays of food, they found Ramirez, Lyn, Marcus, and Valers already eating breakfast together. Marcus eyed them as they approached, signing with a mouthful of food.

Join [us].

Janus pointed over his shoulder as the pair sat down.

"What's going on with them?"

Valers leaned forward.

"I heard some of the Adepts talking about a couple of scouts that have been seen around Valhalla the past few days."

Ramirez met Janus' eyes briefly.

"First I've heard," Lyn said. "I would think Keats or Hawkes would have mentioned something. Or Winters, since she insisted I spend extra time with her for more scout training."

Marcus gestured with a hard biscuit.

"Well, we've hardly had a chance to breathe recently. Maybe we're just out of the loop."

Celes nodded in agreement, and then glanced at Janus.

"You've got that look again."

The others stared at him.

"What look?" Marcus asked.

"The 'there is something bothering me' look Janus gets when he's thinking about something," Celes said.

"Ramirez's got it too." Lyn nodded knowingly.

Collectively, the group looked at Ramirez.

"Spit it out." Lyn punched Ramirez's shoulder.

"The Praetor," Ramirez grunted in between mouthfuls of Passers, looking at Janus.

"What?"

Janus interjected for clarity.

"The morning before we started our advanced training, Ramirez and I ran into the Praetor."

"So that's how you knew that Wouris was going to make us run!" Celes exclaimed.

Ramirez nodded.

"He mentioned that ODIN had recently secured a new deal, and that we would be meeting with our employers in a few months."

"Is that common?" Valers asked.

"The Praetor made it sound like it wasn't," Janus replied.

Captain Rogers strode into the mess, and soon another group of Adepts jumped up and headed out the door.

"Lots of activity," Ramirez mused, finally finished with his mouthful.

"Would our employer send scouts before a scheduled meeting?" Lyn asked.

"Depends," Marcus and Celes said together.

"On what?" Janus asked.

"Two things." Marcus shook his head.

"What are those?" Valers asked.

Celes had a troubled look.

"Who's coming and what's being pla—"

"Cadets! Attention!" Wouris' voice rang across the mess.

The six of them immediately stood up. Wouris came rumbling up, looking irritated.

"All of you are to report back to the barracks immediately, and remain there until further orders. Dismissed."

She turned on her heel and headed out the door.

The common room was full when they returned. Apparently, they'd been the last Wouris found. The cadets swapped rumors, but Janus and Ramirez's story was the highlight. The cadets waited for word from Wouris or the officers, but no one ever came. Eventually, Marcus moved to test the door, only to find it locked. They weren't just ordered back to barracks, they were confined there. And no one responded on comms. Not even Val would give them information.

"You have your orders."

Eventually, the cadets were simply bored. It had been so long since they'd been given a break, they hardly knew what to do with themselves. They mostly felt like they should be doing something more, as they played round after round of Mercy, and occasionally brought up some new theory for what was going on.

"So maybe," Kwandis began, "they're bringing the employer here, and they don't want us to come face to face with them for fear we'll screw something up."

"Oh, come on, Kwandis. Are you suggesting that we're holding some sort of inspection?" Nathans said.

Kwandis looked surprised.

"Sure. Why not? At the factory, we'd have an Overlord visit every few months, and everything would need to be perfect. We'd hide anything that could impact our impression."

Hughes nodded in agreement.

"We're not Adepts yet. Maybe our employer could tell?"

"Inspections weren't uncommon," Marcus said. "It doesn't seem impossible."

"Maybe for people who grew up in a Corporation," Lyn disagreed. "The last thing you should ever do is bring someone unknown to your village. Too dangerous."

Ramirez folded his arms across his chest.

"Too much information."

"I tend to agree," Janus said. "Showing someone where you live is a great way to end up dead."

"Was Cerberus that rough, Janus?" Roderick asked.

"I imagine it has more to do with where in Cerberus you live," Marcus interjected.

"How so?" Roderick asked in confusion.

"But it's a valid point," Celes said, waving a hand. "The reason we live in Valhalla is so that we can stay on the move. It doesn't make sense to bring someone here."

The cadets argued back and forth for a while before eventually returning to their games. After a while, everyone decided to take advantage of the opportunity for an early night, sure that tomorrow would bring answers. Before entering his room, he glanced over at Celes' room, which was already shut, and wondered where she had grown up, and if it was as dangerous.

CHAPTER 22
DEATH

Janus awoke to the sound of blaring alarms.

Ugggh…why Wouris…

Janus stopped grumbling and listened—there was a voice amidst the blaring noise.

"—not a drill—" Val's voice urgently cried. He sat bolt upright. The room was dark.

"—under attack. This is not a—"

Janus leapt from the bed, swiping his hand over his locker, and grabbing his Skadi and communication link. If there was an attack, it should broadcast tactical information. He flipped through the main channels. The grating buzz of static greeted him.

Wearing his synthetic pajama bottoms, he glanced at his armor, then at his blank, unpowered chronometer. He silently slid open his door to the common room.

To his left and right, some of the other cadets peered hesitantly from their own doorways. Marcus seemed more awake than the rest, his head darting about the room. The two exchanged an all clear and met in the middle. Lyn, Ramirez and Celes joined them, soon followed by the rest of the cadets. Janus noted that Celes was the only one actually wearing her armor.

"We need to get organized," Marcus said. "Then we can find out what's happening."

Celes pointed toward the door.

"We have two directions to cover once we leave Sigma three," she said, then pointed in turn to Janus and Marcus. "We'll split up. Janus, you take half; Marcus, the other."

"Agreed," Marcus said, turning to the others. "Hughes, Kwandis, Jones, Zhao, Browning, and Freeham, you're with me. Celes, you're with me too. Alexis, Young and Roderick, you tag along, as well. The rest, follow Janus."

Janus was considering protesting Marcus' snap judgment when the door to Sigma three opened. Framed in the moonlight was an unexpected horror—an ST, looming and monstrous, with a weapon at its side.

Janus felt his heart skip a beat. Instinct took over, raising his weapon before he knew what he was doing. The ST was moving slowly, bringing the Zeus to bear. Janus could feel the recoil of his weapon against his shoulder. There was a loud report, and the ST fell backwards into the hall. The cadets stood and stared, mouths agape.

Janus and Marcus lowered their weapons together. It bothered him how easy it had been. He looked at Marcus. He too was staring at the ST with a mix of shock and disbelief. Janus swallowed, hard.

"Time to go."

Marcus nodded.

The hall beyond the door was deathly quiet and completely dark, illuminated only by the light of the moon. Something was terribly wrong; the barracks had lost power.

Well, Valhalla hasn't crashed… Janus took some solace in the thought.

There were no other STs in the hall. The two groups split silently, heading in opposite directions. Janus took a moment to glance after Celes and Marcus as they journeyed into the dark at the front of the second group.

Celes turned her head and smiled at him.

[Keep] safe.

And she and Marcus disappeared.

Janus' gaze lingered for a moment on the darkness before he looked back to Lyn and Ramirez, who were watching him carefully. He motioned forward, and the group moved as one into the unknown.

They met no resistance, but the emptiness put Janus on edge. Used to the dark of the slums and the need for urgency, Janus found himself frustrated by their slow pace.

"Marcus? You read me?" he spoke into his comms system.

"Loud and clear."

"Anything on your end?"

"Not yet, silent as a grave."

"Let's hope not," Lyn chimed in.

"I'll let you know if we find anything. Keep—"

Marcus stopped suddenly. Janus halted in the hall, listening intently. "Janus, something's going on up ahead. Sounds like a fight in the main hall."

"We'll be right there," Janus said, signaling for the group to turn around.

"No," Celes said in a surprisingly forceful voice. "We can't afford to lose our rearguard. If there's a battle up ahead, you can circle around and hit them from the other side. I know you want to help, but you will help us more by letting us do our job while you do yours."

Janus was torn, but he looked at Lyn and Ramirez. Ramirez just shrugged.

"You heard the lady."

Janus nodded.

He turned to the rest of the group, eyeing them.

"Our family's in trouble," he said. "Let's get moving."

The cadets nodded without hesitation. The Sigma barracks was part of a larger, mostly unoccupied section of Valhalla. The direction Marcus had gone was the route the cadets took in their day-to-day and led straight to the main hall. But the barracks continued further in the direction Janus and his team had headed. It too would lead eventually to the main hall and trunk itself, but first they would have to leave Sigma section and head through Tau. If they found the rest of their roundabout route clear, Janus reasoned, it might mean their enemy knew a thing or two about Valhalla.

The door between Sigma and Tau was heavy, but unlocked and un-powered, and with some help from Ramirez, Janus was able to force it open while Lyn and Naka covered them. It too was quiet. But then, the sudden sound of a Skadi rifle broke through the air. Tau was not completely empty.

Janus hurried down the hall, past darkened and empty barracks, his fellow cadets hot on his heels. Janus could hear the sounds of the intensifying battle, but as they rounded a corner, he had to stop himself from charging forward. Three Adepts were hard pressed by a group of six STs, just in front of the last set of Tau barracks. Janus recognized one of the Adepts as a man named Dunn, with whom he had played more than a few games of Brevis Bellum.

Dunn was crouched behind what little cover he could find, along one of the ribbed supports that ran along the outside of Valhalla. Four of the approaching STs pressed upon him. One Adept was already down, while the other had just been hoisted up by the front of his armor, and was now dangling helplessly from the fist of the leading ST Struggling to break free, the Adept was helpless as the massive hand slammed him into the wall. He went limp immediately.

"Stupid Adept," the ST said.

Advancing in unison, Janus, Lyn, and Ramirez targeted the front two and fired in a burst. The rest of the team stepped forward, and two more

STs went down under a hail of fire. But in their haste, the cadets had made a mistake. It was an uncoordinated attack—no one had shot at the remaining two STs.

With a yell, one of the STs charged, using his powerful legs to leap forward, straight at the cadets.

Janus was surprised by the maneuver, it seemed far too quick thinking and brave for an ST But remarkably, his trained instincts did the job when his mind could not. With the imposing figure bearing down on him, Janus fired once into ST's chest and the armored hulk went down without protest. He stared at the faceless visor for a moment before realizing that the second, and probably smarter ST, had tossed his weapon to the ground and was running full speed away from the group. The young-faced Nathans stepped up.

"I've got him."

He fired twice, two perfect shots, and the ST fell forward, unmoving. Janus turned to congratulate him on his quick thinking, but the look on Nathans' face stopped him.

He lowered his weapon slowly, looking visibly shaken.

Janus felt a pit in his stomach, and avoided looking at Nathans' eyes. Instead, he turned to the group.

"Good work, everyone, but we can't afford to stop."

"I...just...killed him," Nathans stammered, staring at the body down the hall. "He wasn't even armed...he was running away."

Janus turned to look at him again, not knowing what to say. It was a faceless entity, a metal monstrosity that had haunted his childhood and prowled his nightmares. STs were scum, men and women who had sold their soul for a bit of power.

But Marcus... a little voice whispered. It sounded a bit like Clara, or maybe it was Celes. Maybe it was both. Janus pushed it from his mind. Now was not the time. Thankfully, Lyn took over, and said what he could not.

175

"You did what needed to be done," she said. "To save other lives. To a man who wouldn't have thought twice had the situation been reversed."

Nathans looked at her, still in a state of shock, but his eyes reflected his appreciation at her words.

Dunn had come out from his cover and was tending to his teammates as Lyn spoke, but he glanced over at her briefly and nodded.

"We all have to face such things eventually," Lyn said grimly. She motioned with her head at the ST she had killed. Ramirez came up and put a huge, but gentle hand on her shoulder. Janus looked over at her, finding himself more than a little disturbed at her words.

"We need to get moving," Ramirez said quietly. Janus walked over to Dunn.

"How are they?"

"They'll recover," he said. "I'll take care of them. Keep going. ODIN needs you."

Janus nodded, realizing that the other cadets had already lined up to follow. They took off, grim, but determined.

As Janus' team hustled towards the main hall from Tau, Marcus came through his earpiece.

"Janus? Where are you? We could use some support!"

"We're on our way; met some resistance in Tau."

The sound of gunfire echoed from just ahead of them. But this was no minor skirmish going on in front of them. It sounded like an all-out battle.

"Well, you're about to meet a whole lot more! They're everywhere, and I can't raise any of the officers or Sergeant Wouris. You'll be in a good position to hit them from the side; get around their cover."

"We'll be in position soon," Janus responded. "How's your team holding up?"

"So far, so good."

"Good," Lyn interjected. "Because here we come!"

Janus, Lyn, and Ramirez came rushing into the grand hall, firing as they went, diving for cover behind the wide columns that dotted the outside of the vast atrium. A fierce battle raged around the Trunk, the uncountable bodies of Adepts and STs in the thick of it. Moonlight streaming through the red eye of ODIN illuminated dozens of STs all around the hall. Firing from up above suggested that Adepts were engaged along the catwalks all around the Trunk. Janus knew that if they wanted to beat back the STs, they would need to reach the center and secure the Trunk. It was the key to holding the city.

Janus searched for more cover, looking for a way to get there. There was nothing. He had walked around Valhalla for months, and it was only now that he realized how open the grand hall was. Other than a few benches and plantings, the huge distance between him and the canal that ringed the Trunk was essentially a dead zone. And judging from the bodies surrounding it, both Adept and ST, anyone who tried to cross it was suicidal.

Their enemies poured forth from two sections, the Chariot bay and the mess. Adepts still controlled the Trunk, judging by the STs struggling around it. But the enemy was making great strides to the center, using their numbers and strength to break through. Janus could see a group of STs already clustered around one of the doors into the central column, attempting to force their way in. A few of the more intelligent ones had leapt into the canal and were using it as cover.

"Marcus!" Janus said into his comm. "We need to take the canal. It'll give us free reign to move and provide cover. We can hit them on both sides!"

There was a pause.

"Good point," Marcus responded. "I'll go with a few of my squad and take the canal. You cover us. Once it's clear, your team can join us."

"No," Janus said without hesitation. "The STs haven't seen us yet. My team can surprise them."

"And when you do, the STs will fire on you instantly," Marcus replied, "which will provide my team with just the distraction we need to get into the canal, while you retreat back to cover."

"Why don't you both just run out screaming and get your heads blown off?" Celes interjected sarcastically.

There was a poignant pause.

"Good idea, Celes," Marcus said.

"What?" Celes exclaimed.

"No, no, it's true," Janus said. "If we both go out together, it may freeze the STs for a moment while they decide who's more important to shoot. We may be more exposed, but we will be in a much better position to cover each other as we run. Besides, with more targets to shoot at, it's much more likely that at least one of our groups will make it into the canal."

"So there's no downside, really," Marcus laughed.

"Marcus, divide your group up. I'll give the count in fifteen seconds."

Janus turned to face the group.

"Lyn, you're in charge of the team here. Give us cover. I just want a few at my back. Valers, Naka." The pair slid up behind him. "You two up for this?"

"We've got you, Janus," Naka responded.

Ramirez put a hand on Janus' shoulder. "I'm coming too," he grunted.

"You sure?" Janus glanced back at Lyn's grim face.

"Yes," Ramirez stated simply.

Janus nodded.

"Marcus, ready?"

"Absolutely."

"On three."

"One…"

Janus readied himself.

"Two…"

A sharp intake of breath sounded behind him.

"Three!"

They burst from cover, sprinting for the canal. Janus looked across to see Marcus, Alexis, and Young making their own run. He could hear the explosion of fire from behind him as the remaining cadets provided cover.

An ST popped up from the cover of the canal, aiming at Marcus. Janus lined up a shot as he ran. He missed, badly, the round ricocheting off the edge of the trench. But the shot had the desired effect. The ST looked up in surprise, quickly turning his weapon to bear upon Janus. But before the ST could fire, Janus jumped right and fired again. This time the ST went down.

Janus splashed into the shallow river just as a cry went up behind him. Janus turned to see Naka writhing on the ground, just a few meters short of his goal.

Without hesitation, Ramirez effortlessly picked him up with one arm and slung him over a shoulder, carrying him the rest of the way, and diving into the canal.

Janus and Valers cleared the immediate area as Ramirez leapt in, gently depositing Naka as he turned to fire at the incoming STs.

"Check him," Janus said, and Valers bent down to examine their friend.

"Well, he's out cold, but I can't find anything wrong with him," Valers said in confusion. "He's breathing, and he isn't bleeding, as far as I can tell."

Ramirez and Janus exchanged a questioning look.

Not bleeding?

"Stay here with him and watch this area. Ramirez and I will clear out the rest with Marcus and his team."

Valers nodded.

"Marcus," Janus spoke into his comm. "Naka is down, but we think he'll be okay. Valers is staying with him. Ramirez and I will proceed clockwise around the edge."

"After we clear the area between us," Marcus said, "we can bring in the rest of our teams and secure the canal. See you in a few."

Janus looked at Valers.

Sit [tight].

Valers nodded.

Janus and Ramirez splashed through the shallow river, opting for speed over silence.

Just a few STs stood along the shallow canal, and none were expecting an attack from the side. As the last one dropped, the sound of a Skadi rifle came from around the bend and Marcus appeared.

Clear.

Janus kept scanning the area for new STs rushing in as Marcus splashed towards him.

"We're secure for now. Let's get—"

"Incoming!" Marcus yelled in panic, cutting Janus off.

Janus glanced upwards just in time to see a living nightmare hurtling out of the darkness towards them.

The Infernus landed with a tremendous slam, knocking the cadets back, its massive legs clicking and whirring as it compensated for the gigantic force of its landing, the split toes spread wide for balance. As the hulking monster stood up to its full height, Janus suddenly understood why the Praetor's brief demonstration could never communicate its raw power. Janus had never seen an Infernus in the slums before, but he now knew why few spoke of Inferni with anything less than terror.

And this Infernus was indeed terrifying. Its armor was a dull black, but it was given a ghostly blue glow from the hot light of its dual flamethrowers. As it turned its head to look at the three, Janus could see that the helmet featured a huge laughing skull, giving the suit the appearance of death itself. The words 'Merc Killer' had been scrawled onto its right arm, with several notches etched into it.

"Time to roast some mercs." The Infernus laughed, raising its flamethrowers.

Janus' natural instincts took over, and he dove away from the Infernus. But he knew there would be no escape. The canal was too narrow.

It would make for the perfect grave.

A round bounced dangerously close to the Infernus' visor, and suddenly the demon was being peppered by fire from two directions, as the rest of the cadets struggled to take down the monster.

The Infernus shrugged off the fire, but the rounds did divert its attention.

"Pathetic," came the chuckling voice from inside the suit—muffled, yet strangely familiar. "I would have thought you would know better than that."

In a moment, everything clicked into place in Janus' mind.

The Infernus raised his arms high, leaping to the edge of the canal.

"Worthless mercs," the Infernus yelled. "I'll teach you the meaning of fear!"

The monster fired across the hall, and Celes went down with a howl.

"Celes!" Marcus yelled, as both he and Janus sprang into action, leaping towards the hulking monster. The Infernus planted a fist into Marcus' gut, driving the air from his lungs and sending him sprawling across the floor. But as it turned, it paused at the sight of the barrel pointed at its visor.

"Freeze, Wouris," Janus said. The Infernus and Adept stared at each other for a moment. Janus couldn't help but smile. To be the one to figure it out. Clara certainly would have been proud.

Suddenly three rounds peppered the side of the Infernus' head, and Janus glanced left just in time to see Wouris dashing out from around the side of the Trunk.

"Janus, shoot!"

A pit formed in his stomach as the Infernus tilted its head.

"Not quite."

Snatching the weapon from his hands with one arm, it planted its powerful claws into to his side, slashing into him. Janus felt his ribs crack as he was lifted bodily and thrown. Weaponless, he could only watch helplessly as the towering Infernus loomed over him.

Chapter 23
Hard Lessons

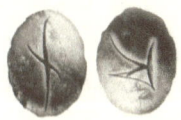

Janus drew in a ragged breath as he prepared for the worst.

I'm sorry, Cla—

"Enough," came a booming voice. The Infernus froze and the hall lit up, illuminating the Trunk and the invading army.

It took Janus a moment before his eyes adjusted to the suddenly bright room. He struggled to his feet, and watched as the Praetor walked casually out of the Trunk, clapping his hands, a smile on his face. Colonel Yalla followed behind him, tending to the fallen. High above him, watching silently from the bridges, were hundreds of Adepts.

"Very good, all of you," Jennings said. "Excellent job. It is great to see such loyal and well-trained cadets defending ODIN."

The Adepts above broke into applause.

The cadets were tentatively stepping out of their hiding places, as the STs began to congregate around the Praetor. Some of them removed their helmets, and Janus recognized familiar faces. Some, he realized, weren't even wearing complete suits of ST armor. Just the pieces that had been visible to the attacking cadets.

"Thanks to all of our willing volunteers who participated in this exercise," the Praetor added.

A particularly squat ST stamped up. Janus knew who it was before Hawkes even pulled off his helmet.

"Yes, well, this particular exercise always seems to have willing participants," Hawkes said with an evil grin.

Lyn led the rest of the cadets from Janus' group towards the gathering crowd. She had an amused, if mildly confused, look on her face.

"What just happened, Praetor?" she asked.

"Just a simple test," Wouris said, walking up. "Designed to see what you've learned, and provide you the opportunity to deal with a battle, and all its repercussions—without the battle."

"But how?" Alexis said from the canal. She was helping a disheveled Young, watching the STs who had been killed get back up, completely unharmed. "We...we killed them. And our friends..."

She paused, unable to speak.

Wouris gave a smile of understanding. "With these."

Celes came walking up, helping Marcus along, and holding a large, oddly shaped round. Janus was surprised to see her up. She turned to the Infernus.

"It got stuck in my armor, but never fully penetrated."

Finally, the Infernus pulled off its helmet.

"That's the problem with these specialty rounds. But they might do more than stun if they penetrated more."

Janus and the other cadets stood openmouthed. It was Colonel Keats.

Lyn gave Ramirez a strange look.

Keats? she mouthed. He shrugged.

"I'm afraid your guess was wrong, Janus," Wouris said seriously from behind the Praetor.

"Yes, Sergeant Wouris was forbidden from participating until the end," said Jennings. "As all sergeants are when their cadets go through this exercise. Although I dare say that Sergeant Wouris would probably make this test even more difficult if given the chance. Overall, you did very well. And Janus demonstrated excellent reasoning, if poor decision-making. Realizing the nature of the test, despite getting some of the specifics wrong shows good battle awareness. But the canal is a common trap we pull on young cadets. It should serve as an excellent lesson to all of you, and a warning about the dangers of sacrificing your mobility. If Keats had been a real Infernus, that river would have been your doom. Sometimes it is better to simply remove an enemy's advantage than to try to turn it to your own. But on a lighter note, it is sometimes surprising the things you learn about people when you least expect it. Don't you agree, Colonel Hawkes?"

Hawkes had a grin on his face.

"Very much, sir. Although anyone who knows Amanda and what she used to—"

Keats narrowed her eyes and gave him a withering stare. Hawkes immediately clammed up.

"So do we have to worry about any more midnight assaults?" Marcus asked with a wince, holding his chest. Colonel Yalla came over and inspected him.

"Medical branch," he said quietly.

"Do you think we would tell you?" Wouris asked.

Yalla walked over to Janus. He lifted his arm to allow the officer to inspect his wound. Janus grit his teeth as the old doctor's fingers probed the area. Yalla nodded approvingly to Keats.

"Mostly superficial. A few bruised ribs, but nothing a small Nanyte injection won't cure."

Janus wondered if he would ever have full rations again.

"You don't have anything to worry about, Marcus," the Praetor said with a smile. "From this point on I want all of you to know that if you hear any warning alarms, they will be the real deal. Besides, it takes us months to put together enough specialty rounds for this exercise. They are hand-made by two of our tech-sergeant weapon smiths, and I think Chiles and Graham would kill me if I asked them to make another batch, no matter how much I outrank them. So, no, you won't get a second opportunity to participate in this exercise."

"So that means you better learn as much as possible from this one," Wouris said, stepping in front of Janus, and staring him in the eye. "Never hesitate. What did you hope to accomplish by not firing?"

"I was afraid I might kill!" Janus exclaimed. The anger in her voice was surprising. But shocking him even further, Wouris grabbed him by the uniform and dragged him over to Keats.

"See this." She knocked on the visor. "All of the armor have had an extra layer added to them."

She grabbed a weapon from a nearby cadet and whipped out a round into her hand.

"See these? Special shattering rounds designed to lose all of their energy before they penetrate armor. You had a better chance of hurting yourself with them than you did Keats. You don't think we thought this through?"

"But…how was I supposed to know that?" Janus asked.

"You're not," Wouris said. "That's the point! You know what your problem is?"

Janus was silent, but shook his head, staring back.

"Arrogance. You had the arrogance to assume that you had actually bested me in battle. That you were smarter than me and the officers. That you knew more than me. Well, guess what, you're not that good. Not yet."

Janus lowered his gaze and remained silent. No one spoke, but he could feel a million eyes upon him.

"As soon as the Praetor dismisses you, you can do a hundred laps around the column before heading to medical to get that cleaned up." She pointed to the slashes across his ribcage. "Maybe it will help you remember the lessons you learned tonight."

Janus looked up; he could see the first vestiges of light trickling through the Great Seal. He sighed.

The Praetor nodded in agreement with Wouris, but after a moment, smiled and turned to the group as a whole.

"I want to reiterate how very pleased I am with all of you tonight. You show great promise. The officers and I are always pleased to see cadets step up and take on the challenge of leadership."

The gathered officers all nodded approvingly at Janus, Marcus, and Celes.

"And commendations to Cadet Lyn for her excellent support. And Cadet Celes for her wise counsel, as well."

He glanced over at Dunn, who stood with his two uninjured companions near the outside of the circle. Janus noted, however, that the Adept who had been slammed into the wall still appeared slightly woozy; realism had been one of the goals of the exercise.

"On a final note, please do not hesitate to discuss with the officers anything you may have felt during the exercise, whether it be a suggestion...or a personal concern..."

Nathans looked up—his face didn't seem quite so young anymore.

"Captain Rogers will be more than happy to listen, and share a story or two. Now, go on and get some brief rest before you start today's training. Dismissed."

Several cadets slapped Janus on the back as they left or gave him thumbs up. Lyn and Ramirez were followed by Celes, who was aiding a very gingerly moving Marcus.

"Don't I get any help?" Janus asked.

"You look fine to me," Celes replied with a teasing smile. "I'm sure you're tough enough to handle it. Besides, Marcus was injured trying to rescue me. You got injured because you were an idiot."

Marcus smiled as Janus scowled.

"Not that either of you were any less stupid, jumping into melee with an Infernus."

Marcus quickly stopped smiling. Celes glanced at Janus, motioning with her head towards the Trunk.

"You better start running before Wouris notices."

And then Wouris' voice cut across the hall. "Cadet Janus! Get yourself moving or I will!"

With a sigh, Janus turned and ran, resisting the urge to clutch his side.

CHAPTER 24
BLOOD POET

The medical branch was busy when Janus finally arrived, but the Adepts running around seemed abnormally stressed and quiet. The lights were dimmed, and lowered shades blocked some of the windows. Despite the obvious gash on his side, the Adepts ignored him. In fact, quite a few Adepts stood around an open door, as if waiting for some unspoken signal.

"Hello?" Janus asked.

One of the Adepts gave him a cold stare, and then seeing his side, relaxed slightly and put a finger to her lips.

Colonel Yalla emerged from a nearby room.

"It's time."

The Adepts filed in, and as they did so, Janus caught a glimpse of a figure lying in one of the beds. Yalla turned to one of his aides.

"Let the Blood Poet know."

The aide saluted formally, and rushed out of the medical branch. Shaking his head, Colonel Yalla sighed, then turned to address Janus.

"Finally come to get that cleaned up?"

Janus nodded. Yalla put a finger to his lips, and Janus followed him quietly into another room. Janus didn't speak until the door had closed behind them.

"What's going on?"

"Sergeant Mura is about to pass. She asked for a few of her close friends to be present."

Janus stared at Yalla in confusion.

"Pass? As in die? Why hasn't she been given an injection?"

Yalla smiled grimly. "They can't fix everything."

Janus shook his head. "Has she received too many injections?"

"Yes and no," Yalla said sadly. "I'd be remiss to give her more anyway, but they won't work in this case."

"Why not? How do they work?"

Yalla smiled slightly.

"That's a great question. I wish I knew the full answer."

"You don't know?" Janus asked in shock. He looked at the glowing blue tubes that emerged from the wall.

"Well, I know pieces, but they are a very complicated piece of technology, and most of my knowledge comes from information that was shared with me, not because I could build them from scratch myself. You'll find that is a common occurrence nowadays with many Daeduluses."

Yalla carefully helped Janus remove his chest armor, and then pulled a small dose of blue gel from the wall. Janus grimaced. Now that he was sitting again, and no longer running, the full pain of his side came roaring back. Yalla probed the area gently, and after a moment, injected the Nanytes right into the wound.

"You should heal quickly, and you shouldn't have any scarring," Yalla said.

"Scarring? Is that a risk?"

190

"Occasionally. But based on your earlier reactions to the Nanytes, it's unlikely. Individually, they aren't very smart. But collectively, they can use signals from the body to decide what to do; like pain or shock. The fewer the signals, they less they can help. That's why they struggle with old injuries, or in Mura's case, issues caused by the body itself."

"So if my wound had already healed completely, they wouldn't do much?"

Yalla nodded.

"In all likelihood, no. That's one of the reasons why we use them as proactively as we do. Perhaps there's a way to reprogram them, or make them smarter, but it is beyond me. Experimenting with them is prohibitively expensive. And unethical. That is one thing that has always been clear from the beginning. Anyone who works with them knows that large doses are dangerous, especially in succession."

Yalla gave Janus a grim smile.

"But it's not all bad."

Janus looked at him curiously.

"Because they can't fix everything, and they can't go out on the battlefield—I still have a job."

Yalla cracked a smile. Janus laughed. He could hardly believe the kindly Yalla had such a grim sense of humor.

"You should meet my aides," Yalla said, as if reading his mind. "They're practically disturbed."

Janus shook his head with a smile. The injection administered, Yalla moved away to deposit the syringe in a box by the door. Janus looked out the window. This one was unshaded, and he could see the sun high in the sky, and white clouds billowing past.

"Yalla?" he said, eyes still on the clouds. "What's a Blood Poet?"

Yalla's smile disappeared. Slowly, he moved back across the room and sat next to Janus, looking out the window with him. He sat quiet for a few moments, before speaking.

"We Adepts," he began. "We rarely perform burials in our line of work. Not out of a lack of respect, but because we rarely have a body. We are often treatable, or dead. And even when a body is left behind, no Adept would wish for their brothers and sisters to die trying to retrieve it. As a result of this, Adept Legions long ago developed their own traditions to honor the dead."

Yalla looked over towards the wall, as if he could see into the next room.

"It's our way of remembering those left behind. The ceremony is led by the Blood Poet. A master of arms, words, and spirit so respected that other Adept Legions, and occasionally even Corporations, recognize their abilities. If the Praetor is our military and societal leader, then the Blood Poet is our spiritual one."

Janus followed Yalla's gaze.

"And the Blood Poet is going to Mura now?"

"Yes. A small ceremony will be performed with her friends, and then, at her request, we will consign her body to the sea."

"So who—"

"Colonel." An aide appeared in the door.

"They're requesting your presence. The Poet is here, and Mura would like to speak with you one more time."

"Pardon me, Janus. I need to go."

Janus nodded, and Yalla disappeared through the open door. Grabbing his armor, Janus slid it back on. His side was already starting to feel better. As he stepped from the room, he saw the hem of a deep red robe disappear into Mura's room, and the door closed. As he left the medical branch, his stomach rumbled, and all dour thoughts left his mind at the promise of a hot meal in the mess.

The next day Wouris wore a much grimmer look.

"Your advanced training is over."

The cadets looked around at each other in confusion. They stood together in formation, facing Wouris in front of the door to the mess.

"This morning, I was informed that the Praetor, under advisement of the officer's council, has elected to move forward with a large contract, and has accepted the first portion of our payment. Due to the size of the operation, all available personnel will be made active for duty. Even cadets."

Wouris struggled to keep her face calm, but her teeth were grinding slowly together.

"This operation will be your first mission, and as such, will determine whether you become full-fledged Adepts. The Praetor and the majority of the officers feel that you are well prepared for this mission and can make a meaningful contribution. Anyone who does not agree may step out now. We don't need any of you becoming a liability. You will be returned to your former Corporations as soon as possible."

Many of the cadets looked around at each other, but none moved. Wouris nodded, then led them through the doors.

The mess hall had been converted into a meeting chamber, with the seats lined up towards the far end of the room. A MuDi had been lowered from the ceiling, and was already running, showing unfamiliar terrain. More and more Adepts crowded into the room, and excitement filled the air. But Wouris leaned against a wall staring stonily at the display.

Janus, Celes, Lyn, Ramirez and Marcus sat off to one side, by the windows. Praetor Jennings entered the room swiftly, sporting a grim look. Wouris stood at attention as he passed, but her expression did not change. The Praetor's appearance silenced the buzz.

"As most of you now know," he began, "ODIN has agreed to a new contract."

There were cheers all around. The Praetor raised a hand for quiet.

"Yes, this is a boon for us. Many of you are aware of the decline in the number of jobs we have had in recent years. The Corporations have been apathetic, at best. This is a critical opportunity for us; a chance to replenish our coffers beyond what trading has been able to do. However, this is not a typical mission. It falls well outside our standard: this is a full-fledged assault upon a Titan Corporation outpost."

The murmuring began again.

"Silence, please," the Praetor commanded. "I realize that such a job hasn't been undertaken in years, and that it is much more dangerous than a standard infiltration operation. I also realize there has been some dissension among the officers concerning my decision to include the cadets in this mission. However, those of you who know me should realize that I would not send out cadets who I do not feel are ready for the task. I consider the safety of my fellow Adepts paramount."

He glanced at Wouris and Keats, who quickly looked away.

"Unfortunately, we cannot pass up a job of such exceptional pay, and let me assure you—the pay is exceptional."

"How much is exceptional?" Marcus blurted out. Colonel Keats stood up, addressing his question before any else could.

"That is none of your concern," she said. "If the Praetor gives the order, it doesn't matter how much money ODIN is receiving for a job."

"Thank you, Colonel." Jennings smiled at Keats. "However, in this case I find it to be a perfectly valid question. We are not a Corporation, after all. To answer: seventy cross-ingots of Immutium alloy, of which, we have already received half."

There was a collective intake of breath from the Adepts, though it seemed many of the officers did not share in their excitement. The majority of the cadets, however, looked around in confusion—Janus included. The number meant nothing to him. Celes must have sensed his question, and leaned over to whisper in his ear.

"That's a huge sum," she said. "That's more Immutium than a Corporation produces in a year. I don't know how much Adepts usually receive for their services, but that's unbelievable."

Lyn popped her head in and gave Celes a puzzled look.

"How do you know that?" she asked. "I didn't even know what Immutium was until we came to ODIN."

"Yes, this is a large payment," the Praetor boomed, saving Celes from the question. "But this is also a special job. There hasn't been an open assault like this in decades. Our employer no doubt feels such a large sum is necessary."

Colonel Hawkes snorted loudly, and Keats shot him an angry look. Jennings acted as if he hadn't heard.

"Major Northcott will now outline the assault and its objectives," the Praetor concluded.

"Alright, listen up. Our intelligence shows that the target is a small, isolated Titan Corporation colony to the north. We understand it is the primary processing outpost for raw materials mined in the Northern Reaches."

The MuDi display shifted, showing a large map with a flashing dot giving the current position of Valhalla. The map moved a thousand kilometers north to display the position of the colony.

"The colony is based on a small promontory with the Siren Sea bordering on two sides."

The MuDi zoomed in to show a model of the outpost, with two beaches on the south and east of the colony. The Major clasped his hands behind his back.

"We have been contracted for two main objectives: first, to disable, but not destroy, the primary processing center at the center of the colony, including the six Hades launchers protecting it."

The MuDi zoomed in to highlight a large factory occupying the middle of the outpost.

"Second, to destroy a research and communications facility at the northernmost tip of the colony. We can only presume our attack is a precursor to another invasion. One that intends to hold the outpost, but does not want to risk any information getting out."

The MuDi moved its focus to a tri-cornered, armored facility at the north end of the colony. Three huge legs supported the wide base of the structure, its concave walls rising upward to a flat top covered with dishes and antennas.

"One full detachment of Adepts will be deployed to disable the mining facility, and another will sweep the outpost to disable the six Hades Missile systems scattered throughout."

The MuDi zoomed out to highlight the six smaller Hades sites on the map, as Keats stepped forward to address the crowd.

"Our intelligence indicates that most of the personnel at the facility are non-military, making it seem unnecessary to deploy so many Adepts. Due to the nature of this mission and the limited timeframe provided by our employer, however, we decided it would be prudent to eliminate the largest threats from the outpost as quickly as possible. When we make our assault, two squadrons of Valkyrie fighters will strike the East and South beaches before our Longboat Personnel Carriers land. Until the six Hades launchers are eliminated, we will be limited in the amount of air support we can offer. After the initial attack, most of our air force will be vulnerable and largely useless."

The MuDi zoomed out further, highlighting two squadrons of Valkyries sweeping across the beaches, one from the South, another from the East. Right behind them, a squadron of Longboats appeared, taking the same route as the Eastern squad of Valks.

"The beaches provide our avenue of entry, as they sit low enough below the hills to grant our forces cover from the Hades sites," she continued. "With the element of surprise, our Longboats can land on the East beach. Our forces will then sweep north and west, eliminating the targets along the way, and circle to meet the Longboats again on the South beach. If things get out of hand, we can offer air support and emergency evac to the West after we take out the missile systems."

"Thank you, Colonel," Major Northcott said. "If anything goes wrong, and the initial evac point is compromised, the alternative evac will be due north of the outpost."

The MuDi zoomed out again and showed the evacuation point many kilometers to the north.

"Don't worry, Major," an Adept said confidently from the front of the crowd. "We're not going to need that evac point."

The Major smiled.

"What's that area between the outpost and the secondary evac point, sir?" Celes asked, looking at the strange grey and black mass just a few kilometers north of edge of the outpost. Many veteran Adepts looked at her, surprised, while others muttered to each other. Celes blushed slightly at the attention. A mustached Adept behind her leaned in.

"No one asks about the evac point," he said. "Bad luck, you see. Research it later."

The Major, however, just nodded his head.

"Actually, the outpost is close to the ruins of Phoenix Corporation. You will have thirty-six hours from the start of the mission to get there should anything happen."

More muttering sounded around the hall.

"What about the comm center, sir?" Roderick asked.

Northcott gave him an angry stare. "I was just about to get to that."

Roderick blanched, and Northcott cleared his throat.

"Unlike the mining facility and the Hades launchers, our initial scout reports suggest the comm center is much less heavily guarded. The cadets, under Sergeant Wouris, will be responsible for its destruction. A sweeper team will follow behind to make sure the job is done properly. The remaining Adepts not directly involved in the mission will remain here on high alert."

Janus scanned the room. None of the older Adepts surrounding him seemed surprised by the decision to keep a complement of ODIN's forces at Valhalla.

Do they fear an attack here?

"Any questions?" Praetor Jennings asked. He waited a beat before continuing. "Good. You will receive further briefing from your respective officers. Cadets will be briefed by Sergeant Wouris. Be ready to deploy at 0400 tomorrow morning. Dismissed."

Janus was lost in thought as the cadets made their way back to Sigma three. His mind wandered from the furtive looks of the officers, to the strange nature of the mission—and its huge reward. But eventually his thoughts settled on Clara, and what she would say about the situation.

Watch those alleys!

Celes cleared her throat, and Janus nearly jumped.

"Is anyone else as bothered as I am about all this?" Celes asked.

"Prob'bly just nerves," Ramirez grunted.

"Of course," Lyn smiled. "If you were bothered by anything, we'd never know, would we?"

"Prob'bly not," Ramirez said simply.

The cadets chuckled, and Janus couldn't help but grin.

"Hey Ramirez," Marcus chuckled, "how'd you get to be so insightful?"

"Well, he certainly didn't get it from us," Celes said.

"Speak for yourself," Janus said with a smirk.

Celes gave him a grin, her voice dripping with sarcasm. "Of course, mighty Janus. I would *never, ever* think of insulting you." She stopped in front of him and gave a mock bow. "I hope you won't take offense at my discourtesy. Whatever was I thinking?"

Janus stopped and put on a hurt look.

"Just because you're a shoo-in to be one of the squad leaders in this mission doesn't mean that people will be foolish enough to follow you," she said. "But you do have potential."

She winked at him, then turned and walked ahead. Lyn and Ramirez followed after her.

Janus shook his head and watched her move to the front of the group. He exchanged a doubtful glance with Marcus, and the pair hurried to catch up.

Wouris met them back in Sigma three. She looked them over as they filed in silently and gathered in a semi-circle around her.

"There will be three teams. Janus, Lyn, and Marcus—you'll be our strike leaders. Celes, Valers, Bynes, Hughes, Kwandis and Young, you're with Janus."

Wouris pointed to Lyn.

"Ramirez, Jones, Holloway, Byron, Kirsten, Roderick. You're on Lyn. Marcus, you'll be leading Naka, Zhao, Browning, Freeham, Alexis, and Nathans. An Adept squad will follow behind you in case you can't get the job done."

Janus looked around at his fellow cadets; the grim looks he saw made it clear they all understood what she meant.

"Tomorrow morning, you will load up into three Longboats," she said, pulling out a map of the Titan outpost. "The two Valkyrie squadrons will assault the East and South Beaches."

She traced the path of the two squadrons with her finger.

"This will be the extent of the air coverage until our veteran Adept squads can take out the Hades launchers. Your Longboats will be hard on the heels of the Valks. You'll drop in"—she pointed to the East beach—"hit the remaining beach defenses, and sweep into the outpost. Move quickly, but don't be afraid to do some scouting as you move through. Most of the buildings are civilian mining structures, so there shouldn't be too much resistance."

Byron raised a hand. "How much is 'not too much?'"

"We'll get an update from our scout teams as we make our final approach, but our last tally was a total of about a hundred STs, and no Inferni at the facility. There aren't many personnel present in the first place, and miners and scientists don't get paid to stand in harm's way. They'll likely start hiding once they realize the outpost is under attack. The only real military presence is the barracks, located here."

She pointed to a building on the Western side of the city.

"Be prepared for enemy reinforcements coming from this direction. Marcus, you'll plant your charges on the structural supports at the near side of the comm center. Move quickly, and position yourselves to support the others."

She again pointed to the map, and motioned to another corner of the communications tower.

"Lyn, your team will place charges on the Southwest corner. It's closest to the enemy barracks, so use your scouting expertise to keep track of enemy movements, and relay those to the rest of the cadets. Janus, your team will have the toughest job; you'll have to move quickly to get here"—she pointed to the farthest corner of the communications facility—"the northernmost tip. After you plant your charges, get moving to rendezvous with the Longboats on the South beach. The Hades launchers, as well as most of the colony's defenses, should have been swept out of the way by our veteran Adept squads by then, so you shouldn't have too much trouble. Once all squads are reported clear, I'll hit the detonator. I will be dropping in with the squad behind you, so if you do run into any trouble, sit tight and we'll come for you. Any questions?"

No one spoke up.

"Good. You all should have memorized the colony's map by now, but you'll get your own hard copy tomorrow morning, in case you've got any jitters."

"Sergeant," said Kirsten. "Why do we carry the plastic maps anyway? We've got our comm links."

"The same reason you memorize it," Wouris said. "A plastic map doesn't run on batteries or clog up with dirt. It won't get crushed during a hectic battle. Never rely on something that is more complicated than it needs to be. It just adds another component for failure. Besides, these aren't completely ordinary maps. Someone toss me a flashlight; Freeham, hit the lights."

The room went dark, and Wouris turned on the light that Hughes tossed her. The group gathered around, their faces dimly illuminated by the glow.

"Here's something else a brightly lit screen doesn't do well."

She brought up the flashlight so everyone could see the bottom of the handle and turned it.

"One, two clicks."

The flashlight went black, plunging the room back into darkness. But after a moment, glowing lines slowly bloomed into view, cris-crossing the map. The faint, purplish traces formed a grid, distinguishing the colony perfectly.

"Bio-luminescence. Reacts to UV light. Glows perfectly well, but is almost impossible to see from a distance, and doesn't give your position away with any extra light. Only lasts for about a week, but still a handy feature if you are ever in a combat zone at night and need an impromptu war meeting. Freeham: lights."

Freeham hit the lights again as Wouris turned the flashlight off and tossed it back to Hughes.

"I understand that you all still have much to learn. Most of you are probably worried by the nature of this mission. But yours is one of the most talented groups we've had in years. I want you to know that I have the utmost confidence all of you will do your jobs, and do them well."

Janus folded his arms across his chest, and saw Celes smiling at him. Marcus gave a wink to her, as Lyn gave Ramirez a thumbs up. Wouris began to pace.

"Don't forget your emergency comm signal if you get into trouble. All you have to do is hit the button. And even though there isn't supposed to be any Infernus presence, don't forget that your armor helps mask and dissipate your heat signature. So don't panic if—"

Ramirez chuckled, causing everyone to turn and look at him in surprise.

"Don't worry, Wouris," he said. "We can handle it."

Wouris' grim look was finally broken, and she smiled.

"Go loosen up for a few hours, eat a good meal, and get some shuteye," she said. "I'll see you tomorrow."

The mess hall was packed that evening. Even still, the cadets found a long table near a window to sit together as one. But by the time Janus had grabbed his food it was a tight fit. Lyn opened up a spot next to Ramirez for him, and between Roderick almost getting pushed off the end, and Lyn seemingly able to contort herself to half her size, he managed to squeeze in. It wasn't particularly comfortable, but it was funny.

He stared around the table. Celes sat diagonally across from him, between Marcus and Valers. Then Hughes and Kwandis. Naka next to Lyn. The others were nearby. Bynes, Holloway, Nathans, Alexis, Young, Jones, Byron, Zhao, Kirsten, Freeham, Browning. He had only been surrounded by so many people one other time in his life, back on the Cerberus lift. That seemed so long ago. And for once, surrounded by laughter, he felt like he knew Clara would have wanted him here. He looked across at Celes. She struggled to eat, switching between contagious laughter and alarm, as elbows and shoulders pushed her further and further from her food. She caught Janus' eye and smiled.

"We're packed like sardines here."

Janus ducked as Ramirez' huge elbow slowly maneuvered to avoid hitting anyone in the head.

"Like what?"

Celes shook her head. "It's a bit tightly packed here."

"Yeah," Janus agreed. "Not like home in Cerberus."

"Obviously, neither of you have been to the hawker's bazaars in Medusa," Marcus said.

"Or the entertainment districts of Hydra," Kirsten added. "Pretty standard fare, really. Right now, this place feels just about right."

"The lifts are occasionally like this," Naka interjected. "Usually around big events and holidays."

"My family is big, so we pack around the table like this every night," Valers said. "What about you Roderick?"

Roderick was practically hanging off the end, despite Ramirez's best efforts to give him space.

"Can't say we were so crowded. But I like the people here more."

"Hear, hear!" Lyn exclaimed. "Ta great friends!"

She raised her glass above her head. Ramirez moved his to shoulder level to clink against hers. Celes gave Janus a subtle nod towards her own drink, and signed **hear, hear**, and Janus smiled in appreciation.

As one, the cadets raised glasses.

"Hear, hear!"

"To victory!" Marcus yelled.

"Hear, hear!" the raucous roar of Adepts came back. Janus turned to see the entire mess toasting the coming day in agreement.

Not like home at all.

Chapter 25
Sharpened Spears

Janus awoke at midnight, the excitement and anxiety of the mission pressing down upon his chest. Clara was counting on him.

He sat up in bed, staring at the wall; no matter what happened in today's mission, he and the other cadets would dress like the veterans they would fight beside. His new Adept armor was stronger and lighter than cadet armor, with more space to hold equipment. Armored plates woven into the suit protected his body, while a tough mesh formed the outer covering. The armor was normally a dull black, but dark brown splotches appeared all over it as he pulled it from its rack. He could feel the tingle of electricity racing through the mesh as it finished its color change. His new suit could change anywhere from a light brown to a solid green. Swapping in a new entropic battery, he checked it over once more. He would get three more camo shifts. He hoped he wouldn't need them.

He wore no helmet. His suit was more for camouflage, gear, and protection from the elements than anything else. It might provide light explosive protection, but a direct hit from a Zeus would be catastrophic. One could survive the loss of an arm, but one always needed a head. He could unfurl a hood from his suit if needed, but the unfortunate reality was that for Adepts, helmets were an impediment they simply couldn't afford.

Out of the wall closet popped another compartment, containing his new Fenris pistol. It too was a dull black with splotches of brown. A stamp of the horse-riding Odin was embossed in the handle. He checked it once over, then rammed it into its holster.

The common room was quiet, lit only by the light of the moon. Janus had just stepped inside when Celes' door slid open, and she appeared in her own armor. The pale moonlight gave her an ethereal glow, and Janus felt his breath catch. She turned to face him, and Janus swallowed as he realized he might have been staring a moment too long. She held a hand up to her chest and signed.

[Looking] good.

Janus exhaled and relaxed. **You [look] ready.**

Celes shook her head with a grin.

"Are you?"

As they made their way towards the mess hall, Janus stopped at a window and stared into the darkness. Valhalla was over the open ocean, away from the coast, and stars filled the blackness in every direction.

"What's on your mind?" Celes asked, standing at his side. Janus took a moment before answering, his gaze not leaving the window.

"Just wondering how Clara is doing right now."

"Clara?" Celes asked, with an edge to her voice. "Who's that?"

"My mother."

Celes' mouth formed a little 'o,' but she remained silent.

"I was just thinking about how she would feel—me getting dragged here, putting my life in danger, doing the things we do."

"And?" Celes asked expectantly. Janus smiled at her directness.

"I wasn't sure at first, when I came here. But that first night in Valhalla, when I saw the stars out there…"

Celes followed his gaze, out to the broad sky where pinpricks of light danced.

"And then last night, when we were all crammed into that tiny space. I realized she would be happy," he said. "Though maybe a little frightened."

"Why?"

"I came from Cerberus. I don't know if it's different from the other Corporations or not, but it isn't a pleasant place. There is so much fog and darkness that you can't see the sky, let alone the stars. Before I came here, I had never experienced the open air, and I had seen the sky only once. Although she never lived outside the city, Clara used to read my books with me, and imagine what the world outside was like. She'd be happy I can finally experience those things, beyond the world she's trapped in, despite whatever dangers there may be."

He was silent for a moment.

"She's sacrificed so much for me."

He became quiet, watching the twinkling lights as they hovered over the horizon.

"See now, that wasn't so bad, was it?" Celes said, smirking.

"What?" Janus glanced at her, confused.

"You don't always have to hold everything in."

Janus returned his stare out the window, folding his arms across his chest.

"Oh come on." Celes laughed. "Let's get breakfast."

The mess hall was dark and empty when they entered. However, the kitchen food dispensers never slept, and one of the machines provided them two bowls of steaming oatmeal. It wasn't anything fancy, but at least it was good and filling.

Half an hour later, Marcus strode into the hall. Catching the pair sitting alone, he made a beeline for them, not even stopping by the mess line.

"Ready to take on our first mission, Janus? We'll show the officers how to do their jobs, won't we?"

"Looking forward to it."

"Bet I plant my charges first." Marcus smirked.

"Oh, we'll take you on," said Celes. "Even if we *do* have to go further than you to get the job done."

"Okay, okay, maybe so." Marcus laughed. "But I don't have you on my squad, Celes. I would say Janus has an unfair advantage."

"Jealous are we, Marcus?" Celes asked.

"No, but you will be when my squad gets the job done first." He smirked. "Double rations or nothing?"

"Let's just make sure we get the job done," Janus interjected.

Marcus' smirk disappeared. He studied Janus for a moment and glanced at Celes.

"Absolutely." Marcus' face reflected his seriousness. "No mistakes, and we all get home tonight."

He stretched out his hand.

"Take care of your squad, and I'll take care of mine. And together we can take care of everyone else."

Janus clasped the outstretched arm, and nodded.

After they had eaten their fill, the three jogged over to the Chariot of Hail. It was brimming with excitement. The Longboats and Valkyries were undergoing a final inspection before the mission. Adepts pulled serviced weapons from large racks on the wall. Others double-checked their equipment to ensure it was functioning properly. A few of the more senior Adepts were practicing their swordplay with unpowered Ghostblades. Janus had never noticed before, but without power, the blades were nearly dull. Ramirez motioned for the three of them to join him near one of the Longboats.

"You may want to grab any special weapons before all the good ones get taken."

"Oh? What have we missed?" Marcus asked with a curious grin.

Ramirez picked up the huge rocket launcher that was leaning on the wall next to him and patted it lovingly.

"Lyn felt that I should be the one to carry the heavy artillery for our squad. I have a pistol for softer targets."

He motioned to the monstrous pistol holstered on his armor.

"Did they give you a cannon instead?" Celes asked skeptically.

Ramirez shrugged. "Whatever works."

Lyn jogged over to join them.

"Wouris says final inspection is in thirty minutes. Praetor Jennings is going ta look over the cadets with her. Do ya have your squads organized?"

She gave Janus and Marcus critical looks.

"I went over everything with my squad last night," Janus said. "But I guess if we have time for one final check…"

"Don't worry, Janus," Celes said. "We've got it all together. I'll grab our rifles. Be right back."

She jogged off towards the weapon racks.

"Well, she certainly is carefree," Ramirez commented dryly.

"Yes, she is," Janus replied with a concerned look.

"She has confidence in her squad leader, is all," Lyn said with a smile.

Janus wasn't sure if that made him feel more or less confident.

When Marcus, Lyn, and Janus had lined up their squads in formation, Praetor Jennings came over to them, Wouris following a step behind. She gave each cadet a once over, securing a strap here, checking a weapon there, until everyone had been inspected.

She took a step back from the group and faced the Praetor.

"Cadets ready for inspection, sir!"

"Thank you, Sergeant. I believe you have already performed that excellently. All of you should get to your assigned Longboats and prepare for departure. ODIN has every confidence in all of you. Good luck and God-speed."

The cadets saluted, and the Praetor returned it, dismissing them.

As Janus motioned his group to the first Longboat, the Praetor pulled him aside.

"A moment, Janus."

Janus gave him an apprehensive look, but signaled his squad to go ahead without him.

"Yes, sir?"

The Praetor narrowed his eyes, his gaze piercing.

"If something goes wrong, the other cadets will listen to you. You've garnered a great deal of loyalty over the past few months."

He paused, watching Janus for a reaction.

"I know you are worried about your mother, Clara," he continued. "You have the greatest potential I have seen in years—I don't want you going into battle distracted. Know that I will make sure she is well cared for at Cerberus, no matter what happens. I think you have earned that. I want you to focus all your energy on this mission. If you think something is wrong, don't be afraid to trust those feelings."

He unclasped the ornately sheathed blade from his belt and handed it to Janus, who looked at it in surprise.

"Take this. You haven't had the opportunity for much training with a Ghostblade; we don't usually allow Cadets to carry them until they have had a full mission in the field. But I think it may help. Not only is it a valuable weapon if you run into trouble, the other cadets and Adepts will listen if they know you carry it. Though whether they follow will be up to you."

209

Janus tested the weight of the blade in his hands, and ran his palm along the engravings, from the red-enameled Odin on the sheath, to the eye that formed the pommel's power readout. It was a beautiful weapon.

"But why?" Janus asked.

The Praetor gave a grim look.

"Are you questioning my judgment?"

"No, sir."

Jennings studied Janus' face.

"Let's just say I don't believe in coincidences." His eyes scanned the length of the sheath, stopping for a moment on a half-moon at the very tip. "But don't let this go to your head. I expect every one of my new cadets to make it back alive. Pride has killed more Adepts than anything else. Don't make the mistake of thinking you always know best. Listen to your squad-mates; they have had just as much training as you. Now get to your Longboat and load up."

Janus' grip tightened around the heavy handle.

"Yes, sir."

The Praetor gave a slight nod. But as Janus turned and jogged towards the Longboat, the Praetor called out to him again.

"Oh, and Janus."

"Sir?"

"I expect to have that back."

CHAPTER 26
THE ASSAULT

The Valkyries and Longboats spent the hours before sunrise moving into position, and as dawn broke, they hugged the ocean swells. A faint yellow glow tinged the horizon as they headed towards the Titan outpost.

Inside, the Longboat was silent, the mission weighing heavily on everyone's minds. Janus stood up and stared out over the ocean through an open hatch, following the rest of the deployment as the Longboats and Valkyries began their run towards the beach. The Valkyries glided like wraiths over the ocean, their multi-chromatic skin changing back and forth between the lighter and darker greens of the ocean waves, making them almost imperceptible to the eye.

Janus tensed as the Titan outpost came into view.

No turning back now.

Glory came over the intercom.

"Two minutes. Get ready."

Janus was glad to have her. They had trained through repeated deployments, and he knew that she would deliver them exactly as she was supposed to.

The Adepts and cadets stood as one. The cadets searched nervously for affirmation from one another amidst their hard-jawed superiors. Celes smiled, and gave the restless group a thumbs up, attempting to calm the cadets.

I'm glad I've got her in my squad.

Glory came over the intercom again.

"Twenty seconds out."

Janus did a silent count in his head.

Fifteen...

Explosions of the Valkyries hitting the beach rang through the fuselage.

Ten...

The Longboat rocked.

"Hades missiles, hold on!" Glory cried.

Five...

The Longboat suddenly decelerated, and the doors were thrown open.

"Hit it!" Glory screamed.

In a moment, Janus was out the door with Celes running by his side.

The sound was deafening, yet everything distinct. The roar of the Longboats as they lifted off, engines straining to get them airborne as fast as possible. Explosions rocking the sand as the Adepts assaulted the last of the beach defenses. The whistle of Zeus fire as it peppered the air around them.

The beach was a mixture of sand and rock. Stony outcroppings dominated the landscape, framing the mining colony rising above them in natural walls. The bunkers and buildings they could see burned and smoked. The Valkyries had done their job.

Janus' feet pounded the earth, kicking up a spray as he ran. Suddenly, an ST emerged from behind a rocky hill, aiming at another squad down the beach. His heart quickened. Two reports sounded from just beside him. As the ST collapsed under Celes' salvo, Janus turned his attention to two more STs hustling up a nearby boulder carrying a tripod. They tumbled over as Valers and Bynes eliminated them.

As they moved up the beach, pressing forward, firing as they ran, Janus felt everything and nothing. The heat from his companions' fire; the cold emptiness when an ST fell. They were like the soulless automatons on which he practiced. They received no more consideration than for the brief seconds they threatened him or his squad. While he ran, his mind felt strangely disconnected, instinct and training guiding him effortlessly across the rocky expanse. For once, he did not hate the STs. They were simply an obstacle to overcome.

One hated a nemesis, not an obstacle.

More STs came flooding from a camouflaged bunker that had avoided the Valkyries' fury. Janus pulled a Loki Variable Grenade from his armor, adjusting the power of the blast as he ran. Watching his enemy scramble to put themselves into some semblance of a formation, he briefly registered that the STs seemed confused. Unsure. And then he lightly tossed the grenade into the small ditch that held the hidden bunker.

The nearest ST displayed a surprising instinct. His hand shot out to catch the twirling weapon. He opened his hand, and brought it close to his face in curiosity.

Janus registered only a brief flash, and the feeling of a hot wind as it ushered him forward.

Reaching the outskirts of the colony, Janus looked to his left and right. Other Adept squads were already moving along inside, and Marcus' team was disappearing around a corner, a swathe of motionless STs around them.

Janus took a moment to collect himself in the cover of the buildings, feeling his heart slow.

The colony was strangely quiet. Distant explosions sounded like far off thunder. Gunfire buzzed like insects. Janus raised his hand, motioning the squad to slow, settling the pace from their frantic run across the sand.

They were between two low buildings just inside the reaches of the colony. Both buildings were of a crude, hastily constructed quality, mostly made of rusting sheet metal. Many were no more than one or two stories, but here and there, older, taller buildings of steel and glass stood. They were closely packed together, and all had the same feeling of decay.

"Celes, tell me what's happening," Janus said, motioning her up top. Celes nodded, and Janus gave her a boost up to the edge of the roof. She hung briefly, peeking over the edge before quickly pulling herself up. She disappeared for but a moment before popping back over the edge and rejoining the squad.

"I see the target, two kilometers, west-northwest. Two Adept squads are already deep in the city. Seven more right behind. The cadets are all at the back of the pack. The factory is almost due west. Lyn's squad is on the right. Byron's her spotter. We signaled each other, so they know where we are. Marcus is further out on our left, and he's got three STs advancing on him at eleven o'clock. There's a tall building between them, so I don't think he sees them coming."

"Hughes," Janus said, turning to the rest of the squad. "Raise Marcus. Let him know what's coming. Bynes, let Lyn know we've got her left flank, and we want her to watch our right. Valers and Kwandis, take the left. Celes, you and I will take point. Keep an eye out. I'm counting on you to keep us moving towards the target. Young, cover our rear. Let's not be surprised by any smarter-than-average STs."

Grim faces nodded back at him.

"Let's move quickly, but don't do anything stupid."

The faces cracked slightly into smiles.

"Move out."

He set up a steady pace, sticking to the alleys and side streets to avoid the more exposed main roads; leapfrogging forward with Celes. It was remarkably easy. For its great size, the outpost seemed almost deserted. Wouris was right; the residents had gone to ground.

Many of the buildings were for storage or mining purposes, but the occasional abandoned bar or store popped up as they went. The colony must have thrived at one point, but looking at the peeling paint and rusting walls, those days were long gone.

One of the veteran Adept voices crackled over the group radio band in Janus' ear.

"Omega Squad, Alexander's Army, here. Hades launchers are more heavily guarded than original intel would suggest. First launcher at mission grid Charlie three. Requesting additional squad support to ensure timely destruction of launchers, over."

"Alpha Squad, Valhalla's Valor, here," another Adept responded. "We're coming up on your position now, Alexander's. Out."

The radios went quiet, and silence pervaded the outpost. Janus weaved his way silently through the buildings, slowed only by his caution, as they saw not a soul. A strange fluttering began to take hold of his gut, and with less than a quarter of the distance left to the communications tower, Janus called a halt. He stopped in a small enclosure at the corner of four buildings with good sight lines. A huge, rusting excavator was visible through the narrow alley, its claw-like shovels waiting silently for the elements to claim it.

Celes speedily climbed an old rain gutter after a few quick pulls to see if it would fail.

"Squad one," Janus whispered into his headset, "Wouris' Washouts, to squad two. How goes it, Lyn?"

"I don't know Janus," Lyn's voice responded. "I really don't know. We've had no trouble at all so far. I saw a couple STs heading east, but they were way off, and disappeared before I could have Jones take them out. I heard the report that the Hades launchers are pretty heavily guarded."

"Yeah, me too."

"It's really bugging me, though," she continued. "I mean, I've seen some huge mining equipment, and a lot of it, but it's all so old. It's been years since it's been used. I can't imagine anyone would want anything here anymore. It isn't supposed to be this easy, is it?"

Janus allowed his eyes to roam around to the taller buildings that poked up here and there over the low rooftops.

"I know what you mean."

"Hey, relax, both of you," Marcus' voice cut across the radio.

"It doesn't seem odd to you at all, Marcus?" Lyn said.

"Of course it does, but the Praetor isn't in the business of making bad calls. Besides, if my time in the ST corps taught me anything, Corporations aren't known for their amazing decision-making. Territory and status means more than practicality. If someone wants this rock, and wants to overpay for it, it's fine by me."

"I can always count on your confidence, Marcus," said Lyn.

"Of course you can. Anyway, why would they devote more men to this useless piece of dirt than they already have? This facility is fairly old, there can't be much left of value. We're here just to make a statement, stir things up a bit."

"And if we're not?" Janus asked simply.

"Then just think of how valuable whatever we find here must be," Marcus responded immediately.

Lyn chuckled. "You're an inspiring opportunist, Marcus."

"Thank you."

"Alright, enough. We have a job to do," Janus said. "Lyn, where are you?"

"About three hundred meters from the target, southeast of your position. Byron and Celes appear to be having a merry little conversation with hand signals."

Janus glanced up. Celes was hidden behind a small chimney, making tiny, frantic motions with her hands towards the distant spotter.

"It's a good thing you've got us, too," her voice cut across the conversation. "Behind me. Second building on the left. Third floor window, second from the right. ST"

"Am I clear for a look?" Janus asked.

"Don't. He's moving, and may have already spotted us. Although he doesn't seem to want to engage."

"Do you have a shot?"

"Only with a big risk."

Janus shook his head and then jumped on the radio. "Lyn, Marcus. Did you get that?"

"You should keep moving," Lyn said. "That ST can't do much. And if you get a move on, he won't even be able to relay your position to others. They already know we're here, it won't compromise the mission in any way."

"We've both got the same feeling Lyn," Janus said. "Something's up. You know we have to check it out."

"Maybe he realized what a bad idea it would be to attack," Marcus interjected. "If I was an ST, I'd be scared too, knowing we're out here."

"We can't ignore it," Janus said seriously. "I'm going to find out."

He signaled for Celes to drop down.

"No," Marcus said. "My team will do it. That ST may be watching you."

"And if there are more?" Lyn asked hesitantly.

"We'll let you know in a couple. We're going in."

"Be careful," Celes whispered.

The radio went silent. Janus quickly moved his team forward, and into a position under a nearby archway. Gunfire erupted to their left, but quickly faded away, impossible to pinpoint. Several tense minutes passed.

"Marcus?" Lyn's voice came across the radio. "Do you read?"

More silence.

"Marcus, do you copy?" Lyn said nervously. "What do you think, Janus?"

Janus stared at the top of the building.

"Just wait."

"Are you sure?" Lyn said.

"Yes," Janus said. Celes and the other cadets looked at him nervously. Janus looked at Celes as he spoke into the radio. "Marcus wouldn't have been caught off guard. We would know."

Another minute passed. Lyn's voice came over the radio again. "Janus, I think—"

"Clear," Marcus' voice said. Celes blew a sigh of relief. Janus peered around a roof corner at the third-floor window. The helmet still sat in the window.

"Rats," Marcus said.

"What?" Janus asked in confusion.

"It was just an empty helmet on the table. A rat got inside and started poking around. It ran off when we came in. The building's completely empty, but these upper rooms have some fancy digs. Bunch of faded old furniture. Covered in dust, but still pretty nice."

Janus shook his head and looked back at the team. The relief was clear on their faces.

"Well, that's good news," Lyn said.

"Hold on," Marcus said cautiously. Janus' eyes shot back up to the window, the top of Marcus' head just visible.

"What?" Lyn asked, with a hint of nervousness.

"Six STs between you and the comm tower," he said.

Janus felt oddly relieved at this proclamation.

"Relative positions?"

"Where are you Janus?"

"The arch, directly northeast of your position," Janus replied.

"Got it. And I've got Lyn, too. Two on a rooftop, three buildings northwest of you, Janus. Twenty-five meters, maybe. One on a roof near Lyn, twenty meters or so to the north. I can just make out the other three on the ground in a recess between the three on the roof."

"Can the STs on the rooftops see each other?"

"Yes, but their view is obscured to their South. The three on the ground can see the two on your side, Janus, but they're blind to the one above—make it eight STs. Two more just popped up in an alley on the left—get back!"

Marcus' head disappeared from view as the window disintegrated under a hail of Zeus fire.

The wall was peppered with rounds, which took noticeable chunks with every impact.

"Marcus!" Celes said.

"I'm fine, I'm fine," came the hasty reply, the sounds of exploding walls in the background. "But we've definitely been spotted. We can't offer much support."

"Don't worry!" Janus responded hastily. "Get to safety, and then keep moving. We can handle the STs. Finish your part of the mission."

"Will do. The two new STs are to the left of the set of two on the rooftop. Get there quickly; they weren't moving when they started firing. With any luck, you'll catch them with their pants down."

"Thanks, Marcus."

"Good luck!"

The sound of the Zeus was fading fast in the background. Janus hastily came up with a plan, and turned back to address his team.

"We need to hit the rooftop STs at the same time. Then we can seize the high ground over the rest. Celes, climb up behind that chimney there." He pointed to the north. "See if that gives you a shot on that single ST"

She immediately turned and scrambled spider-like up the wall behind her.

"And find a spot for me too, I'm coming up. Lyn?"

"Yes, Janus?"

"Can you and Byron find a position to attack the other two on the roof? I want to set up a cross-fire."

"We're on it."

"Ramirez, take Holloway. Kwandis, Hughes, and Roderick, move in on the three in the middle. Jones, Valers, and Young, you three hit the pair on the ground to my left as soon as the action starts. That should distract them and give you a chance to surprise them from behind. Kirsten, Bynes, watch our back and flanks. We're probably going to attract attention. And be ready to move up at a moment's notice. Wait for my signal."

Using a corner where the arch intersected the building with the chimney, Janus vaulted himself to the roof, catching the edge and hauling himself up. Sliding catlike through the shadows, he came up silently behind Celes.

"How're we doing?"

"What took you so long?" came Celes' playful reply, although she remained watching the ST from her hiding place. "The others are nearly in position. There is a good spot behind that generator over there. If you stay below the lip of the building, the STs won't be able to spot you."

Janus nodded, then took off, moving silently and keeping low. When he reached his destination, he peered around the defunct generator atop the building. The two STs were crouched behind a low wall, watching the window where Marcus had appeared, seemingly unsure how to proceed.

220

The other lone ST was pressed against the tiny shack that provided roof access.

Janus activated his comm link.

"One of them has red chevrons on his shoulder. A sergeant, I would guess. I'll take that one."

"Roger," said Celes. "Everyone's in position."

"On my mark. Three...two...one..."

Byron's voice cut in over the radio. "Hold!"

Janus paused, waiting for Byron.

"We've got four Inferni that just boosted in from out of nowhere. Should be coming into your view...right..."

Janus heard the Inferni before he saw them, but their unmistakable red armor couldn't be missed as they hurtled in from overhead to land among the startled STs. The ST sergeant seemed tiny next to the huge Infernus, and he began making rapid gestures towards the building.

Lyn's voice cut across the radio nervously. "Maybe we should just go around."

Janus could understand her sentiment, as one of the Inferni seemed to look right at him with an evil, red gaze. But it only lasted a moment before the Infernus had continued on.

"Janus, time..." Celes worried voice came in.

"We don't have time, Lyn. Besides, we can't let those Inferni just roam around. New plan: Ramirez, you've got the heavy artillery. Get up here. You'll hit the Inferni. Young, get up here on watch. Celes, Byron, re-sight on those Inferni. If Ramirez can't take them all, I need you to finish the job. The rest of you stick to your original targets."

"And what about the STs with them on the roof?" Celes asked.

"Lyn, take the one on your side. I've got the two on the left."

Janus tensed, watching Lyn slip around a corner to get into a new position.

"Ramirez?"

There was a grunt of acknowledgement over the radio.

"Mark!"

Ramirez popped up from behind a wall and launched a rocket straight into the mass of Inferni. Three of them went flying like bowling pins, but the fourth leapt out of the way, and disappeared into the alley behind the building. The sound of Skadi fire that followed suggested the other three had not landed safely. The two STs had been knocked back from the explosion, but appeared unharmed. The first stood in a daze, and Janus quickly eliminated him, but the second—the sergeant—rolled off the roof to the left, using his companion's body as a shield.

Janus turned from his quarry just in time to see Lyn's target topple off the roof with a burst of fire in his back.

A cry went up from below. Janus rushed to the edge to see Valers knocked unconscious against a wall, and Jones wrestling the sergeant for control of her weapon. The sergeant had surprised them from above, and turned the skirmish in his favor, pressing Hughes to deal with the remaining two STs on his own.

Janus cursed himself for missing the sergeant as he ran along the edge of the rooftops, desperately trying to reach his team. He took aim as he ran, and eliminated one of the two STs, but not before the sergeant had put Jones on her back with a kick to the gut and smashed Hughes into a wall, stunning him, and sending his weapon flying. Standing over Jones, the sergeant raised a menacing foot, preparing to crush her beneath the weight of the suit. Catching a glimpse of Jones over the back of the sergeant, Janus could see the surprise and terror on her face. Janus' mind was racing. If he fired a shot, he might hit Jones through the suit. There was only one option.

With a running leap, Janus threw himself off the side of the building, unsheathing the Praetor's Ghostblade as he fell.

What happened next was a blur. He felt the blade slice through the air as he brought it down over his head. Then without any additional resistance, its spectral blue cut a swathe down the middle of the sergeant. One moment, the armored soldier towered over Jones; the next, he toppled in two, shorn from head to foot. Landing lightly, Janus rolled, and flipped himself over Jones' prone body. Using his momentum to add to his strength, he hurled the weapon straight into the chest of the remaining ST Janus sighed with relief as the suit fell backwards into the dirt and lay still. It had been a risky move, but it worked.

He was just about to turn to help Jones up, when the final Infernus came crashing down in front of him.

The menacing monster raised its huge clawed fist, flames licking its arm. Janus struggled to get his rifle from his back, but he knew it was too late.

Keats was not in the suit this time.

As the flames began to curl forth from the devastating weapon, time seemed to slow. Janus could see himself oddly reflected in the glistening red. He briefly registered the expression of anger stamped upon his face.

I'm not supposed to die like this. Clara needs me. My squad needs me. This isn't supposed to be the end.

Janus felt angry and disappointed.

But then a strange sight greeted his eyes. The Infernus' visor splintered, cracking slowly from the center. Janus could see every spidery line as it traced itself across the helmet. Suddenly, as if time had no consistency, the giant warrior slumped over and collapsed to the ground. His adrenaline still pumping, Janus slowly turned around.

He couldn't help but smile as Celes lowered her rifle, and let out a deep, nervous breath.

Chapter 27
Ivory Tower

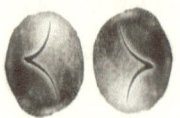

Retrieving the Ghostblade from the fallen ST, Janus quickly broke the cadets into three groups. Valers had mostly recovered, but still staggered slightly, clutching his head. Jones was nursing her arm. With assurances they would be fine on their own, Janus ordered them to the evac point. He would have to make do without them. Lyn disappeared with Ramirez and the rest of her squad around an old, rusting drill as Janus watched Jones and Valers limp away. They were swallowed up by a cloud of smoke and dust. With a touch of Celes' hand upon his shoulder, Janus turned away, and resumed his silent march towards the communications tower, the others close behind.

The tower was far larger than anything else in the complex. The MuDi had failed to do it justice. It stood well above the surrounding buildings. Three spine-like pillars anchored each corner, straining to support the weight of the place. At the top of the flattened roof, a gigantic wire dish and antenna protruded into the sky.

The bright walls shone in the sunlight. It was clearly the greatest military asset in the area. It practically screamed *target!*

Janus motioned his squad forward. As the team moved around the tower, the outpost buildings began to thin. Janus signaled them to move further away to avoid being spotted by the patrolling guards. When they reached the far side, they hid at the edge of the forest that surrounded the north end of the outpost. Janus sent Celes up a tree to give them a better view. She scanned the building with the scope on her rifle.

"The west entrance is well guarded," came her voice over the comm. "Multiple Inferni. No easy way inside to plant the charges, and who knows what's waiting in there."

"Squad one, Wouris' Washouts, to squads two and three," Janus replied. "Where are you, Marcus? Lyn?"

Marcus responded first.

"We're near the east side. We've got some heavy defenses here. Looks like another fight to get in."

"It's the same over in the south," Lynn cut in. "We're looking for a way to get our charges planted. Any ideas on how to get the job done?"

"Do we even need to get inside?" Celes cut into Janus ear. "What about the base of the pillars?"

Janus studied the rising columns more closely. Obscured by brush, the bases were difficult to discern, and it took him a few moments to find a good view. Upon closer inspection, however, Janus could see that he'd initially underestimated the strain that the weight of the armor bolted onto the building would inflict—the pillars bowed outward, practically bursting.

"Those columns look like they were constructed to support a building half as heavy as this one," he said. "I think you're right, Celes. If we plant the charges at the base of those pillars, they'll fall easily. I doubt we'd even need all three."

"Easy," Lyn said. "We'll be out of here before it even starts ta rain."

Janus glanced up; there was hardly a cloud in the sky.

"You sure about that?" Janus asked.

"Positive. Ramirez agrees."

"Well, in any case," Marcus laughed. "While those dolts are guarding the entrances, we'll just walk up to the pillars, and bring the whole place down around them."

"Alright then," Janus said, smiling at Celes. "Good plan. Let's get to it."

Planting the charges was almost too easy. Janus wondered if the dumbest guards had been left to protect the place, while the rest had gone to ground. Hughes crawled for several agonizing minutes to plant the charges, but Janus honestly wondered if he needed to bother. Of the three STs closest to them, Janus had been tempted to shoot the one in the back of the group, just to see if the others would even notice. While he contemplated this thought, another Adept voice came over the headset.

"Omega Squad, Alexander's Army, here. It took some effort, but the Hades launchers have been taken out."

"Nice work, Omega. Air support is on route. Evac will be available to the south and east. Valhalla out."

Janus smiled.

Maybe being an Adept isn't that hard after all.

When Hughes finally crawled back into hiding at the edge of the forest, Janus ordered them to get a quick pace going to the evac point. The rest of the team still on the ground assembled to begin their crouched jog back along the hem of the woods. He was just about to get moving himself when he realized that Celes had not shifted from her position in the tree. She was still staring at the tower.

"Celes?" he said expectantly.

"That's odd."

"What?"

"The communications dish. It's pointing the wrong way."

Janus stopped, and turned to look back at the tower. "What do you mean?"

Celes turned around to face the team, away from the tower.

"This is a Titan outpost. And Titan is that way," she made a motion with her hand to the west, out over the cadets. "But the dish—"

"Is pointing east," Janus said. "Low over open ocean."

Celes nodded.

Marcus' voice rang out over the radio. "Hurry up, Janus. We can't wait all day. Wouris wants to blow the joint. Wherever you are, get moving."

Janus signaled in sign for the team to return to the evac point, glancing out over the forest to the west. Dark clouds were gathering, creeping towards the sun.

"We're on our way."

"Janus, where are you?" Wouris cut in. "Are you clear?"

Still turning over this new information in his mind, he kept glancing over his shoulder as he ran.

"Squad one is clear, and we are moving back towards evac. Blow it when ready."

Buildings rushed by. He wanted to be as close to the evac point as possible when the tower went down.

"Alright, blowing in five," Wouris said. "Slow count."

"Sorry, Marcus," Janus finally responded. "Just preoccupied."

"Five…"

"Well don't be," Marcus said. "That's a good way to get your squad killed."

"Four…"

"Besides, those oafs are pretty thick. Why would we want to go into the tower and face the guards…?"

"Three…" Wouris voice was like a strange mantra in the back of his mind.

"When we can just blow it up from outside?"

Janus froze.

"Marcus, what did you say?"

"Two…"

"I said, why even go inside when it's so easy to blow it up from out here?"

"One…"

Janus turned and looked at the communications center. Something clicked into place.

"Wouris, wait!"

"What is it, Janus?" Wouris sounded concerned.

Janus pulled an about face, and sprinted back towards the communications tower. Celes reacted immediately, running along beside him. The other cadets were right on his heels.

"What is one of the most important tools in a battle? For an outpost on the fringe of Corporate control?" he asked, panting into the comm link. "Communication! Do you really think no one at this outpost considered the weight on those supports? Why would any competent commander leave such a critical structure with such a glaring weakness?"

"Corporate commanders aren't known for their brilliant battle tactics," Wouris said. But the tone of her voice betrayed her false confidence. "Our intelligence showed that this was a minor outpost with a very small population of military personnel compared to the researchers and miners."

"So why such a huge communications tower, then?"

Janus stopped at the edge of the city once more, the tower's west entrance clearly visible across a small tract of open land leading to the plateau. Six Inferni and two STs stood by the entrance. Janus studied them. They appeared to be waiting for something. The Infernus commander continually checked his left arm, almost like he was checking a watch. After a few minutes, he shook his head at his compatriots, and signaled them towards one of the burning Hades launchers within the city. They leapt away, easily clearing the distance as they jumped from rooftop to rooftop. Only the two STs remained. Janus took one last look and turned to his squad.

"Celes," he said. "Get on that roof, and take the right man. I'll take the left. The rest of you, establish a position, and wait here for my mark."

Celes grabbed his arm, giving him a hard look. "What are you doing? The charges are already planted."

"Just trust me."

"I do," she said, "but you heard Wouris. What do you expect to find?"

Janus didn't answer. Instead he silently crept to the corner of the building on his left, minimizing the distance to the communication tower. As he did so, he spoke into the group channel so that every one of the cadets and Wouris could hear.

"Why has it been so easy to infiltrate this outpost? We met plenty of resistance on the beach, but then nothing."

He paused to check if Celes was ready. She sat hidden in a shadow on top of a building, but he could see her thumbs up.

"And where are the non-military personnel? We haven't seen anyone. Surely we would have caught some of them by surprise in our dash here. Not everyone could have escaped the outpost when we attacked."

He took a deep breath and dashed around the corner, out into the open. The two STs looked up at him in surprise, but hardly had time to even raise their weapons before they met a quick end from a deadly hail of Skadi fire.

"Why, for a mining facility, is there only rusting, decrepit equipment? Why is such an important asset set-up in the wrong direction?"

Janus lowered his weapon as he hurtled over a rock, easily clearing the distance to the entrance in a matter of moments. He slowed as he reached the door, searching for a way to open it, and was surprised when the door opened automatically for him.

"What the…" Celes muttered into the headset.

Janus peered into the darkness behind the door and hesitantly stepped inside. As he left the morning sunlight, his eyes adjusted to the darkness and he saw the inside of the communications tower for the first time.

It was completely empty.

No equipment, no personnel.

Nothing.

High above, a clap of thunder shook the sky.

CHAPTER 28
THE ANGRY SWARM

Janus pounded out of the tower, pushing his emergency comm and yelling into the ODIN command frequency.

"Abort mission! Titan knew we were coming. I repeat, abort mission!"

Janus heard Praetor Jennings come over the command frequency. "All squads, high alert! Janus report!"

Janus was breathless as he sprinted across the plateau, back towards the city and Celes.

"Sir, the tower—it's empty—there's nothing inside."

"But why sacrifice so many personnel and the Hades launchers if they kn…"

The Praetor's voice dropped away.

"All squads, emergency action! It's a tra—"

Janus twisted his head in shock as the frequency filled with a squealing static.

Out of nowhere, a rocket came streaking from behind, obliterating the rocky boulders before him. Nearly knocked off his feet, he kept running through a shower of stony flecks, not even looking back until he stumbled into the outlying buildings. When he did, his heart dropped.

Behind him, the forest was going up in flames. From deep within the trees, dozens upon dozens of Inferni burst into the sky, easily leaping over Janus' head, and into the city. Behind them came hundreds of STs, emerging from the fiery brush, Zeuses raised. It was a nightmare. Screams and yells sounded within the city as the Inferni struck hard, explosions mixing with the crash of thunder from the gathering storm. Smoke and gunfire filled the air, as the Inferni laid waste to everything before them. The cacophony of noise surrounded Janus like a prison.

He swallowed his fear and ran hard. He had to rejoin his squad. But where to go? Enemy Troopers appeared in all directions, and Janus was forced to zigzag through the streets, ducking from building to building. He weaved through alleys, as the ramshackle metal structures around him echoed with thunder and fury.

Finally, he caught a glimpse of the familiar faces of Kwandis and Hughes, pressed against a building a few meters ahead. Keeping low, he stopped, signaling frantically. But they didn't respond. An explosion shook the ground from somewhere nearby, and Hughes slid slowly sideways until his head hit the ground. Kwandis remained slumped silently against the broken stone wall.

Janus paused only for a moment to reflect on how peaceful they looked. Then he ran on.

The screams of surprise were no more, but the firefight and explosions had not abated. The dark grey solidified overhead, mixing with the rising smoke. Janus moved as fast as he could, but even then, the Inferni stayed far ahead of him. It was a race, the Inferni in the lead, their presence slowing him down, while a crushing wave of STs followed on his heels, forcing him onward. His breathing was heavier, his movements thick and jerky as the adrenaline pumped through his veins. There was no rest. The journey back was infinitely longer. He focused on moving south, but was driven east, west, and north by the mass of Titan troops. Jumping into a window, he passed through an abandoned residence. It looked relatively well tended, like it had been lived in and only recently lost. Simple lamps, chairs, lockers, and beds for miners looked fresh and new. But when a nearby explosion made him dive to the floor, he turned over to see a ceiling caked in dust and cobwebs.

The cheap wooden door now swung loosely on its hinges. He peered around it, through the splintered frame, and spied a reassuring sight. Young and Bynes were pressed against a wall across the street, catching their breath. He could see the life heaving in their chests. Janus signaled them, and they returned it with exuberant relief. The pair motioned down their alley, and Janus rushed to join them. He was jumping through the window when a rush of air made him look up. To his horror, an Infernus ploughed into the alley, and Janus dove towards the middle of the street. There was a sudden, intense blast of light from the alley, and then all went quiet.

He ducked into the next building, a pub filled with glasses and bottles of empty drink. Leaping over the bar, Janus pulled a variable grenade from his armor, turning the cylindrical weapon's power to its maximum output.

Flying out of the side door and into the alley at the end of the thoroughfare, Janus arrived just in time to see the Infernus scratch two more notches on his arm. Janus felt his blood boil. He grabbed a second grenade, and hurled both at the Infernus with all his might.

"What are you doing?"

Janus looked up in surprise, deftly hiding the broken tile he had found in the folds of his rags.

"Nothing."

He eyed Clara. She was standing on top of a rotting wooden box. She leapt down to him, squishing through the mass.

"Give it to me."

"Give what?" Janus asked innocently.

233

She towered over him, her eyes narrowing. Janus sighed, and handed over the tile. It was sharp on one end. She swiped it from his tiny hand, and held it in front of him.

"And what were you planning on doing with this?"

"Drive the rats away."

She shook her head. "And you think a pointy rock will do that?"

"They're cowards. Show a bit of backbone and they run."

"They run from Troopers. And they run from other, stronger gangs. But they don't run from people like us."

Janus kicked his foot in contempt, knocking over an old can nearby.

"Well, they should."

"Why?" she asked.

"It's not theirs." He paused, not looking at her. "Why should we give up our stuff?"

Clara sighed.

"No, it's not their stuff. But the world isn't always fair. And there are more important things than a few scraps and our pride."

"Aren't we supposed to stand up to bullies?" Janus asked in a huff. He stared at the dirt. "They killed the flower. It was jus' trying to survive."

Clara shook her head in exasperation. But she sat down next to him and rubbed his head.

"Yes, they did. But you can't stand up to bullies—you can't survive—if they kill you."

She tossed the tile away, and then grabbed him by the cheeks.

"I know you want more, Janus. I know this place is terrible. But that doesn't mean you pick fights."

"They're picking fights," he interjected. "Not me."

"Sometimes, you need to know how to let go, Janus." She smiled. "Sometimes, you need to know how to lose."

Janus picked himself off slowly from the ground. His head was ringing. In the heat of battle, he had forgotten how powerful a single variable grenade could be, let alone a pair at the maximum setting. Melted glass and steel pooled on the ground below crumbling buildings. The Infernus was utterly gone. Janus held his head, and picked up his Skadi. A fragment of sheared metal cut deep into the power cell. He tossed the weapon aside and checked for his pistol. It was gone; just a broken strap remained. No doubt lost sometime before.

"What are you trying to do, kill me?"

Janus whipped around, and immediately felt a surge of relief. Celes was standing behind him, a grim look on her face.

"Celes…" He wasn't sure what to say.

"He got what he deserved. Your Skadi destroyed?"

Janus nodded, pulling the Ghostblade just an inch out of its sheath. She held up her pistol.

"Seven shots," she said, and motioned behind her. "Come on, we need to get out of here before any more surprises show up."

Everywhere Janus and Celes turned, STs and Inferni swarmed the streets. The pair caught sight of an Albatross carrier between two buildings, dropping more troops into the outpost while releasing a flurry of Peregrine scout craft. They were pressed from all sides; staying ahead of the merciless assault was all Janus and Celes could do.

"How are we going to get out of this one?" Celes whispered to Janus in a strangely calm voice.

They were in a crawlspace beneath some kind of food storage shack, opened up by an explosion. Janus watched the boots of a squad of STs run by from underneath a rotting sack of grain.

"We have to make it to the primary evac point at the south beach," Celes said. "The Praetor will probably send a wave of Valkyries to open up a hole before the majority of the Titan troops arrive from the north of the city. The Longboats will be right on their heels, just like our assault, to pick up as many surviving Adepts as they can."

Janus shifted a pile of PSRs that had spilled from a crate to give him a better view to his left.

"But with so many incoming enemy troops, if we miss the ride the first time…" Janus said.

"We would have to go to the emergency evac point," Celes whispered. "Straight through enemy lines."

Janus shook his head. "Then we'll just have to get to the beach before Titan overruns it."

CHAPTER 29
TIDE OF BATTLE

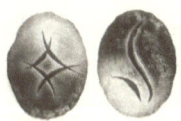

Pulling themselves from the crawlspace, Janus and Celes darted on. They had to hurry—some of the Titan sweeps had already pulled past them, putting them right in the middle of the enemy forces. Dark clouds loomed overhead, but Celes pulled Janus deeper into the shadows as a Peregrine hovered above them, watching for signs of Adept activity.

We're taking far too long, Janus thought. *The Longboats will leave before we even get close to the beach.*

Janus had a bitter taste in his mouth. No matter where he and Celes turned, STs awaited them, strangely aware of where they would go, where they would hide. He could only watch as Titan slowly tightened the noose, leaving only desperation to fuel their resolve.

With less than a hundred meters to go before they reached the edge of the outpost, Janus and Celes were forced to stop. The Titan line had passed them as it finished its sweep, pushing the main ODIN force back to the few trenches and bunkers that dotted the beach, and leaving Janus and Celes to watch from afar. Now, the Titan forces massed for a final assault upon the entrenched Adepts, pausing at the edge of the outpost.

A stillness settled over the beach. Not even the rain fell.

The pair stood atop a crumbing roof, hidden by shadows and smoke, watching as the Adepts of ODIN readied their final stand. Inferni landed near the edge of the outpost, while troopers checked their Zeus rifles. The Adepts were surrounded, hemmed from all sides, and separated from the Titan army by only a short stretch of beach. Above, a few Peregrine scouts hovered, waiting for some unspoken signal.

Celes and Janus could feel a strange hesitation. Something made their foe pause. A show of respect for a cornered animal.

Janus, caught up in the moment, realized he had been holding his breath. As he exhaled, the first wave of Inferni stepped onto the beach. The rain came down again—hard.

A low rumble echoed from high above, and Janus looked up, expecting to see traces of lighting between the clouds. Instead, missiles suddenly streaked forth from the dark clouds, striking into the Titan air forces and the edge of the outpost, scattering STs as they ran for cover. The Adepts let out a ragged cheer as the Valkyries and Longboats burst forth from the low clouds.

Celes turned to Janus, her face obscured by the downpour.

"Come on, we've got to go while they're in disarray. It's our only shot at the beach."

Janus nodded, and they both leapt down to the street below. They rushed along toward the scattered troops. A missile streaked into a group of STs, killing some, and stunning the rest. Their sudden absence left a gap in the wall of resistance that had blocked them. Janus quickly grabbed Celes by the hand, and steered her towards the hole. They ran full out, putting all of their energy into clearing the gap and reaching the Longboats.

As they passed the last building, a huge fist came out of nowhere, and plastered Janus right in the chest. The wind whooshed out of his lungs as he was knocked to the ground, hitting his head against the side of a building, and gasping for breath.

His head was fuzzy, and the thickening rain clouded his vision. He could hear the sounds of battle on the beach, as the Adepts fought for survival. A huge figure loomed over him. Janus once again felt the odd sensation that time was moving more slowly around him. He tried to scramble away, and felt the figure reaching for him, grabbing, ripping the sheath from his back.

"Not so fast, merc. Thought you could escape?"

Janus flipped himself over, and the ST lifted his visor so Janus could see his sneering face. Janus had trouble understanding the trooper; he seemed to be elongating his words unnecessarily.

"You mercs are gonna die," the ST sneered, standing over Janus, his lips curling contemptuously as he formed the words.

Janus' head was clearing. Celes was struggling against another soldier. Her arms were pinned; she simply couldn't beat the strength of the suit. Her pistol lay some distance away. The Ghostblade, however, had landed just behind Janus' armored opponent. Some of the stunned STs were standing up, slowly reaching for their weapons. The sneering Trooper reached down and picked up a Zeus rifle from one of his dead comrades. Its form came sharply into focus.

Then, the ST brought the weapon to bear on Janus' forehead, and slowly pulled the trigger.

Janus instinctively whipped his head to the side, feeling the shockwave of the round as it passed, burying itself deep in the ground. He quickly flipped his arms behind his head, and rolled between the trooper's legs. The man was still turning to face Janus as he snatched up the Ghostblade, swinging the weapon around in a blinding arc.

It bit into the trooper's waist in slow motion, the metal armor separating before the glowing weapon. The Ghostblade split the ST like a warm marshmallow, clean, and instantaneous. He'd sheathed the weapon before the soldier had even toppled over in two.

The other STs were grabbing for their weapons, watching him with surprise, as Celes struggled mightily against her captor, who was barely able to hold on to her thrashing body. It would be an impossible task to take down so many with his Ghostblade. Janus' eyes fell on the Zeus rifle that had been dropped by the sneering ST. Picking it up, he leveled it on one of the rising Troopers.

The kick of the Zeus sent him slamming back into the wall, and the barrel of the weapon skyward. But the ST dropped like a rock. Janus felt as if he'd just broken his shoulder, but steeled himself against the pain. He braced a leg against the wall, and aimed at another rising ST With every shot, he felt his spine compress. Within moments, only one remained standing—the ST who held Celes hostage.

She had finally been completely overpowered by the Trooper, who held both of her arms behind her with one gloved hand. Celes grimaced as the ST squeezed her around the neck with his free hand, using her as a shield from the Zeus. Janus kept the weapon raised as he followed the Trooper, who slowly backed around a corner. The Trooper crouched as low as possible behind her, and was tightening his grip when a round caught him in the side of the head. He fell over, leaving a gasping Celes on the ground. A sopping wet Wouris stepped out from behind an open crate of rusting shovels.

"Everyone alright?" she asked, searching their surroundings for more foes.

"Wouris!" Janus exclaimed, holding his side as he went to help Celes. "Are we glad to see you."

"Yeah, me especially…" Celes gagged, rubbing her throat, and getting up slowly.

"I told you I would come running if you got into trouble. I don't like to waste time training cadets just to let them get killed."

"That's a good policy," Celes gasped, smiling weakly.

Wouris smirked. "Let's get to the beach or we'll miss the boat."

A loud roar of engines made them look up in surprise. Janus snatched up the Ghostblade, and they hurried to the edge of the outpost. As they cleared the last buildings, the Longboat engines sounded another roar. Crouching behind a rock, Janus, Celes, and Wouris watched with dismay as what remained of the ODIN fleet sped away, pursued by the regrouped Titan air force, leaving a beach littered with dead Adepts, Troopers and a rising tide.

CHAPTER 30
THOSE LEFT BEHIND

Janus was in a state of shock as the Longboats disappeared from view. They had failed to get to the beach in time, and now were faced with the almost impossible task of getting out of the outpost and to the emergency evac in less than thirty-four hours. Janus' ribs would make it harder; at least a few were broken.

Wouris pulled them back into the city.

"We need a moment to come up with a plan. Let's take a breather in here."

Her voice was calm as she steered them into the building just beside where Janus and Celes had been ambushed, a warehouse filled with empty wooden boxes marked 'drills.'

Janus took a deep breath to help him focus, and doubled over in pain. After a moment of firm reassurances to Celes that he was fine, the three sat grimly upon the wooden boxes, thinking about their next move.

Wouris motioned Janus over to her. "Let's take a look at your injuries."

Janus winced as they pulled off his armor. Celes gasped. Janus' chest was an angry purplish-black from the punishment he received from the ST, and the kick from the Zeus.

"We won't be able to move quite as quickly with an injury like that," Wouris said.

"I'm fine." Janus lurched to his feet, and immediately fell over, grasping his side and feeling woozy.

"Easy now." Celes smiled at him. "No need to be the hero all the time."

"Okay." Janus grimaced. "So maybe we need a plan that doesn't involve a whole lot of running and jumping. Ideas?"

"Actually, I do have one," Celes said brightly. Janus and Wouris both looked at her in surprise. "Wouris, you've studied STs more than I have; they're not particularly bright about security, are they?"

"No, they're usually just good for taking orders."

"And you've used an ST suit before, so you understand how they work?"

"Well, they're not that hard." Wouris shrugged her shoulders. "I mean, look at the people who use them."

Janus looked at Celes as if she were insane—he knew immediately what she was thinking.

"You want us to be prisoners while Wouris escorts us through the Titan defenses in Trooper armor?" he said.

"Yes."

"While you and I are completely defenseless," Janus added.

"Why not? Then we could move you slowly. If we had to run, you wouldn't be able to make it."

"Where would we get a suit?" Wouris asked. "All the ones here have holes in their heads. Or no heads at all. Someone would be bound to notice that."

"Not you too, Wouris," Janus said.

"Well, not every suit has a hole in the head." Celes motioned to the Ghostblade. "One of them has a perfectly good helmet. And if we put that helmet on one of the other suits…"

"We've got a perfectly good suit." Wouris snapped her fingers. "Good plan, Celes."

Janus folded his arms across his chest. "You guys could just leave me behind. I'm sure I could make it."

Wouris and Celes rolled their eyes in unison.

"Oh drop it, Janus," Celes said, exasperated. "You're coming with us. One way or another."

With that, she gave him a dangerous look. Janus coughed nervously, but said nothing.

Getting the suit off of the two dead Troopers proved to be a much bigger chore than actually getting Wouris into it. It was a loose fit; Wouris' smaller frame was obviously not made for it. Once inside, however, she looked like a full-fledged ST Slinging their remaining weapons over her back—which consisted only of Wouris' Skadi and pistol, Celes' pistol, and Janus' blade—she soon had Janus and Celes moving a slow march in front of her.

The rain slowed to a stop as the three moved through the ramshackle structures, leaving behind dripping roofs and walls, muddy puddles, and an ever brightening sky. They passed small clusters of STs, who largely ignored them. It was odd, seeing them this way. They laughed and joked with each other, completely at ease and flush with success.

Clutching his ribs, Janus tried not to glance back at Wouris, but to look instead like a defeated prisoner. It wasn't particularly difficult, given his current condition. Unfortunately, it also attracted the attention of a squad of Inferni, who approached the three with interest. Wouris hastily gave Janus a particularly nasty shove in the back, which sent him sprawling in front of the group of laughing Inferni. He rolled over in pain, and Celes helped him up.

"I swear she's enjoying this..." he muttered.

After they cleared the Inferni, Celes spoke reassuringly in his ear.

"I'm sure she's just trying to make it look as convincing as possible."

A sudden, hearty shove caught Celes off guard, knocking her into a puddle of mud. She came up sopping wet and snarling.

"Oh, she is going to pay for this..."

"You shouldn't talk so loudly," Wouris whispered to them. "You might be heard. I don't want your plan to fail."

But the mirth in her voice made her words less than convincing.

Ahead of them, the communications tower rose above the edge of the forest. Wouris took them on a path away from it, not wanting to be any closer than necessary. With the edge of the forest in sight, Wouris suddenly shoved Janus and Celes down a side street.

"Quick, this way. They've got a checkpoint up ahead, and we need to find a way around. Get down here before we're—"

"Hey you!"

Janus and Celes made to stop, but Wouris pushed them further into the alley, keeping them moving. A short, balding officer in a light green uniform was marching over to them, pointing a finger at Wouris. Janus took a quick glance around. The five STs at the checkpoint watched the spectacle with mild disinterest. Another platoon of STs was marching by, and a few Titan Peregrines hovered overhead.

Wouris kept marching, ignoring the man.

"I said, 'Hey you!' Where do you think you are going?" He leapt in front of the trio.

"Prisoners..." Wouris grunted and glanced at the man's chest. "Uh, sir."

The man muttered under his breath and rolled his eyes. He looked thoroughly displeased to be there, let alone traipsing through the mud.

"It's Overlord Hodges, to you." The man paused. "Prisoners? I didn't think we were supposed to take any."

Janus grimaced at the way he said it so casually.

"Just movin' 'em," Wouris mumbled. "Orders."

The little man looked skeptical for a second.

"Who gave that order?" he demanded, examining the state of his boots, which were rapidly sinking into the mud. Janus could feel the weight of many eyes upon them. But before Wouris could come up with an answer, the man waved his hand.

"Oh, never mind. I'll find out later. The Executor may have reasons. Just take them to the barracks for processing."

"Yes, sir." Wouris saluted. She shoved Janus and Celes forward, marching the pair north, but stopped as the man cleared his throat. Wouris turned to look at him.

"It's that way," he said irritably, pointing to the west. After a moment to appear suitably dumb, she responded.

"Uh…yeah, right. Sorry, sir."

The little man was muttering to himself again. "Where do they get…well, get moving," he said exasperatedly, shaking mud from his shoes.

Wouris turned the group around and headed west. But they barely made it two steps.

"Wait," Hodges said suddenly, his face smug. "I've changed my mind. Give me your ID number; I'm going to run this by command."

Janus and Celes anxiously looked around for escape routes. The passing patrol marched closer.

"Uh, uh, command, sir?" Wouris asked slowly. Hodges' smile grew larger.

"Yes, I think they'll want a word with a Trooper of your…caliber."

The Peregrine scouts shot off south. The skies now clear, Wouris began to shake her head slowly back and forth.

"Pathetic…"

The little man seemed taken aback.

"What?" he demanded angrily. "What did you say?"

"I said," Wouris watched the passing platoon round a corner and disappear from view. "I'm sorry. I lied to you earlier. These two aren't prisoners at all."

The man's anger fell away to confusion, and then surprise, as Wouris slammed her Zeus rifle into his head. He collapsed in a heap. The disinterested STs sat bolt upright. Wouris quickly slung the weapons off her back and tossed them to Janus and Celes.

"I think they finally realized something is wrong," she commented dryly.

The five STs fumbled with their weapons. In a moment, Janus, Celes, and Wouris had dispatched them with hardly an effort. Unfortunately, at that moment, a second patrol rounded the corner.

"Oh, son of a…nothing left for it now."

Wouris tossed her Zeus, picked up Janus and Celes in each arm, and began bounding for the forest. Janus grunted in pain. The incoming patrol ran straight to the fallen STs. They hadn't seen the three yet. Wouris ran straight through them, and was out of the group before they knew what happened.

Janus counted the distance in his head. Forty meters to the forest. He could hear cries of dismay from the patrol.

Thirty meters, angry shouts. *Well, it was worth a shot*, Janus thought.

Twenty meters. Rounds peppered the area around them, and Wouris zigzagged.

Ten meters. Sounds of pursuit—the STs were after them now. They reached the smattering of trees that formed the fringe of the forest.

Five meters. The trees were becoming dense now, the brush thickening. Janus and Celes covered their heads as the branches cut into their faces. Wouris' long stride did not slow, the tough suit easily able to bull its way through the dense forest.

The Titan STs, hot on their heels, easily followed the trail of broken brush and branches. Peregrine scouts rushed overhead, blocked from view by the forest canopy.

Wouris broke from the brush into a large open field, and increased her speed. She leapt over the small creeks and rivulets running through the dense grass, gaining distance from the pursuing Troopers. No Titan soldier could match her foot speed. But she could not escape the Peregrines; now able to pursue their prey directly, they swooped into the clearing. STs dropped from above in front of the group, while the pursuing Troopers finally broke from the forest and began to fire. Janus and Celes returned fire from their awkward positions, unable to get clean shots through their watering eyes.

Janus yelled to Wouris over the sounds of the Peregrine's engines. "We might be able to lose them in the Phoenix ruins."

"Right," Wouris replied, as she broke right to avoid the incoming Troopers. The three passed again into the forest; the Peregrines left behind, relying on the slower STs to guide them.

The forest exploded in front of them; the Peregrines were eager to not lose their prey. Wouris hurtled through the smoke and over the small crater. Wood and dirt rained down upon them, and Janus and Celes covered their heads to protect themselves.

"Maybe we won't need to lose them in the ruins if you can keep this up, Wouris," Celes yelled.

"I could keep this up all day," she panted.

A burst of flame torched the area in front of them, and Wouris was forced to do a quick hop around the newly kindled fire.

"Or maybe not," Celes continued, looking grim.

Inferni crashed into the forest, torching the area with their flamethrowers, clearing paths for the pursuing STs while attempting to corral the escaping trio.

Wouris was slowing, the breakneck pace taking its toll on her. An Infernus landed ahead of them, but Janus and Celes were ready this time, peppering it with fire as Wouris closed the distance. Timing their shots with Wouris' loping stride, they zeroed in on the monstrosity's helmet as it turned to bring its weapons to bear. A loud crack sounded as the fiend crumpled just steps in front of them.

Wouris stumbled as she leapt over the Infernus, and the group went sprawling to the ground. Celes collided painfully with a tree, while Janus had a near miss with a rock. Wouris lay panting, but managed to struggle to her feet.

"I don't think I can go much further," she gasped.

"I don't think you'll have to," Celes said. "Look!"

They were on the edge of the forest. Spread out in front of them rested the gigantic ruins of Phoenix Corporation.

Chapter 31
Phoenix

Phoenix was a burnt shell of its former glory.

The three stood on a hill overlooking the remains of the Corporation. Blackened, shattered buildings stretched out before them as far as the eye could see, rising above an eerie fog that had settled into the cracks in the early morning air. Some towered far overhead still, forcing them to crane their necks to peer towards the top, while others had been shorn nearly in half. Broken highways stretched in and out of the fog, disappearing into the depths of the city below. Here and there, golden accents shone in the sun, pressing through the decay of the passing years, and the ashes of the destruction.

The three descended speedily into the dead city, the sounds of pursuit echoing strangely through the destroyed landscape. Once they had reached ground level, and began to traverse the broken streets, the blackened buildings seemed to come alive. Twisted metal clawed at them as they ran, as if the place was possessed by its former power and fury. Debris littered the ground. Blasted rock filled craters, and shattered trains, trucks, buildings formed mountains. With every step, the fog swirled about them, like the city was breathing, just waiting for its moment. Janus shivered as his body struggled to adjust; it was colder than the grave.

Celes led the way, slowing slightly so that Wouris could catch her breath as the sounds of pursuit died off amongst the silent monoliths. Their armor slowly turned to a dull grey, matching their surroundings.

Janus was amazed by the size of the ruins. He had spent his life exploring the different parts of the slums of Cerberus, and he still had never even come close to knowing all of its byways. Phoenix was exponentially larger. Buildings as wide as Valhalla emerged along huge ruined boulevards. Even crumbling, their sizes were enormous, and every so often, one would climb higher and higher, before disappearing completely in the clouds and mist. Phoenix could have housed Cerberus several times over, and in one fleeting instant, Janus had a vision of a place filled with thousands upon thousands of people as far as the eye could see. And then the vision was gone, insubstantial as the mist.

"It'll take some time to cross the ruins to the evac point," Wouris said, interrupting Janus' reverie. "We need to find a place to rest before we continue."

"Well that shouldn't be too hard to do in a place like this," Janus noted.

The sounds of the STs and Inferni behind them grew louder, although it was impossible to tell where they were amongst the echoing maze. Used to the trash-filled Cerberus slums, Janus felt in his element within the ruins. He led them deeper into the city, expertly finding paths through the strewn wreckage, pausing only to get his bearings or to listen to the echoing pursuit. The STs struggled to follow them.

The Phoenix ruins felt familiar, and Janus soon discovered a lift station, not all that different from Cerberus, but considerably more ornate. A great, golden wing sprouted from the side of the nearby building, encompassing the station like a protective mother. Another golden wing lay broken and shattered upon the ground. Raised gold and red enamel peeked out from the blackened exterior and scorched walls, forming fiery patterns all around the outside of the station. It looked like some great, un-hatched egg.

But whatever it had been, it certainly wasn't now. The great column that supported the lift's ascent to the higher levels was broken clean in two, the main entrance sitting just beneath its remains. A jagged hole had been opened in the side of the station, and Janus clambered up to it. Peering into the dark, he was surprised to see that this was not the bottom. The lift station seemed to have collapsed into some kind of underground cavern. Wouris was intrigued by this, but Celes seemed unsurprised.

"Most Corporations have maintained a few underground bunkers in secret, to house important Executors or equipment in case of a battle."

Janus looked at Celes with confusion. "How do you know that?"

She cleared her throat hesitantly.

"Perhaps," Wouris jumped in, "*you* should have studied the Corporations better, Janus. Although the locations of the bunkers generally aren't known, we have been aware of their existence for some time. It should be available in the ODIN computers. You can study it when we get back."

"Shall we look into it?" Celes said with an upbeat tone. "Any place designed to house Executors probably has equipment and supplies we can use, plus it will give us a safe place to rest."

They descended into the dark cavern, using the broken and splintered lift as a stair, hopping from piece to piece, their eyes struggling to adjust to the gloom. The mist spread its tendrils everywhere. Finally, after they had gone an indiscernible depth, their feet hit bottom.

The dim light of the cavernous room revealed a forgotten splendor. Plush red and gold carpets, couches, cushions, all covered in a fine layer of dust. Beautiful oil paintings of long-forgotten men and women—some in carriages, some on horseback, some standing behind oaken desks with glowing computers—still hung on the walls, but they had faded, unprotected from the elements. The remains of a sultan-like spa were crushed beneath the huge slab of the lift, fountains and faucets long since run dry, leaving only dusty and moldy baths. They pulled out their flashlights, illuminating even more of the bunker. A computer station in the far wall remained unpowered. Next to it, a sliding door was stuck partially open.

"This lift wasn't the main entrance to the bunker," Celes said, looking around. "It was supposed to act as protection for it. An attacking army wouldn't be likely to destroy their only means into the upper levels of the city."

"They obviously didn't plan for a scenario where invasion wasn't the goal," Janus said reflectively, letting his flashlight wander the room. He stopped the beam on the half open door. "Let's see if we can find a supply room through here."

Janus was in awe of the wealth and excess that greeted him as the three wandered through from room to room. Grand beds with soft linens and hundreds of plush pillows. Huge, multileveled pools with waterfalls, and bridges to cross them. Great dining halls, with massive marble tables that could seat dozens before white tablecloths and utensils covered in a fine layer of gold. Massive ballrooms with mirrored ceilings and false outdoor balconies, designed to entertain hundreds. And rooms more fantastic still, filled with strange devices whose purpose Janus couldn't imagine. The further they walked, the more there was to discover. It was as if the place would never end. The opulence was overwhelming, and the rooms had everything—except people. They had been claimed by their true masters: dust and time.

Janus felt the slightest twinge of vindication.

They finally discovered a large supply room, past a set of massive kitchens. The back half of the storeroom had collapsed, and a thick, musty smell filled the trio's nostrils. Large fridges and freezers, unpowered for years, contained nothing but mold. Shelves and shelves of parts and replacement necessities stood next to crates of hoarded treasures. A small hole disappeared into the building above, the crashed single-man lift below it likely one of the many secret entrances to the bunker.

"Look at these."

Wouris pointed out a weapons locker on the far wall. Janus and Celes joined her. Inside the locker were four large and ornamented Security Suits. The suits had a silvery sheen, and etchings filled with gold spread across the ceramium plates. Each had a solid gold Phoenix emblazoned upon each shoulder.

"Elite Infernus suits. For the Executor's guard," Wouris noted, putting a hand on the suits. "Good, still functional."

She eyed Janus and Celes.

"And close enough in size. We can use these to get to the evac point in no time."

Large silvery wings extended from each helmet, and each claw was shaped like a talon. The suits still possessed their angular form, but the heavy plate armor had been etched to look like bird feathers. They were not so much terrifying as imposing.

While Janus stared in fascination at the suits, Celes discovered a medical locker to their right, and started pulling out supplies. Before Janus knew what was happening, she was beside him again, pulling at his armor.

"I'm fine, Celes," he said, pushing her hands away.

"Look, you're no good to us if we have to carry you out of here."

"I dealt with worse when I lived in the slums. I'll heal just fine."

Celes gave him an exasperated look.

"Don't be stupid. You might be just fine, you might not."

"I'll be fine."

"Well, at the very least, you'll heal faster if you let me bind those ribs up," she snapped.

Janus looked slightly abashed. He sat down, grumbling, on a piece of ceiling debris. "Fine," he said. "Do whatever you want."

"Good," Celes said. "I'm glad to know you don't always act like an arrogant idiot."

Wouris chuckled from her spot against the wall.

"What are you laughing at?" Celes snarled.

"Nothing," she said. "Nothing at all."

But a smile still lingered on her lips.

She walked the room while Celes worked, stopping to stare at a pipe that ran vertically along the wall. Janus noticed her linger.

"What?" he asked, wincing as Celes wrapped his torso.

"This pipe—it's an old water line, but it's dripping," she said. "There must be an intact water source somewhere down here. It's amazing that it's still running. Toss me your waterskins. I'll fill them up. We should hydrate while we can."

Janus gingerly pulled out an empty sack with a filter on the end and tossed it to Wouris. She found a valve along the pipe, and filled the three skins, tossing two of them back to Celes. The water was cool and refreshing, and tasted good.

When Celes had finished binding his ribs, Janus stood slowly, and walked over to the half of the room that had entirely collapsed, looking for more supplies. He felt much better, and no longer quite regretted every breath. But he kept silent, instead letting his flashlight roam over the huge wall of broken tristeel and plasment. It was like a whole building had sunk into the ground.

"Looks like most of the dry goods were crushed, so we don't have any extra food." Highlighting a small hole at the base of the wall, he held his flashlight steady. "Hold on, there might be something behind here."

Janus got to his knees and peered into the darkness. The light from his flashlight was quickly swallowed up by the space. Celes and Wouris joined him, adding their light to his. The hole stretched forward into a small tunnel.

"Well, let's check it out!" Celes said excitedly, her discontent gone at the prospect of adventure.

"Do you think that's the best idea?" Janus glanced up the crumbling wall.

"We might need more supplies," she said. "And who knows what else might lie in this bunker? Besides, this passage hasn't collapsed yet!"

Janus glanced at Wouris. She looked skeptical, but shrugged. "She might be right."

"I'm the smallest, so let me see if I can squeeze through first," Celes said. She handed her rifle to Janus, attached her flashlight to her ear and, crawling on her hands and knees, crept into the hole. She called back to them, her voice faint.

"It is really tight back here. No way you'll fit through with the ST armor on. But it looks like it opens up afterwards. Hold on."

There was a pause.

"Okay, I'm through," came her faint voice. "Oh."

Another pause.

"This is interesting," she called back. "You'll want to take a look at this."

Janus and Wouris shared a curious look, and he quickly helped her out of the armor. Soon they too were crawling into the hole, the light disappearing behind them as the tunnel twisted and turned through the wreckage. Dust rained down upon them, and Janus glanced skeptically at the roof of the passage. Finally they emerged into a dimly lit room. Janus looked around for the light source, locating it on a small panel sticking out of the wall, adjacent to another door. But this door was totally different from the ornate, ornamental affairs of the rest of the bunker. It was much larger, and extremely solid, seemingly built to withstand a huge blast. It bore the Phoenix Corporation emblem, an imposing fiery bird rising from the flames with its wings outstretched. The adjacent panel was damaged, a large hole in it. A twisted piece of concrete and steel debris lay nearby.

The three moved forward to examine the door, and to their complete surprise, the glowing panel sprung to life.

"Iden...tion please. Stand...circle..."

A glowing circle appeared in front of the door.

"Odd," Celes mused. "This still has power. There must be a secondary set of fusion generators for the bunker. Perhaps the same thing supplying the water."

"The collapsed ceiling must have cut off the rest," Janus noted. "Maybe we can open these doors. There's bound to be something valuable behind them."

Janus felt a curious excitement begin to take hold of him, like those times so long ago, scrounging in the slums.

"Or something extremely dangerous," Wouris said simply. "Either way, we should find out. Let's take a look at this ID panel. We might be able to get around the security system."

Celes nodded, and pulled some small tools from her suit, carefully examining the glowing panel. Wouris joined her, and together they probed the hole in the device for a solution to the shut door.

Janus took a closer look at door itself, in case Wouris and Celes were unable to open it with finesse. He quickly ruled out forcing it open. The doors were far too solid to be wrenched open with muscle, and an explosion in the already small and weakened room was out of the question. He wasn't even sure it would work anyway. Celes and Wouris' voices were a whisper.

"What if we cut the wiring here and..."

Janus moved forward to examine the edges of the doors for a weakness, stepping into the illuminated circle on the floor. As he did, a mechanical stalk descended from above him, revealing a disembodied, eye-like device. It bathed him in a soft green light, circling him slowly. The panel spoke in its broken voice. "Scan...prog...ess. Stand by..."

Celes and Wouris both turned to watch.

After a few moments, it spoke again.

"...an comp...lcome Execut..."

The sound of heavy locks disengaging could be heard behind the door, and then it swept open, blasting Janus with a rush of air. Beyond the door lay total darkness, the noticeable thrum of machinery echoing in the distance.

Janus laughed. "Well, that was easy."

Celes stood up, looking confused. "What did you do?"

"I just asked it politely."

Wouris looked sheepish.

"I guess it would have made sense to just test whether the ID machine still worked or not, first. It's obviously been damaged."

"What, don't you think I'm Executor material?" Janus asked boldly.

Celes gave him a shove. "Yeah, we'll all just bow down to your superiority."

She stepped into the circle with him, and the strange eyestalk scanned her as well. "...ror...no matc...sequence fou...notation ma..."

Celes looked at the scanner.

"Odd. I wonder if—"

A strange roar emanated from the hall; distant, but imposing. It was so loud Janus almost covered his ears. Glowing blue lines appeared on the floor ahead of them, guiding them forward.

"Enough," Wouris said emphatically. "Let's check it out. Before something else happens."

Chapter 32
The Hive

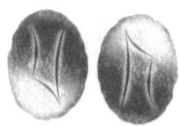

The three moved as silently as ghosts, the faint sounds of machinery floating down the hall. Their surroundings were pitch black, only the glowing lines showing them the way forward. The floor sloped downwards, leading them deeper underground, until suddenly, another door with the Phoenix emblem blocked the way. Its panel glowed green; it was unlocked. The sounds of machinery could be heard much more clearly now, and as the second door slid slowly open, the noise became nearly deafening.

A blast of heat swept across Janus. He gaped in amazement.

Stepping slowly out onto the balcony before him, he found himself overlooking a huge, automated factory. Innumerable conveyors and cranes carried hundreds, even thousands, of Security Trooper suits and weapons. Great presses molded new Infernus armor, which were then moved along to be cleaned and hardened in giant vats of chemicals. Every few moments, a new suit would rush by, disappearing into the mass of machinery and metal that seemed to stretch indefinitely in all directions.

"I've never seen anything like this," Wouris said, flabbergasted.

"Do you think it has been running all this time," Celes asked in awe. "Under the ruins of Phoenix?"

"Let's find out."

Janus cocked his head for them to follow as he descended a set of stairs to their right. Wide catwalks stretched across the factory floor, which seemed to be a mass of gears and molten metal, following the trail of conveyor belts to where the Infernus suits disappeared. The suits separated into two directions, and Janus went right again, following one set as the others vanished behind them.

The factory was immense, and Janus did his best to soak it all in, pausing to watch as myriad Daeduluses with heavy, metal arms screwed prefabricated jump jets in the feet and back of each Infernus. One conveyor had a line of Zeus rifles slowly filing along it, all disappearing through a dark hole in the wall of the factory. The din made speech impossible. Janus pointed to another heavy door across from several catwalks.

[This] way.

The deafening roar rumbled through the factory again, and Janus was forced to cover his ears. The three froze at the screeching and clanking of metal, as the cranes and belts ground to a halt. Janus could see an unfinished suit lodged in the assembly line, not too far from where they stood. A warning buzzer sounded somewhere in the distance. But after a few tense moments, they realized that no one was coming, and opened the heavy door with a quick button press.

Soft blue lighting illuminated them as they stepped inside. This room was noticeably cooler and quieter than the one they had just left. It appeared to be a small control room, with dozens of screens showing different parts of the factory floor, and other equipment displaying temperatures, parameter controls, errors, and automatic repairs that were underway. A huge red warning screen highlighted the area that had gotten stuck.

"Look at this," Celes said. She pointed to another screen, on the opposite side of the room. A series of numbers, laid out in small lines, looked to be ticking slowly upward. Beside it stood a second door, labeled 'Storage.'

"It looks like there are factories all around the outside edge of the facility," said Celes. "Initial production started on 545-11-28. That's over 50 years ago. It was paused on…576-03-23, and resumed 584-05-09."

"And if this production quota of fifteen hundred Zeus rifles a day is accurate," Wouris said, looking upward, and doing a quick calculation in her head, "that's nearly twenty-five million Zeuses alone."

The three looked together at the second door. It was Janus who finally opened it. For a moment, there was nothing but a wall of darkness beyond. Then far above, huge lamps began to glow faintly, slowly illuminating the jaw-dropping sight.

A vast sea of weapons and suits were stacked in rows hundreds high, all within a gigantic underground warehouse. Columns of scouts and fighters stacked vertically in rows. Janus peered over a rail; the room was impossibly tall.

"Incredible," Wouris gasped. "There's enough equipment here to supply the world's largest army. A force this big might have a shot at taking on all the other Corporations."

"Too bad it's useless without an army to go with it," Celes noted.

Wouris walked to a hanging fighter. They were simple affairs, with one large engine in the back, a tiny cockpit, and two wings sweeping forward. The only noticeable marking was a single Phoenix emblem on the right side of the vehicle.

"These are Siren class fighters. I haven't seen one of these in years. They are highly effective against other fighter craft. Carry a lot of ordinance, good speed, but almost no armor. They disappeared when Phoenix fell. No other corporation could afford to produce so many throwaway fighters."

"Throwaway?" Janus asked. "What kind of general allows their people to be sacrificed?"

"The Phoenix Executors did. They were the largest, after all."

"It's amazing they lost," Celes said.

"Not necessarily. Sometimes you aren't as strong as you think you are…" Wouris trailed off, glancing towards Janus.

"Come on," said Celes. "Let's finish looking around."

They followed the catwalks to another production floor, this one feeding the storage room with Sirens. This factory was cooler than the first; it just assembled the final components. Passing the Sirens as they were built, Janus could see what Wouris meant by throwaway. They were essentially engines with wings, designed for maximum payload with a minimum of anything else.

But nothing was more surprising to Janus than the very size of the underground facility. Through the haze of cranes, assembly lines, and metal, he could see the factory stretched further and further; it was designed to equip a massive army.

"Celes raised a good point earlier," Janus said to Wouris. "What's the point of all this without an army to use it?"

"Phoenix was destroyed," Celes interrupted. "Perhaps there was an army to use it before."

"So how is the factory still running? What's supplying its furnaces with materials? Could Phoenix really have fielded such a huge army?"

Wouris shook her head.

"I don't know. They may have had the citizens to fight, but every soldier you have on the front lines is one less working the fields. The Corporations already have large standing armies compared to their populations. I don't think even Phoenix had the capability to pull more of its citizens as soldiers. Besides, the other Corporations would have quickly realized what was happening." She swept a hand around at the factory. "They may not be able to see the production, but they would see the end results. I don't think Phoenix would have been able to produce an army fast enough to use all this."

"So, then," Celes asked, giving voice to Janus' unspoken question. "What was the point?"

CHAPTER 33
THE WHITE-HAIRED MAN

The factory finally seemed to be coming to an end as they reached another heavy door marked "Cold Storage." Beyond the door lay another long passage, sloping downwards, ever deeper into the facility. The air grew cold again, and they finally reached a thick, heavily insulated door, again marked "Cold Storage." Janus prepped himself for a blast of cold air, and opened the door.

The space beyond had totally collapsed. A massive building from the surface had sunk deep into the ground, filling the area, its many floors creating layers of rock and dirt, ringed by an old metal catwalk, the only surviving element of what the room must once have been. The rest of the massive space was crushed beneath the Phoenix superscraper. The air around them was freezing, and seemed to be generated from the depths of Phoenix itself, rising up the collapsed column to fill the ruins above. It was difficult to see in the thick fog. The catwalk protested as Janus carefully placed his weight upon it.

The three ran their flashlights over the wall of earth before them, the light granting the fog a ghostly quality. Faint gleams along the surface caught Celes' eye, and Wouris crouched at the edge where the building slid into the cavern, disbelief upon her face.

"Immutium!" she breathed, her voice elated. "The area's laden with it. It's a literal treasure trove. It must have just filled this cavern before! It isn't a natural substance though. I wonder what Phoenix was using it for?"

She scooped up a handful of Immutium and dirt, and put in one of her waist pockets.

"Maybe Chiles or Graham can give us an idea if we take a sample back."

"Well," Janus said, nodding. "When we get back to Valhalla, maybe we can send some forces to collect—"

He froze. Voices echoed from the mist in front of him. He flicked his palm in an exaggerated movement so that Celes and Wouris could see.

Contact.

Peering over a rail to his left, he could just make out the shapes of two STs below them, walking along a bridge beneath their platform. Janus strained to hear them.

"…why we're here or working with them."

"Orders are orders. Who knows what the HAMs want with this place."

Janus silently flipped over the rail, hanging by his legs to get a closer look at the soldiers.

"I hate repair jobs," said the first. "These factories just won't keep running. And I hate being sent out to the edges. It takes forever to get out here with all the collapsed passages."

"Just be glad we were out this far already," the second one interjected. "This is the short leg."

Janus squinted at the pair of STs through the fog. It was almost impossible to discern anything about the suits, but just before the pair disappeared completely into the mist, an emblem glinted in the light of the other's headlamps.

Using his legs to flip himself back over the rail, he signaled to Celes and Wouris, giving them the all clear.

"Cerberus!" Janus whispered excitedly.

"Well, I guess we're not the first ones to find this place..." Celes whispered back.

Right. Wouris signed. **Stick [to hand] signals. [No telling how] many there [are].**

Janus and Celes agreed. They moved swiftly along the dark catwalk. It would take an exceptionally skilled—and very lucky—ST to realize anything lurked in the shadows.

Beyond the catwalks, they were forced to crawl through perilously small passages, until finally they emerged into a room with three doors, leading in all directions. Janus opted for the one that descended deeper still.

Leaving the heavy mist and darkness behind, the trio passed through shattered glass doors, into what appeared to be a laboratory, or what was left of one: broken consoles, smashed machinery, stray tubing, and oozing vats filled with strange blue goo.

Electrogel. Janus signed.

Wouris responded with quick flashes of her hands. **[These] labs [look like they were] destroyed [from the] inside.**

Celes signaled with one hand in response. **Bomb.**

Wouris nodded.

Janus noted the damage only got worse as they moved deeper. Some rooms were nothing more than blackened glass and twisted metal. Whoever had destroyed the labs had known what they were doing. And they were thorough.

They heard more voices—faint but getting stronger. Moving deeper into the vast, many-roomed laboratory, they caught glimpses of men and women in some of the broken rooms. Not all were armored STs. Some even appeared to be civilians—scientists, perhaps—wearing uniforms of

266

green and brown. They were picking through the debris, salvaging equipment from those labs that had received the least damage. Others directed STs, shoulders emblazoned with Cerberus sigils, who carried huge crates of equipment in and out of the area.

Danger. STs. Two. Right. Celes signaled.

Roger. Move left.

Janus' hand flashed quickly. He watched the two STs as they loaded an empty crate with materials scrounged by another. The crate was close to overflowing with salvaged circuits and parts. The STs lifted the huge load and began trudging back from whence they came.

Celes switched from shorthand to the longer form of signaling.

Where [are] they going[?]

Wouris moved forward so that Janus and Celes could see her hands.

[That's what] we [are] going [to] find out.

It didn't take long for them to reach their goal. They stood on the highest level of a multileveled room full of salvaged equipment, partially melted computer stations, and warped glass. STs, Inferni, and unarmored officers swarmed the room like ants.

Janus, Celes, and Wouris wisely pulled themselves back. In one corner stood a large stack of crates stamped with the Cerberus emblem. Black ash covered the floor, muffling the sound of their footsteps against the constant clunking of ST boots. With a tiny lull in the STs streaming in and out of the tunnels below, the three quickly made a move, crossing the short open space, and retreating into the darkness of the highest corner of the room. Janus could just barely make out a raised platform that jutted out on the ground floor.

An Infernus rushing across the open space caught his attention. Its armor bore the purple and black Cerberus emblem.

"Honorable Executor Delacroix!"

A voice full of contempt responded to the Infernus' statement. "Speak."

"Three new shipments of Immutium have arrived from the Southern Cerberus facility as per your request. Overlord Middleton wishes that you know she sends her warmest regards to your operations."

A man strode into view on the raised platform. He wore black armor, layered with plates in a manner similar to ODIN Adept armor, but an attached cape gave him a more regal look. Inlaid silver and green thread formed circular patterns along the corners of the cape, while jade green epaulettes were covered with the white hair that flowed down to his shoulders, hiding his face. He placed his hands on the railing of the platform and stared at the officer from his position. The fearsome-looking Infernus took a step back.

Delacroix's voice lightened slightly, but the underlying contempt was still present. "Excellent. Unload the Immutium into Section 3B. Take the rest to the factory levels, Overlord Halifax will see to it there."

"Sir, you don't want the Immutium moved to Section 4D? What about our delivery?"

Delacroix laughed. "Oh, I don't think the Adepts of ODIN will need the rest of their payment."

"Yes, Honorable Executor." The Infernus bowed politely, backed up several steps, and then hesitated, as if he had something else to say.

"Is there something else?" Delacroix asked, an edge to his voice

"My Lord, Overlord Middleton regrets to inform you that all further shipments have been temporarily suspended due to some unwanted attention from the SPARTAN Mercenary group. The SPARTAN citadel has been seen north of Lightemann's Ridge."

Delacroix began to slowly descend the flight of stairs that connected the platform to the main floor, keeping his face down as he did so. He stopped halfway and stared at the Infernus.

"Tell Middleton." He paused. "That she should put her affairs in order, and quickly, or she will answer to me. Do you understand? Now go."

The Infernus, who continued to back up as Delacroix had descended, saluted.

"Yes, my Lor—Honorable Executor Delacroix!" he fumbled over his words, and then turned and ran back into the tunnel, disappearing from view.

Delacroix surveyed the bustling Cerberus STs from his vantage point. But they all seemed intent to avoid his gaze, and sped by faster. Even the flow of officers moving back and forth between the platform and the floor seemed to stop, as if they were afraid to intrude upon him.

Placing his hands behind his back, Delacroix slowly descended the rest of the stairs to the main floor. Janus struggled to get a look at his obscured face, fascinated by the dominance of the figure before him.

A green uniformed, but unarmored man ran up to Delacroix, and saluted. "My Lord Delacroix."

Delacroix tilted his head towards the man, who quickly held out a video feed.

"Overlord Halifax wishes to speak with you, Executor. The interference down here was too great to reach you directly."

Delacroix nodded as the man hastily backed away, and then fled the scene.

"What is it, Halifax?" Delacroix's smooth voice said into the transmitter.

"Sir, belts six, ten, and fourteen have stopped working again. I've sent some men to repair the system, but it looks like, from preliminary reports, it will take some time to get them back up and running."

Delacroix's voice remained eerily calm. "Halifax, I want those belts back online within the hour."

"I don't think that's possible, Executor. We are working with limited personnel and resources. The factory was never intended to be run at these levels."

Delacroix's voice rose suddenly. "Don't tell me how this factory is supposed to run! I know what it's supposed to produce!"

The workers in the room froze, looking for escape routes. Delacroix glanced around, and the workers immediately started working at double speed. He calmed slightly.

"I need our production maxed, Halifax. Every hour we lose is another opportunity for discovery, and I have spent too long to have this taken away! I'm already getting reports that Middleton is under increased scrutiny, and it has taken too much time to get the facility back up and running as it is. We cannot afford to wait. What do you think will happen once we are discovered?"

"The factory will be fixed within the hour, Executor."

"Good."

Janus watched Delacroix sigh, and pick up a beaker that had been carelessly dropped to the floor. He turned it over in his hands slowly.

"It's not how you start—"

"My Lord!"

A different Trooper ran up, his armor brand new and unmarked, like it had just come off the line.

Delacroix looked up swiftly from the beaker. "What?" he barked.

The trooper quailed under the eye of the Executor.

"Uh…my Lord, uh…our guards have just reported that Titan Security forces are sweeping the area above the bunker for a small group of ODIN Mercenaries."

"What?" Delacroix's voice exploded. All activity in the room stopped.

"What are you telling me for? Seal up all the entrances. We cannot be discovered here."

"Of course, Lord Delacroix!"

The Trooper quickly ran off. A flurry of officers flew by the Executor and quickly directed the working STs into action. Celes touched Janus on the arm; he turned his head quickly, startled.

Time to go, she signaled with two hands.

Janus nodded. He looked back at the Executor, who now stood alone in the center of the room. Delacroix took one last look around the lab, and then hurled the glass beaker into the wall, uttering a howl of rage.

CHAPTER 34
PARTING GIFTS

Janus and Celes hurried behind Wouris as she led them on a furious dash back along the catwalks.

Evading the flurry of activity, however, did not prove difficult. The STs seemed single-minded in their task—to reach their designated positions and seal the entrances; not to search. And unencumbered as they were in their lighter, smaller armor, it did not take long for the three of them to quickly outdistance the STs as they raced through the complex.

Janus flashed a word to Celes and Wouris as they ran.

Typical.

Wouris shook her head and Celes smiled.

When they finally returned to the darkened hall that connected the factory to the supply room, they found the door already open, and the two STs they had passed earlier leaning against opposite walls, complaining to each other.

"Stupid Captain Burroughs," said the first. "Doesn't seem to care that this stupid entrance is sealed up. 'Overlord Middleton wants all entrances secure.' 'Overlord Middleton will be angry with us if we don't follow orders.' Damn, I hate him."

"Tell me about it, 'Neff. First we're sent to repair that stupid old belt, and now we're guarding a collapsed entrance. Why are we working with those people? Burroughs doesn't even know; he just follows Middleton's orders. I mean, what do they want with this old factory anyway? It's been producing a ton of suits that can't be custom fitted. They're cheap, they're low quality. How are we supposed to use them? It's absolutely pointless!"

"Oh, don't get me start—"

There was a loud pop, and both troopers slumped over and fell to the ground, lifeless.

Janus stared at the pair. They were just soldiers with a string of bad breaks. But as he looked at the Cerberus emblem across their shoulders, he couldn't stop thinking of Clara, and Middleton.

Two less pawns for Middleton. Two less thugs in the slums.

But he couldn't help look over at Celes, who wore a grimace.

"Perhaps, if only we'd been a bit faster," she said.

"And perhaps they might have caught us," Wouris interjected. Celes bit her lip, and then nodded.

The three took a few moments to dispose of the evidence of their infiltration, using the ST's own Zeus rifles and a sprinkling of some of the Immutium from the collapsed cavern to create the appearance of a fight. It seemed believable enough to Janus; STs weren't known for their mild tempers, and the promise of even small riches would likely be enough to set a pair of them off.

"Good," Wouris said. "That should cover our tracks well enough."

"Do you think they'll believe they shot each other?" Celes said. "Seems a little unlikely to me."

"They're STs," Janus said. "They'll likely be found by STs. I don't think they'll look too closely. Besides, the tunnel is supposed to be blocked; I don't think they'll even consider someone coming this way."

273

"It will do well enough," Wouris said. "Let's get out of here before we run into any more."

It was morning when they finally exited the bunker, clad in the three Infernus suits they'd found. A full night had passed while they journeyed underground, but they were soon bounding with ease towards the evac point. Wouris, however, motioned for them to slow, as if suddenly remembering an important detail.

"One last thing before we go."

She pulled out a detonator. Janus and Celes looked curiously at her.

"I've been testing it periodically, but the signal was jammed during the assault. While we were underground, the signal couldn't get through anyway. Decided I should leave it alone for awhile."

She pushed the button, and a huge ball of flame erupted to the south.

"Oh dear," she said. "Apparently they forgot to disarm the charges before they turned off the jammer."

Celes smiled.

"Come on," she said. "Let's go home."

CHAPTER 35
RETURNING

Being inside an Infernus suit was a novel experience for Janus, and Wouris was constantly reminding him to keep his altitude low as they jumped through the trees. They had great speed, and were likely well outside the search area of the Titan forces. But it would only take one scout noticing an unrecognized Infernus emerging from the trees to bring a massive force down upon them.

Janus flicked between his different vision modes, fascinated by the infrared of the monstrous suits. Infernus armor, unsurprisingly, ran hot, and Wouris and Celes' outlines shone brightly, even among the trees. He wondered how well he would have shown up in his Adept armor, but he wasn't particularly keen on finding out.

While the suits gave them great speed, it couldn't speed the passage of time. It was just after noon when they arrived at the evac area.

"Evac won't arrive until nightfall," Wouris said to them. "We'll settle down in that stream. Get all the way into the water; leave just enough uncovered to keep your air exchanger open."

The next few hours were dreadfully boring, as Wouris insisted on radio silence except for critical messages, which meant that Janus' afternoon consisted of staring uncomfortably at Celes' just visible visor, unable to speak or move.

Finally as night fell, the familiar sound of an ODIN Longboat roared overhead, and Janus heard Wouris' voice break the silence.

"Longboat, come in. This is Wouris, over."

"Wouris, this is Longboat Zero-Delta," Glory responded. "Glad to hear you're still kicking, over."

"It's good to see you too, Glory. We're ready to go home, over."

"Roger that. Where are you? I'll drop down to pick you up. Over."

"We're in the river. Don't panic when we emerge, out."

Trudging from the water, Janus couldn't help but chuckle as he heard Glory let out a low whistle.

Lyn, Ramirez, and Marcus greeted them eagerly when they jumped onto the Longboat as it hovered by the shore. Glory deftly adjusted the engines, keeping the craft from tilting from the sudden weight.

"We knew ya would make it!" Lyn exclaimed, as Ramirez and Marcus helped them out of their large suits. "Can't say we weren't worried, though."

With her armor off, Celes quickly gave each of them a hug, her arms lingering around Marcus as she looked at Lyn.

"Well, you weren't the only ones!"

"I wasn't." Marcus smiled at Celes. "I knew they couldn't get you that easy."

He released her and turned to Janus, extending his hand.

"All of you."

Janus nodded in respect as the pair clasped hands. "I'm glad you all made it out. Who else?"

"We did pretty well, considering," Lyn said, with a meaningful look. "Ramirez and I made it out with Holloway and Kirsten. Jones and Valers made it back to the beach before it got too crazy. We ran into Marcus along the way, and he had Zhao, Alexis, and Nathans with him. We lost Byron on the way out; his Longboat got hit on the fly. Roderick got taken out on the run back to the beach."

"I lost Naka, Browning, and Freeham to a squad of Inferni," Marcus said.

Wouris grimaced.

"They went down fighting, though," he added.

"Marcus really did you proud, Wouris," Lyn piped in. "His squad saved Rolan's Rangers. But...we don't know what happened to Bynes, Hughes, Kwandis, or Young."

Janus shook his head. "They didn't make it."

"Right." She nodded sorrowfully. "The Praetor will be happy to know all of you made it though; especially you, Janus."

Janus raised his eyebrows. "He wants his blade back."

When the Longboat finally landed in Valhalla, Janus couldn't help but feel a sense of relief. Along with Celes and Wouris, he'd experienced an unpleasant, but brief bout of shivers and vomiting on the flight back. Before they had even disembarked, Colonel Hawkes ordered the three of them to proceed directly to the infirmary. Ramirez, Lyn, and Marcus were given no such order.

"We haven't been hungry since we got back," Lyn said. "So many people missing or dead. Now that you're back, I'm feeling better."

Their stomachs growling, Janus and Celes watched the other three head for the mess.

"Come on," Wouris said. "The sooner we report to the infirmary, the sooner we can eat."

When they arrived at the infirmary, they found Praetor Jennings waiting for them. He quickly sized up the group, then nodded for Colonel Yalla to proceed.

"I want you all prepared for a debriefing at 0800 tomorrow. In the Torch. Sergeant, I would like to see you immediately following your examination."

Janus and Celes saluted, and stood to attention.

"Yes, sir."

Wouris followed suit, eyeing Janus and Celes to ensure they didn't break form.

"Sir."

"Go on," the Praetor said, with a casual wave. "Get fixed up."

By the time they left the infirmary, it was nearly 2300 hours. Yalla had given them a clean bill of health, unable to explain their bout of sickness, but glad to say that Janus' ribs were healing remarkably well, even before the Nanytes. Wouris bade them good night, and headed off to see the Praetor. Both Janus and Celes were tired, but the need for food moved them slowly in the direction of the mess.

As they entered, they were met with a chorus of cheers. Adepts stood up and patted them on the back as they passed. Bewildered, Janus and Celes headed over to where Marcus, Lyn, and Ramirez were sitting. All three were smiling broadly at them.

"What's with the celebration?" Janus asked.

"Eh, we couldn't sleep." Marcus grinned.

"More like everyone's happy to have you back alive. They couldn't believe anyone else made it. That, and the fact that everybody loved Wouris' little finishing touch to your adventure," Lyn said. "Hey, you still have that?"

Lyn pointed to the sword still on Janus' back.

"Oh, I guess, yeah." Janus looked surprised. "We saw the Praetor in the infirmary, but he didn't ask for it, and I didn't think to give it back. I don't know what to do with it. I can't just throw it in the weapons locker."

"I'm sure he's a bit preoccupied," Celes said. "Maybe he'll ask for it at the debriefing tomorrow?"

"Debriefing?" asked Marcus.

"The Praetor will want to know everything we heard on the trip back in the Longboat," Ramirez said.

"Good point," Marcus conceded. "Which reminds me—don't stuff yourselves tonight. The Praetor gave every remaining cadet full Adept status with the condition that we continue our training. We spent the day with Keats and Hawkes before we were permitted to travel to the evac point."

"Why did the Praetor let you do that, anyway?" Janus asked with concern. "He didn't know anyone would make it back in the first place. Why let you three risk coming along?"

"I realize growing up in Cerberus probably made you less than sociable Janus." Marcus grinned. "But even leaders have feelings."

"After such a huge loss," Celes said, "for the Praetor to look confident someone was going to make it back? It would be a huge morale boost."

"Hey," Janus said, giving Marcus a look. "I'm perfectly sociable."

"Besides," Celes said, giving Janus a smirk, "the Praetor probably figured that if anyone was going to make it out, it would be you."

Marcus' grin vanished, while Ramirez and Lyn laughed.

"Careful," Marcus grunted. "His head doesn't need to be any bigger than it already is."

Lyn yawned. "Well, I think I'm off to bed. I want as much sleep as I can get before another training session like the one we had today. I think Keats and Hawkes want us to be able to take on the whole of the Titan Corporate Forces if we ever go up against them again. We'll probably be training during your debriefing, so fill us in afterward."

"Will do," Celes said.

"Good night," Lyn said as she rose.

Ramirez rose with her, waving goodnight to the rest of the group.

"I'm going to grab some food and do the same," Janus said, standing up from the table.

Marcus glanced at Celes, and stifled a big yawn. "I guess I'm off then," he said, resignedly.

"Yeah," Celes said.

"See you in the morning," he said.

"See you."

There was a moment of quiet, before Marcus turned, and walked out of the mess.

CHAPTER 36
DARK HORIZONS

With a set of hideous alarms, and a sudden flooding of bright light, Janus came miserably awake.

"On your feet!" barked a familiar voice.

Janus blinked groggily, the room an unfamiliar blur.

"Val? What time is it?"

"Not me," Val replied.

Janus shook his head, trying to snap himself out of his stupor.

"What? Who?"

"I thought this might happen."

"Wouris…?"

Janus was confused, sitting up in bed. His door was open.

"You've got half an hour before debriefing. Get up, or the Praetor will have my hide."

Janus saw her shadow leave his room.

"Oh and remember," she called back, "it's Sergeant Wouris to you."

Twenty-five minutes later, Janus was jogging into the center of Valhalla. He was still a cadet until the Ceremony of the Ascension, but he was now allowed to wear the ODIN symbol emblazoned on his shoulder, matching the huge seal that glowed brightly above him in the morning sun. He had his pistol belted to his waist, and the Praetor's Immutium Ghostblade on his back. Celes ran up behind him from the mess, and they took the lift up to command, which was designated by two runes:

Odin's Torch. It was the third beacon of Valhalla, and it sat at the very top of the Trunk. The crown of the great tree. It housed Command, Valhalla's nerve center. The Praetor was the only person with a residence on that level, but few would argue the chief officers did not live there, each of them spending so much time in the Torch. Every important decision that impacted ODIN was made within its heavily armored walls.

Wouris was waiting for them at the entrance. She gave them a quick inspection, and nodded in approval.

Heavy doors slid open to reveal a blur of activity. They had stepped directly onto the main bridge, which was abuzz with the Adepts who piloted and watched over Valhalla. Hundreds of monitors stretched across the room, tracking everything from power consumption and activity levels, to scans of the skies and flight control, ending in a huge panoramic window that revealed a dazzling view.

Valhalla was hovering above a long coastline under a cloudless sky, slowly moving south. The Adepts were constantly relaying information to a fierce-looking, grey-haired woman, whom Janus assumed to be the one in charge. Janus had heard stories about her—Captain of the Watch, Major Tuorneg, the commander for all of Valhalla's control deck crews. Some of the older Adepts he'd spoken to compared her to an ancient seafaring captain in demeanor, at home on her ship, rarely leaving to step ashore. Other than the Praetor, she was probably the only one who knew all of Valhalla's intricate inner workings. She lightly sipped a coffee as she perched over a MuDi in the center of the room, maintaining a hawk-like eye over the myriad displays and stations.

"Don't get in anybody's way," Wouris whispered, nudging them forward.

Janus walked slowly between the stations, careful to avoid disturbing any of the Adepts, listening to their chatter, and watching their screens.

"Engineering, we're seeing inconsistent spikes in engine three's power."

"Roger, LB zero-three-alpha, you are clear for departure."

"Water purifier zero-four is on the fritz again."

Janus walked to the huge window and stared out. It was breathtaking. The views from the various levels of Valhalla were incredible, but from the command deck, they were truly spectacular. The bridge formed a wide ring around the crown of the city, and Janus was given a full view of tall white clouds to the west, and broad rolling plains far to the east. Seabirds wheeled below, using the huge mass of air pushed by the gigantic city to lift them ever higher. Janus looked at Celes and smiled; she too seemed to be agape at the view.

Cerberus might be taller, but it didn't afford views like this.

"Captain, scouts report a storm front forty kilometers south-southeast, bearing one-seven-six."

Janus turned to look at Major Tuorneg, and realized that she had been keeping a close eye the two of them.

"Adjust bearing to one-eight-five, keep us off the coast," she responded. Her eyes roamed the room, watching every minor detail. Every so often, her gaze would resettle on the pair.

At a signal from Wouris, Janus and Celes carefully made their way to the back, following her into a round, glass-walled meeting room. A MuDi rested in the middle of a circular oak table in the center.

283

Praetor Jennings then appeared on the bridge, had a brief word with Major Tuorneg, and strode easily into the room. With a wave of his hand, the walls of the room became opaque, and the doors slid shut.

"Glad to see all of you made it back safely." The Praetor seemed to be in a much better mood this morning. "At ease."

The three relaxed.

"Sergeant Wouris has already filled me in on most of the details of your little adventure, but I would like to hear the stories from your own perspectives, as well. Before we begin, however"—he turned to Janus, and stretched out his hand—"I believe you have something of mine."

Janus removed the Praetor's blade from his back, and handed it to him. He felt oddly light without it.

"Excellent." His mood became more serious, and he motioned for them to sit around the table at the center of the room. "Now, if you would, please tell me about the mission."

So Janus began the long tale, with Celes filling in parts as he went along. The Praetor listened carefully, asking questions only for clarification. When Janus had finished, the Praetor nodded.

"Janus, I wanted to thank you, by the way."

"For what?" Janus was confused.

The Praetor smiled sadly.

"The few seconds you gave us probably saved many lives. Our casualties could have been far worse without your warning."

Wouris nodded at Janus.

"Several of the officers reported your warning saved them. Everyone was glad to hear that you made it back."

"Indeed." The Praetor stood and put his hands behind his back. "Now, however, one question remains foremost in our minds: How did Titan know we were coming?"

"And what about the Cerberus forces in the Phoenix ruins?" Celes said.

"Yes, that too is a concern. Anytime a Corporation goes through so much for secrecy, it's cause for alarm. With the state the Adept Legions are in, we can't afford to have any one Corporation gaining too much power. But we have at least one clue. The report you overheard about the SPARTAN citadel near Lightemann's Ridge. It's part of a mountain range located southeast of Phoenix."

The MuDi in the table switched on with a touch of the Praetor's hand, and displayed a two-dimensional view of Valhalla's current position, as well as a view of the mountains in question.

"I had Major Tuorneg set a course for it this morning."

Wouris leaned forward as the MuDi popped up into three dimensions and displayed the ridge.

"If we search the area surrounding the ridge, we may be able to find some answers to the question of Cerberus' activities."

"It seemed the wisest course of action, as we have no other leads." The Praetor nodded. "It is likely that the facility under the Phoenix ruins will be on high alert for some time. In the meantime, it will take us three weeks to reach the ridge."

Janus and Celes looked up from the map, surprised.

"Three weeks?" Celes said.

"Yes," the Praetor said. "Until we have a better understanding of the forces at play here, I'm not taking any chances. We're taking a roundabout route, with scouts running out ahead to make sure there are no more surprises in store for us. The search will take some time; we will have to do it carefully so we aren't detected. Our slow arrival will give time for our forward scouts to get a general idea where the Lightemann facility is located. While we travel, you will rejoin your fellow Adepts to continue your training. Any questions?"

Janus spoke up.

"Actually, I have one, sir."

"Yes, Janus?" The Praetor gave him his full attention.

"Do you think Cerberus hired us to distract Titan from their mining operations, so that their own operation would remain undiscovered?"

"We can't be sure, but the possibility has crossed my mind." The Praetor thought carefully for a moment before continuing. "This Delacroix fellow is troubling. If he is a Cerberus Executor, he's playing a dangerous game."

"But what else could he be if not a Cerberus Executor?" Celes asked.

The Praetor shook his head in dismay.

"I'm not sure."

Chapter 37
Technique

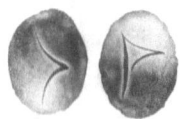

"The others are already training," Wouris said to Janus and Celes as the lift descended from the Torch. "Normally, you would be placed under the command of another Sergeant after graduation to full Adept status. However, since you did not have an opportunity to fully complete your training, the Praetor has left me in charge of you for the time being."

Sunlight filtered down from the skylights above, giving Valhalla a comforting glow. Wouris pointed over the edge. Far below them, Janus could see Ramirez' huge figure looming above the rest of the cadets as they trained.

"I believe Captain Rogers is overseeing your squad-mates for now," Wouris continued. "You will train with him until tonight."

The lift slowed, stopping at the bottom of the Trunk. Janus and Celes got off, while Wouris remained behind.

"I need to talk to Colonel Keats and Colonel Hawkes. So train hard—you know now what's at stake."

The lift sped away, leaving Janus and Celes to join the others.

As they approached, Ramirez was squaring off against Jones and Valers. They circled him, preparing to strike from opposite sides. With a cry, Valers leapt to attack from behind, while Jones rushed him from the front. It might have gone well—if Ramirez hadn't whirled around, grabbed Valers by the ankle in mid-air, and tossed him mightily over his head into Jones in one smooth motion. The pair skidded painfully across the floor of the hall in a tangled mass. Slowly extricating themselves from each other, Valers shook his head in dismay.

"Ramirez, I'm glad you're on our side."

Watching Jones and Valers fight made Janus' stomach churn, a mixture of happiness and bitterness.

"Hey!" Jones said, when she noticed Janus and Celes watching from the sidelines. "Look who's back to train!"

Valers and Jones jogged swiftly over. Ramirez stayed put, exchanging an understanding nod with Janus.

"We really owe you one, Janus, and you too, Celes. I never really got the chance to thank you for saving our lives the other day." Valers shook Janus' hand. "We owe you."

"Big," Jones added. "If you ever need us…"

"We'll be there," Valers finished.

"And next time, we won't be taken out so easily." Jones pounded her fist into her palm.

"We're just glad you guys made it back okay," Celes said with a grin. "Why don't you show me what you were practicing just now?"

Janus excused himself, and wandered past the remaining cadets, watching Lyn absentmindedly as she ducked, weaved, and flipped in an elegant dance, avoiding blows from Holloway and Kirsten. As he looked around now, he realized how many faces were missing, faces he could imagine there still—Byron, sparring with Young; Roderick, with an irate Captain Northcott yelling in his ear to aim higher; Browning, Freeham, and Bynes, the three of them begging him to join in a game of Brevis Bellum. Naka would undoubtedly be laughing his warm, friendly laugh—maybe at Holloway and Kirsten as they struggled to fight Lyn, maybe at himself if he had been here to fight her; and Hughes and Kwandis—they had been inseparable. Even in death.

All of them gone—almost half the cadets—in an instant. It hadn't really registered with him before. He felt angry. He had failed. He had let his squad down. No, not his squad—they were supposed to be his family. And yet he felt oddly detached. He knew all of them, but he didn't really *know* anyone of them. Where did Naka come from again? Medusa? Hydra? What was it that Kwandis hated, that thing Hughes always did? Was it mixing her Passers together, or slipping 'radishes' on her plate? Or was that Freeham? How much did he know about those who survived? But to ask would be to invite questions. About himself. About his past. And he didn't really want to talk about that.

Could he have warned them sooner? Could he have saved their lives? After all, of all the cadet squads, he had lost the most. He didn't even know how some of his team had died. He could feel the bile welling up in his throat. He had seen loss in the slums, but never felt it on his own. Crying didn't help. Not when survival was on the line. He swallowed hard, and clenched his fists, searching for something to take his mind from the pain.

Some distance away, he spied Marcus working with an unpowered Ghostblade. As Janus approached, Marcus acknowledged him with a simple nod, but did not stop his exercises. Janus stepped in front of him, too close for Marcus to comfortably swing. They stared at each other for several moments.

Wordlessly, they both took a fighting stance.

In a flash, Marcus launched himself at Janus, swinging the dull blade. Janus ducked and weaved, struggling to stay just in front of the weapon, occasionally deflecting the flat of the weapon with a brief touch. It was tiring, and painful, as occasionally, Marcus connected. Each swing was forceful, with little restraint. But Janus didn't mind. The pain was focusing, and distracting.

"How did they die?" Marcus asked in heavy breaths.

289

Janus was surprised by the question, but the hefty blows didn't stop.

"Young and Bynes were hit by an Inferni. I don't think they suffered. Hughes and Kwandis—I don't know."

"Because you weren't there," Marcus said.

Janus stopped, and was hit by the full force of Marcus' swing, tumbling to the ground. He stared up at Marcus, who lowered the Ghostblade to his side.

"You left them behind."

Janus scowled, and sprang upright, fists clenched. "I had to."

"They expected you to lead them," Marcus said. "Just like Naka and Browning and Freeham expected me to save them. I watched that Infernus take them out. I wasn't fast enough."

Janus unclenched his fists. "If I had been faster, maybe no one would have died."

"I should have picked up on that trap. I was a Trooper. I shouldn't have left anyone behind."

Janus stared at him for a moment, then raised his hands again. "Why aren't you swinging?"

Marcus met Janus' eyes. And raised the blade.

They sparred for what seemed like hours, only stopping to switch who carried the Ghostblade, and who struggled to stay away.

Long after the sun has passed its zenith, Wouris reappeared. Rogers nodded solemnly to her, and disappeared as she addressed the cadets.

"At sunset, we will hold the ceremony for our lost comrades. You will form up as a platoon at 1820 around the Trunk in formal dress, at which time we will proceed to Platform A for the Blood Poet's Ceremony."

There was neither anger nor sadness in her words, but they gave Janus chills.

"Anyone late will receive two weeks' confinement, reduced rations for three months, and be placed on inactive status for the next mission. Dismissed."

Chapter 38
The Blood Poets' Ceremony

Formal dress was not much different from standard attire, especially for a new Adept, as a matter of grim practicality. Janus' armor featured a red stripe along the right side of his torso, and the ODIN symbol embroidered in gold thread on his left breast. He met up with the other cadets in the main room of Sigma Three.

An air of nervousness hung over them. Not one cadet had witnessed the ceremony before. It would be a final farewell to friends who would never witness it. No one wanted to mess it up.

The sun was low on the horizon as they departed, deep orange light piercing the windows of Valhalla. Unconsciously, Janus and Marcus took the lead of the marching column, and the others fell into formation behind them. The Adepts jogged in silence, their thoughts wandering, as their subconscious minds guided them to the center of the floating citadel.

When they entered the great hall, however, Janus stopped. Several surprised cadets collided with him, and a few irritable cries rang out, before a general hush quickly fell over the group.

The Praetor and Wouris were talking quietly in front of the Trunk. And despite their whispers, they commanded all the attention of the hall. Praetor Jennings wore gold armor, detailed blue and silver etching covering the full breadth of the suit, creating the combined appearance of an ancient knight, and an Adept soldier. The etchings formed images of Adepts in battle, and Janus realized that each plate told a story in a single picture, fitting perfectly together, exposing only enough of the black suit beneath it to let the Praetor move smoothly.

But the Praetor paled in comparison to Wouris' striking garb. She was robed in deep red velvet, trimmed and inlaid with gold thread. The long flowing robe was elegant, even as her frame and hands disappeared within in. An incredible number of medals and awards were pinned to her front. For the first time, Janus truly understood why she commanded so much respect within ODIN. If the number of medals on her chest were any indication, she should have left her Sergeant's position long ago.

"She's..." Celes whispered just behind him, awestruck. "She's ODIN's Blood Poet."

The cries of surprise alerted the Praetor and Wouris to the squad's presence, and both turned to the halted column. Wouris and Jennings waited patiently for the group to cross the floor.

"Praetor. Sergeant," Janus said, saluting them both.

"Janus." Praetor Jennings smiled. "It is proper for you to refer to Sergeant Wouris as the Lady Poet or Master Poet while she is performing her duties."

"Yes, sir." Janus looked at Wouris. "Uh, sorry. Lady Poet."

"Good. Now, as the Master realizes," he spoke a little more loudly, turning once again to Wouris, "one's Blood Poet duties should take precedence over any other necessities. I have given you a great deal of leeway on this before, Lady Poet, but on this matter, you will hold to my orders. I am sure your former cadets are quite capable of proceeding to the Ceremony under cadet Janus."

"Of course, Praetor." Wouris bowed slightly. Although she had clearly lost whatever disagreement she had been having with the Praetor, there was no disrespect in her voice. She turned and strode purposefully away from the column.

The Praetor sighed and smiled, then turned back towards Janus. "You are capable of getting to Voyages within the next ten minutes, I presume?"

"Yes, sir."

"Of course, sir," Marcus spoke up. "We will be there, you can count on that."

Janus looked at him in annoyance.

"Good. I will hold you to that cadet Auras," the Praetor said. Janus was momentarily confused, but the Praetor did not pause. "Once that task has been accomplished, you, cadet Soltis, and cadet Janus will join Colonel Hawkes at the rear of the formation."

Janus suddenly realized that the Praetor had been referring to Marcus and Celes, and that he had never heard their surnames before. He wondered, too, if they had just realized he did not have one.

"Sir…" Celes began.

"Yes, cadet…" He trailed off as he turned to her. "This is a formal ceremony. Do you think another address is warranted?"

Celes hesitantly cleared her throat, and glanced behind her towards Valers, catching eyes with Janus as she did so. "No, sir."

Janus looked toward the ground in embarrassment.

The setting sun turned the sky a deep red as it began its final slide below the horizon. A cool evening sea breeze played along the nooks and crannies of the metal platform that made up the Chariot of Voyages. At the edge of the platform, a large raised dais had been constructed for the Ceremony, covered in a red felt. A single, plain pedestal rose from its center.

Joining the silent mass of Adepts, the former cadets solemnly lined up in the rear of the formation. Janus tried not to fidget while he waited for the Ceremony to begin. He did not have long to wait, however, as Colonel Hawkes appeared, and pulled Marcus, Celes, and himself from the gathering with a single silent motion of his hand. Leading them around the outside edge, Hawkes placed them alarmingly close, at the front right corner of the gathering. To their left waited Lieutenant Forrenza, who seemed completely at ease. Grunting in satisfaction, Hawkes quickly disappeared back into the formation. A chill breeze blew across the platform, but Janus felt very hot and uncomfortable in his new location. A quick glance told him Celes and Marcus were equally alarmed.

When the sun touched the horizon, the Ceremony began. A pathway opened through the middle of the massed Adepts, and the officers of ODIN appeared in a slow, marching processional. Each officer wore black armor with red torsos and shoulders, and carried a tall lance with a broad, red standard, the ODIN warrior symbol emblazoned upon it. On top of each standard was a burning brazier. At each row of Adepts, two officers stopped, forming a burning pathway down the center of the platform.

Then the senior officers appeared, draped in red capes. They did not carry standards, but wore sheathed Ghostblades. They climbed the steps to stand behind the pedestal, and stared out over the ocean, their backs to the crowd. Janus felt ill at ease. He had never seen so much respect given for the dead, and he had never been so directly responsible for their passing.

The Praetor appeared at the edge of the gathering. He walked alone, silently bearing the gaze of the assembly. He too climbed the dais, joining the senior officers, and staring out over the open ocean.

Six sergeants materialized, moving at a slow march between the burning standards. They bore a single, empty Adept suit suspended between them by six sheathed Ghostblades. As the sergeants marched, Janus lost sight of them for a moment in the crowd, and when they appeared again, Janus could see Kwandis' still body. He struggled not to break formation. Each time an Adept blocked his view, the body changed. Hughes.

Young. Bynes. Roderick. Janus looked away—he surely was not the only one seeing visions of the dead.

The procession halted before the pedestal, and draped their silent burden on top of it. The officers at the platform's edge performed an about face, turning towards the empty suit, and raised their sheathed blades in salute. They held themselves stiffly at attention, neither swaying nor shifting. Only the Praetor did not turn.

At that moment, the gathering became deathly still. Wouris had appeared, and she was absolutely entrancing. Her red robes had become deep blood in the setting sun, while the inlaid gold filigree glowed in the last rays of the day. She seemed to float along the path of burning standards. As she approached the pedestal, the honor guard of sergeants took a step back. She mounted the steps to the dais, walking around the pedestal so that she faced the Adepts. As she did so, her hand hovered above the empty Adept armor, as if the suit had an invisible occupant. Her face bore a look of incredible sorrow.

She turned once to look at the Praetor, her eyes full of pity. He seemed acutely aware of her gaze, but did not turn to look, instead bowing his head. In that moment, Janus came to understand why Wouris remained, and would be forevermore, a sergeant.

Celes grabbed Janus' hand softly. Janus looked down in surprise, but Celes had already given it a squeeze, and let it go.

"Sorry," she whispered. "It—it must be so painful, to send Adepts to their deaths. Not everyone can do it."

Janus nodded.

Wouris returned her gaze to the crowd, but now the look of sorrow was gone, replaced by a calm demeanor that swept over the Adepts. Amplifiers caused her voice to resonate throughout the night sky.

"Sisters and brothers. Soldiers of ODIN. Tonight we stand together in remembrance of those who fought valiantly beside us in battle."

Wouris closed her eyes, and the senior officers stepped forward, each intoning the names of the lost. There were so many. They were spoken in no particular order, a cadet honored alongside a veteran, both remembered for their sacrifice, each familiar name an unexpected stab to Janus' heart. Occasionally, it sounded as if one of the officers would stumble over a name, but the others would continue forward, and soon the missing voice would rejoin the others.

When they had finished, Wouris' resonating voice washed again over the crowd.

"Some of you may wonder why those we love and cherish are taken so suddenly away. Let me tell you this: never forget them, but never ask why they fought and died. They fought for the same reason those who came before us fought. For the same reason each of you continue to fight."

And then, from deep within her, the most mesmerizing and beautiful voice Janus had ever heard rang out in song:

There was a time,

Not long ago,

When a rare few were sublime,

And the people cowed below.

Harsh existence,

That was certain.

For fiends brook no resistance,

Behind the gilded curtain.

Then one day,

Some arose,

Wanting to know freedom,

Stood to say,

Simple prose,

"We leave your foul kingdom."

Wailing, crying,

The rulers fought.

Despite the many dying,

Their deceptions were for naught.

Broke free, we did,

From Corp'rate shroud,

And those who cowered and hid;

Today we stand, strong and proud,

And with every breath,

Every lifeline cut,

To Corp'rate curse, we say:

'Tis better for death,

For no matter what,

"We will not live that way."

CHAPTER 39
ASCENSION

The last note of the poem died slowly in the twilight, and Janus noticed the officers' braziers had gone out in the wind.

"Never forget them," Wouris said, "nor the reason why they fought."

"Never forget!" the officers intoned.

"We honor you, Lady Poet," the Praetor said solemnly, turning to face the expectant Adepts, and bowing his head slightly.

Wouris smiled, bowing fully, but keeping her eyes focused on the Praetor.

"No, Praetor, we honor you, for having the courage to lead us into battle."

She straightened.

A slight smile came unbidden to the Praetor's lips, and a single glistening tear ran down his cheek. He mouthed 'thank you,' but quickly regained his composure. Wouris gracefully left the platform, escorted by the six honor guards. The Praetor watched her go. When she and the guards had fully disappeared, he spoke to the Adepts.

"And now, let us begin the Ceremony of Ascension!"

Immediately, the officers relit their braziers, but now they spouted blue flames. Each officer drew their Ghostblade, and held it aloft. An ethereal blue glow filled the air. The Praetor's voice resonated through the crowd.

"When faced with the heat of battle, there are those who rise above the rest. We have honored some of them tonight." He paused, glancing at the memorial pedestal. "Now, we honor those who will continue to lead us to victory, so that the sacrifices of those who have fallen will not be forgotten."

Captain Rogers and Major Northcott stepped forward. Rogers produced a small dark cherry wood box.

"There is not a single Adept here who did not fight bravely," the Praetor said, "who did not make Titan pay for what they did to our brothers and sisters in battle. However, only a select few fought with such ferocity and valor to deserve, and preserve, the sanctity of the awards we honor them with tonight."

Rogers marched over to the Praetor, and presented the open box to him, while Northcott called out in a booming voice.

"For uncommon bravery and skill in battle, and for their efforts in returning so many safely in a battle where so many were lost, we award the Order of the Shining Lance to Lieutenant Cecilia Forrenza, and Adept Marcus Auras."

Forrenza clapped Marcus heartily on the back, and Marcus grinned.

"Congratulations, Marcus," Janus and Celes said together. Cries of encouragement sounded from behind them. Rolan's Rangers had not forgotten Marcus' actions.

Marcus strode forward at the Major's motion, and stood at attention in front of the Praetor, who plucked a small silver lance from the box, pinning it to Marcus' left breast. The Praetor made a motion for the pair to stay. Marcus smiled from behind the Praetor, clearly enjoying the moment.

Janus could see two more sets of honors resting within: three bronze stars, and a set of silver bars.

"For special services to ODIN, we award Adept Celes Soltis, Adept Janus, and"—he paused as Wouris reappeared next to Janus, dressed down into red armor—"Sergeant Wouris the bronze star, for their part in alerting ODIN forces to the Titan trap, and for the discovery of vital information below the ruins of Phoenix."

He looked out over the crowd.

"And for providing a damn fine morale boost."

The crowd and most of the officers laughed. Both Wouris and the Praetor gave him a disapproving look, but he merely shrugged, and grinned.

Celes, Janus, and Wouris stepped forward as one to present themselves to the Praetor. He pinned the award on each of them, although he struggled to find a place to put it on Wouris. There was a general applause from the crowd, and Janus thought for sure he could hear someone whistling. Janus shifted uncomfortably. Lingering doubts gnawed at him. Marcus smiled and clapped, clearly proud of his friends.

"Good ole Lyn," Celes whispered. Janus smiled slightly as another whistle sounded.

"And now we have one other special honor tonight," The Praetor said, turning to face the crowd. "Sometimes on the field of battle, individuals go above and beyond what is required of them, putting themselves in danger, making difficult decisions, and doing whatever is necessary to ensure that their brothers and sisters here at ODIN come home both safe and victorious.

"Many of you also know that it is sometimes difficult for us to find officers here. It only takes one battle for most to realize they do not want to be responsible for those left behind. But when we"—he pointed to the row of officers before the crowd—"see those of you who demonstrate the traits necessary to lead, and lead well, ODIN cannot afford for you to sit idly by—even if you may not feel ready."

He glanced at Wouris. "Lady Poet."

Wouris took a step forward.

Northcott brought forward the cherry box with the silver bars, and Wouris carefully reached in to pick them up. She stared at them hesitantly for a moment.

"Adept Janus," she said, suddenly turning to face him. "I, the Blood Poet of ODIN, hereby promote you to the rank of Lieutenant."

She put a bar on the side of his neck.

"But—" Janus was stunned.

"Never forget your duty to your sisters and brothers," Wouris cut in, pinning the second bar to the other side. "Lead them well. The other sergeants and I will be watching."

Janus was at a loss for words. He looked around at the grim faces of the officers, the sergeants, and the crowd. He felt as if he could see out across the ocean, all the way to the slums of Cerberus. It was like he could see Clara standing on a trash pile, watching him, and whispering faintly to him.

Sometimes, you need to know…

And then he looked Wouris in the eye. "I will not fail them."

The crowd broke into cheers. The officers looked palpably relieved. Lyn whistled louder, and even Ramirez was smiling. Celes beamed at him. Marcus wore a look as hard as stone.

"It is the resolve of these individuals that drives us onward!" the Praetor cried as the cheering died down. "But we must not forget what we suffered only a few days ago. We must be ready to face some hard questions. And we must always be ready to fight."

There were murmurs of agreement from the crowd.

"Why was our assault met with such force?" the Praetor's voice rose. "Because throughout the world, no warriors are as feared as Adept warriors! And of all the Legions, which one has the most devoted officers?"

The officers banged their standards twice upon the ground and shouted.

"ODIN!"

"The most powerful weapons?"

The Adepts responded:

"ODIN!"

"The greatest reputation?"

"ODIN!"

"The most fearsome warriors?" he roared.

"ODIN! ODIN! ODIN!" the roar came back.

Janus let out a cry of victory. He was an Adept—he was an officer!

And far off, beyond the bend of the horizon, Lightemann's Ridge waited.

— END OF BOOK I —

A Thank You to My Readers

To all who have just read this book, thank you.

Thank you for your time, your dedication, and your support. Each and every one of you has contributed greatly to the joy I find in writing, allowing me the opportunity to shape the world you live in, if only for a brief time. Few things are more exciting to a sci-fi writer.

Creating this novel has been a journey filled with intensity and emotion—days both high and low. Knowing that this work is in your hands is incredibly significant to me. There are many great books out there, and many other distractions. Time is precious, and I'm thankful for all that you have given me.

For more on The Phoenix Fallacy, or to contact me, please visit www.phoenixfallacy.com and find me on Facebook @phoenixfallacy. No matter how you felt about Janus' adventure, I encourage you to review it online. Help other readers decide if this book if worth picking up and sharing.

Most of all, I hope you enjoyed the journey, and that we will have more opportunities to travel together soon.

Sincerely,

Jon Sourbeer

About the Author

A computer programmer by day, and a writer by night, Jonathan Sourbeer has long been a fan of technology and science fiction, drawing from a wide variety of experiences for his work. This includes (among others) a stint in corporate finance, a degree in physics, providing op-eds for the *Wall Street Journal*, running a half-Ironman with Navy Seals, and diving the Great Barrier Reef.

When he's not writing or working in tech, you can often find him rock climbing, building electronics with his father, or trying to be a better cook. He currently resides in Seattle, Washington.

www.ingramcontent.com/pod-product-compliance
Lightning Source LLC
Chambersburg PA
CBHW021207250626
47155CB00008B/2714